D0962228

THE TIMELESS ONE

THE REVENGE OF
MAGIC
THE TIMELESS ONE

JAMES RILEY

ALADDIN

NEW YORK LONDON TORONTO SYDNEY NEW DELHI

ALADDIN

An imprint of Simon & Schuster Children's Publishing Division
1230 Avenue of the Americas, New York, New York 10020
First Aladdin hardcover edition October 2020
Text © 2020 by James Riley
Jacket illustration © 2020 by Vivienne To
All rights reserved, including the right of reproduction in whole or in part in any form.
ALADDIN and related logo are registered trademarks of Simon & Schuster, Inc.
For information about special discounts for bulk purchases, please contact Simon & Schuster
Special Sales at 1-866-506-1949 or business@simonandschuster.com.
The Simon & Schuster Speakers Bureau can bring authors to your live event.
For more information or to book an event, contact the Simon & Schuster Speakers Bureau
at 1-866-248-3049 or visit our website at www.simonspeakers.com.
Jacket design by Laura Lyn DiSiena © 2020 by Simon & Schuster, Inc.
The text of this book was set in Adobe Garamond Pro.
Manufactured in the United States of America 0820 FFG
2 4 6 8 10 9 7 5 3 1
Library of Congress Control Number 2020940784
ISBN 9781534425811 (hc)
ISBN 9781534425835 (ebook)

For my dad

THE TIMELESS ONE

- ONE -

FORT FITZGERALD HAD TRAVELED TO other dimensions, flown with dragons, and fought off ancient horrors. He'd saved the city of London from a boy under the spell of Spirit magic; he'd held the sword of King Arthur—one of the Arthurs, at least—and made deals with the queen of the faeries.

One thing he'd never done, though, was raise a pet.

Sure, he'd always wanted one. He'd begged his father for years to get a cat, but his father had always refused, saying he was a dog person. So Fort eventually tried a different approach and asked if they could get a dog, only for his father to claim he'd always been a cat person, and just not into dogs. It'd been an ongoing battle that Fort had no chance of ever winning.

Well, at least until now, ever since Fort had arrived home after being expelled from the Oppenheimer School to find a surprise in his old room at his aunt's apartment—a surprise that Fort needed his friends to help him with *urgently*.

And so, the same night he arrived back at his aunt's place, without even having had enough time to unpack or, more importantly, actually spend time with his newly returned father, Fort opened four circles of green light in the cavern beneath the original Oppenheimer School—teleportation portals to four separate places.

Fort stepped through the first one, carrying a large green duffel bag that a few hours earlier had been filled with clothes but now had strange mewling noises coming from it. He winced at the sound as he looked around the cavern, barely lit by the glow of the portals.

This wasn't going to cut it, he decided. They'd need a bit more illumination, so he cast Heal Minor Wounds but didn't release it from his hand. The blue magic of the spell played off the surrounding rocks, giving just enough light to see by.

Behind him, the teleportation circle led back to his bedroom at his aunt Cora's apartment, and Fort looked at it with a long sigh. As excited as he was about the little newcomer in the duffel bag, a huge part of him wished he could be in that apartment, spending every possible minute that he could with his dad.

They'd barely had any time together, between getting his father released from the TDA after days of debriefing and medical checks. And then they'd been watched on the military transport the entire way home, until finally they'd been handed over to Fort's aunt.

Even now, he worried that he'd walk back through that portal and find out it was all a dream, that his father was still gone, taken by the Dracsi. Fort had to constantly remind himself that his dad was home, awake, and *safe*, and that he wasn't going anywhere. The reminder sent a shudder of relief through Fort.

Granted, it wasn't like everything else was okay. Cyrus was still missing after a fellow Carmarthen Academy classmate of his, William, had used Spirit magic on the silver-haired boy, forcing Cyrus to send himself somewhere else in time. Not to mention that Fort, Rachel, and Jia only had a year to find the Timeless One—the Old One of Time magic—and defeat him using Excalibur, or they'd be prisoners of the faerie queen of Avalon for the rest of time.

Oh, and where was Excalibur now? No one knew. Ellora, another Carmarthen Academy student, had jumped away in time with it, in order to keep the sword out of Colonel Charles's hands. That had been a smart move at the time, but now they had no idea where or when she was, or if she'd be coming back with the sword.

At least Merlin, a mysterious old man who seemed to be the mythical wizard from the King Arthur stories, had offered to train Rachel and Jia to fight the Timeless One. He hadn't mentioned training Fort, which had stung a bit, but Fort tried not to think about it with all the other things to worry about. Still, all the training in the world wouldn't help Rachel and Jia without Excalibur.

And yet, for all of that, Fort had his father back. Even just reminding himself that his father was here, home with family, made the rest of it feel like it wasn't so bad, that they'd be able to work it all out. It also didn't hurt that he was about to see his friends again after missing them for a few days, including one whom he hadn't seen for even longer in person—

Sierra Ramirez passed through the second portal from where she'd been hiding in the UK, looking tired but still thrilled, her eyes on the duffel bag in Fort's hands. Of course she'd already seen its contents from inside Fort's head using her Mind magic, but that didn't seem to dim her enthusiasm at all. "Fort!" she shouted, and gave him a huge hug, avoiding the bag.

"Sierra!" Fort shouted in return, only to get all the air

knocked out of his lungs as she squeezed him tightly. Even without any air, he couldn't believe how great it was to see her. He'd been so used to talking to a Mind magic version of Sierra that he had forgotten how much better it was to see her in person. There was no one he felt closer to, not even Cyrus, considering how much of Sierra's life he'd felt like he'd lived through her memories, back when he'd first arrived at the Oppenheimer School.

"It's been so long!" he told her when he could breathe again.

"I was in your head, like, twenty minutes ago," she said, grinning widely. "All I did since then was reach out to the other two, and show you where they'd be so you could open portals."

"I meant since we were together in person," he said, blushing a bit.

Sierra laughed, then hugged him again. "I know, Fitzgerald. I'm just messing with you! I can't believe how good it is to see you for reals too, instead of just in our minds—"

"Is this the big emergency?" said a voice, and Sierra immediately pulled back, turning to find Rachel Carter passing through her portal. "More importantly, where is—"

She was interrupted as Jia Liang arrived, throwing nervous glances back through her own teleportation circle. But as soon as Jia saw Rachel, both girls brightened and hugged with even more excitement than Sierra and Fort had. Fort rolled his eyes.

"You two just saw each other, like, a week ago," he said.

"Shut it, Fitzgerald," Rachel said to him over her shoulder.

"A lot has happened since then," Jia said as she pulled away from Rachel. "*You* two got expelled, and now they won't even let me go to class." She shook her head. "They're guarding me constantly, because Agent Cole thinks I'm going to steal a book of magic or something."

"Tell her we did that already," Rachel said, her tone joking but her face showing she wasn't thrilled about how Jia was being treated.

"I can't stay for more than a few minutes," Jia told them, giving Rachel an especially apologetic look. "I didn't want to take the chance of a guard walking in if we opened a portal to my room, so I told them I had to use the restroom. They won't wait long before checking on me." She glanced back through the portal behind her, where the ugly green tile of a bathroom in the second Oppenheimer School gave Fort unpleasant flashbacks.

"So what couldn't wait until tomorrow, Fort?" Rachel asked, her eyes on Jia.

"Um, here's the thing," he said, looking down at the ground, suddenly less excited about showing them now that he'd heard about what Jia was going through. "Remember when D'hea, the Old One of Healing, was going to destroy the world because he thought all the dragons were gone? We didn't know at the time that Damian actually *is* a dragon, so I convinced him to just make a new one out of magic. . . ."

Rachel began to groan loudly, while Jia just stared at him with her eyebrows raised. Meanwhile, Sierra had covered her mouth with her hand but wasn't able to hide her laughter. "Are you serious, Fort?" Rachel said. "You and I *just* got expelled. Jia's basically a prisoner—"

"I mean, Dr. Ambrose is sneaking me the Healing book every so often," Jia said.

"And you brought us here to share that you've got a *baby dragon* in there?" Rachel finished, pointing at the bag. "Is that what you're saying?"

A tiny *meep* escaped from the bag, followed by clawing noises.

"Well, kind of?" Fort said, and Sierra burst out laughing.

"Wait until you see this thing!" she said, laughing harder. "It thinks Fort is its daddy!"

Rachel snorted at this, while Jia reached up to cover her mouth, just like Sierra had a moment ago. "Come on, Sierra, this isn't funny," Jia said, but her voice broke a bit as she tried not to laugh.

"She's right, Mindflayer," Rachel said to Sierra, her own mouth twitching violently. "It's incredibly serious. I mean, does Fort even know how to change a diaper?"

This set all three of them off, laughing so hard that they missed the very annoyed looks Fort was giving them. "Hey, *all right*," he said, setting the bag down. "It's not funny, okay?"

"Fort, tell them what you named it!" Sierra said, having trouble breathing now.

"What?" Jia shouted. "You have a name already?"

"Please tell me it's Fort Jr.!" Rachel said.

Fort rolled his eyes. "First of all, it's a *she*. I think."

This set off even more gales of laughter.

"But her name isn't important!" Fort shouted over them. "What am I supposed to do with—"

"He named her *Ember*!" Sierra said. "Is that not the most adorable dragon name you've ever heard?"

Rachel and Jia both stopped laughing long enough to shout "Awwww!" at him, but that was the least of Fort's concerns. He should have warned Sierra, but there hadn't been time.

"*Don't* say her name, Sierra," Fort whispered, not liking how the duffel bag had stopped moving. "Ever since she learned it, she's been—"

A *whoosh* sound from within confirmed his worst fears as a small flame began to spread through the duffel bag.

"Nice!" Rachel said, quickly snuffing it out with a magical gust of wind. "You didn't say she was already breathing fire!"

A low growl emerged from the burned section of the bag, and slowly a scaly black head about the size of an apple pushed out. Ember's black scales glinted in the light of the green portals, and her red eyes stared suspiciously at Jia, Rachel, and Sierra. Behind her, wings the size of her body unfurled, and she briefly stretched them before wrapping them back around herself protectively.

Rachel gasped. "I take it all back—she's the cutest thing ever, and I *want* her." She leaned down, extending a hand. "She's like the size of a house cat. Come here, Ember!"

"No!" Fort shouted as Sierra quickly stepped out of the way, knowing what was coming. Ember pulled in a deep breath, ready to send out another plume of fire, but Fort picked up the bag before she could unleash her flames on Rachel and turned the tiny dragon to face him. "No, dragon, we do *not* set people on fire!"

The dragon began to purr, rubbing her cheeks full of fire against Fort's hand. He patted her head awkwardly. "Good girl, Ember. Good girl!"

Immediately she released a plume of fire several dozen feet long off over his shoulder, the heat of which almost caused him to drop the bag.

"Whoa!" Rachel said, scooting back from where she'd been squatting. "Looks like someone is cranky!"

Ember's eyes darkened, and she turned back to Rachel and Jia, smoke rising from her nostrils. "She would have burned down my aunt's apartment if I hadn't teleported her flame away," Fort said, spinning the duffel bag so she couldn't see his friends. "I think she might be hungry." He picked her up to look her in the eye. "No more fire when people say your name, okay? *Okay?*"

She stared back at him for a moment, then licked him sloppily on the face.

"What do dragons eat?" Jia asked. "If it's people, I'm not okay with that."

"Damian always liked hamburgers," Sierra said, then

coughed to hide another laugh as Fort shot her a dirty look.

"That was in his human form," Fort said. "D'hea, the Old One of Healing, said dragons ate gold and silver." Ember slowly climbed out of the bag and up onto Fort's body, digging her claws painfully into his chest to climb up to his shoulder. From there, she curled her long neck around his protectively, her eyes still watching the others with suspicion. "Is that something you can magic up, Rachel?"

"Gold and silver?" Rachel said. "You think I wouldn't have done that for some spare cash if I could?"

"It must be possible," Jia told her. "Your magic is all about elemental control, after all. We probably just haven't found the right combination of words."

Rachel looked at her thoughtfully. "Maybe, but I don't know that I have any spell words for changing something into something else."

Jia wrinkled her nose. "This is why the books are so frustrating. I know a few different words for that, but if I tell them to you, you won't be able to remember them. We need to figure out a way around that."

"*Hello*, baby dragon over here!" Fort said, waving his hand. Ember raised her claws and mimicked him, giving the others an even dirtier look. "I can't exactly wait around for you to figure out how to turn rocks into gold. I need to feed her something soon, and then, I don't know, get her somewhere safe to hide, like a cave or—"

"Hey!" Rachel shouted indignantly, as Jia looked just as shocked. "Are you joking? You can't just abandon a baby animal like that!"

"She's a *dragon*!" Fort said, as Ember growled at Rachel. "I'm pretty sure she can take care of herself!"

"She's a baby and seems to think you're her mom!" Rachel said. "You *have* to take care of her, Fort. She doesn't have anyone else!"

"Seriously, Fort," Jia said. "The fact that she's a dragon makes it even more important that you watch over her. Think about what kind of panic there'd be if someone found her. Or even worse, if Colonel Charles got ahold of her."

Fort opened his mouth to respond but had no idea what to say. He couldn't keep a *dragon*, not in an apartment . . . not even if he was still at the Oppenheimer School. If he somehow was able to keep Ember hidden, she still needed to eat, not to mention probably go for walks or something. And what about when he started school again? He couldn't take her there, not without setting off mass hysteria.

"See?" Sierra said to him. "This is what I've been saying. She's *yours*, Fort. Think of her as a pet."

"Actually, that's a great idea," Jia said, and held up her hand. It began to glow with blue Healing magic, and Ember hissed at her warily, but as the magic filled the little dragon, she quickly calmed down, then fell asleep on Fort's shoulder.

"Hey, what'd you do?" Fort said, trying to make sure his dragon was okay.

"I put her to sleep—calm down," Jia said, unleashing a second spell. As the blue light passed over the slumbering dragon, Ember's black scales began to morph into fur. Her ears pulled in, becoming more of a small triangle on top of her now rounder head, and whiskers pushed out of her snout.

And just like that, a small black kitten snored quietly on Fort's shoulder. Apparently Jia's spell took age into account, because Ember was even smaller as a cat than she'd been as a dragon.

"There," Jia said with some satisfaction. "That should solve all your problems."

"Um, what?" Fort said incredulously, not even able to count the number of ways that was wrong.

"Now you can keep her at your aunt's place with no problems!" Jia said, then glanced at Rachel. "See? That's just *one* of my changing spells. We really need to figure out how to swap spell words, so you can use it to change lead into gold or whatever."

"Totally," Rachel said. "And I'm glad we were able to solve your problem for you, Fort. You're welcome."

"Um, what?" Fort said again. "This doesn't solve *anything*—"

"Since we're already here for Fort's fake emergency, let's quickly cover the actual important stuff," Rachel continued, ignoring him. She held out her hand to count on her fingers. "One, we need to find Excalibur, from whatever time Ellora sent it to; two, we need to track down Merlin, so he can train Jia and me like he promised, which is a problem since Damian destroyed Merlin's cottage, and we might not be able to find him now; and three, we'll need to somehow locate the Timeless One, the Old One of Time magic, who could literally be anywhere or any*when* in time. And we need to do all of that within a year, or the faerie queen will basically imprison us in her world for the rest of our lives." She paused, then looked up at Ember, asleep. "Oh, and four, I'm going to need to cuddle that cat ASAP!"

- TWO -

WHOA!" FORT SAID. "HOLD ON. Just because Ember's now a cat doesn't mean this is all solved. She's still a dragon, and eventually she's going to go back to her normal form. Plus, we didn't solve the problem of what to feed her!"

"She's a literal cat now, so you should be able to feed her cat food," Jia said. "If Damian can eat hamburgers in human form with no problems, then she should be fine too."

"And you know who'd probably know what to do with her?" Rachel asked. "*Merlin*. Which means we're back to the important stuff."

"Wasn't he just, like, a hologram?" Sierra asked. "From what I saw in Fort's memories, it was a machine of some kind that he was using to appear. If that got destroyed with the cottage, I'm not sure we're going to find him that easily."

15

"I think he was communicating from another time," Jia said. "It was a bit confusing, and there was a lot going on. Still, he invited us to train with him, so maybe he'll find *us*—"

A door closing back through Jia's portal made them all go silent. Jia's eyes widened, and she immediately slipped back through the glowing circle, waving her hand at them all to say good-bye.

Fort quickly closed the portal behind her, and Rachel sighed loudly. "Ugh, this is the worst," she said. "I *really* hate that she's stuck there. She sounds miserable."

"I could get her out if you want," Sierra said. "Well, unless that horrible Agent Cole woman is wearing one of my amulets, which I'm sure she is." She paused. "Still, that didn't stop me when Colonel Charles wore one. We never did figure out how I could do all of that, did we?"

Fort recalled the moment when he and Sierra were trapped in Colonel Charles's office, Sierra's mind in the body of Dr. Opps. The colonel had known it was her and used one of her own Mind magic items on her, trapping her in Dr. Opps's body, which had been incredibly painful, and stopped her from using her magic.

And yet, somehow, she'd broken free and used Mind magic she hadn't ever learned, some kind of telekinesis, to destroy the amulet around Colonel Charles's neck. So much had happened since then that Fort had almost forgotten about it.

Rachel, though, barely seemed to have heard. "Thanks for keeping us in contact, Sierra," she said, staring off into space. "She's just so lonely there now, stuck in her room. She only ever sees Dr. Ambrose and that Sebastian jerk, who told her that Agent Cole is having the healers start learning spells that Dr. Ambrose banned previously. Things are falling apart there."

Banned spells? The only one Fort had heard about was Ethereal Spirit, which turned the caster into a ghost, basically, and let them pass through solid objects. That kind of magic in Colonel Charles's and Agent Cole's hands would definitely lead to bad things.

But that was going to have to wait. First they had to figure out what to do with Ember, find Merlin, find Excalibur, make sure Rachel got trained with the sword, find the Timeless One so she could defeat him . . . there was so much to do that the Oppenheimer School just wasn't the worst problem right now.

Though who knew how long *that'd* last.

"I'll keep you two connected as much as I can," Sierra told Rachel, who gave her a thankful smile. "At least Jia will have you around whenever she wants."

"You're a lifesaver," Rachel said. "Where are you, anyway, when you're not meeting with us here? Still in the UK?"

Sierra nodded. "I, um, am tying up some loose ends," she said, looking down at the floor. "You know, the book of Spirit magic needs to be found. And we never did locate the Time book."

"Not to mention there's an insane dragon somewhere out there still, since Damian got away," Fort said, and frowned as Sierra winced. "What?"

"Nothing," she said, and his frown deepened. Considering how close they'd become since he'd accidentally gotten connected to her and seen her memories while she'd been in a coma when he'd first come to the Oppenheimer School, it seemed odd for her not to be telling him something. But whatever it was, it could wait.

"Let us know if you find the books, and we'll come grab them," Rachel told her. "Or if your magic detects anything about Merlin or the Timeless One, of course. Or Ellora."

"Or Cyrus," Fort said. "William used Spirit magic on him, making Cyrus send himself somewhere else in time, but it should wear off eventually, I'd hope. So wherever Cyrus is, hopefully it's where he wants to be."

"I'm sure he's fine," Sierra said as Ember stirred on Fort's shoulder, and he absently reached up to scratch her chin. She stretched as he did and settled back in. "For all we know, he'll be waiting for us whenever we find Merlin."

"I *really* need one of those," Rachel said, staring at Ember on Fort's shoulder. She shook her head, as if pulling herself out of a daze, and clapped her hands. "Okay, then we've all got our jobs. Fort, you take care of Fort Jr. there for now. Then as soon as we can both get away, we'll go to Merlin's cottage, or whatever's left of it, and see what we can find."

"It might be a few days," Fort said, still rubbing Ember's chin. "I'm starting at a new school tomorrow. You know, the nonmagic kind."

"Already?" Rachel said, her eyebrows flying up. "You just got home!"

"I think my dad just wants things back to normal," Fort said with a sigh. "And that includes school. I wouldn't have minded waiting a few weeks, just to deal with everything else first."

"He just doesn't want to go back to math class," Sierra told Rachel. "I offered to Mind magic him into knowing everything that his teacher knows, but for some reason, he said no."

"You'd probably wipe my memories by accident," Fort said. "Then *you'll* have to change a dragon's diapers."

"I'll just Mind magic someone into being a nanny," Sierra said.

"You two are so strange," Rachel said, looking back and forth between Fort and Sierra. Then she turned to Ember and grinned. "But *you*, I want to eat for *dinner*!"

With that, she petted the cat on Fort's neck, then stepped back through the portal to her bedroom at her parents' house.

"I'll help you with your dad and aunt," Sierra said as Fort closed Rachel's portal. "You know, make them think Ember's a stray you found, so they're okay with taking her in. If you want me to."

Fort nodded. "That'd be good. I still need to figure out what I'm going to do with her, but at least this will be easier than living with a dragon baby."

Something sharp attacked his ear. "Hey!" he yelled, reaching over to pull Ember off him. "No biting, young lady!"

"You know, I'm not sure she speaks English," Sierra said with a smile.

The cat stared at Fort for a moment. "Volai hrana," she said, then closed her eyes and fell back asleep.

- THREE -

ORT AND SIERRA SPENT THE NEXT TEN
minutes trying to wake Ember up, not even sure if
they'd really heard her speak for real. But while they'd
managed to annoy her a bunch, she hadn't repeated whatever
those words had been and instead just ended up shooting fire
at them so they'd stop irritating her.

How she could still do *that* as a cat, Fort didn't even want to
know, but it wasn't going to make his life any easier.

Now, an hour later, Fort lay on his bed, staring at the cat
noisily inhaling wet cat food on the floor in front of him. He'd
sent Sierra back to the UK and teleported himself to the grocery store to pick up food for the dragon, which apparently
was working out okay. Ember had instantly woken back up as
he opened the can, and had laid right into three of them so far,
making Fort glad he'd bought as much as he had money for.

But as busy as she was eating, she still hadn't said another word, if she actually had to begin with.

Fort shook his head, pretty sure he'd imagined it. How could Ember have spoken, after literally just being born earlier that day? There was no way, not even for a magical creature.

Except she *did* understand her name already, which was pretty much impossible for any human baby. Not to mention the fact that she breathed fire, so maybe comparing her to other, nonmagical animals didn't make any sense.

But even so, she'd just emerged from her egg, like, six hours ago. And she was a *cat*. How could she be speaking?

"Ember?" he whispered. "Do you understand what I'm saying?"

Ember completely ignored him, working on her fourth can. Fair enough. Ignoring him *was* fairly catlike, especially with food around.

He sighed and rolled over onto his back, staring at his ceiling. Sierra claimed she wasn't getting anything from reading Ember's mind. But who knew if Mind magic even worked on animals, let alone dragons, who were literally *made* from magic? Maybe they were resistant to magic, or their thoughts were so foreign that Sierra couldn't even sense them.

"I hope you *can* talk, Ember," Fort said, sighing heavily as he lay on his bed. "Then you can tell me what to do with you."

"Oh, I thought we were keeping her," said a voice, and Fort almost fell off the bed in surprise. He turned over to find his father standing in his door with a smile. "Sorry I didn't knock," his dad said, "but I wanted to meet your stray officially."

In spite of being surprised, Fort couldn't help but smile back, still not believing that his father could be standing here, in his doorway. He'd wanted to come back and spend more time with his dad but wasn't quite sure what Ember would decide to do, even as a kitten.

At least things had worked out well with Sierra convincing both his father and Aunt Cora that Ember was a neighborhood stray and had shown up at Fort's window, meowing to be let in from the cold. She'd even pushed them to agree when Fort pointed out that he could use a pet after everything he'd gone through, which was nice, because the last thing Fort wanted to do at the moment was argue with his dad.

"Her name is Ember," Fort said to his dad, who slowly approached the cat and squatted down where she ate. Fort watched them both warily, waiting for the moment that he'd have to rescue his father from a plume of fire, but the cat just looked up briefly, hissed loudly enough to panic Fort, but then thankfully turned back to her food.

"Huh," his dad said as Fort's heart rate slowly returned to normal. "Not so friendly, I see."

"She hates everyone," Fort agreed. "You should have seen how she was around . . ." He trailed off as he realized he couldn't exactly admit that Ember had met his friends. "Um, around the neighbors, according to Aunt Cora."

"Well, she's a cat," his father said, leaning back against the wall a few feet away from Ember, which made Fort feel a little less anxious. "That's pretty typical, I'm told. Me, I was always a dog person."

"Oh yeah?" Fort said, smiling. "So you'd be okay with us getting a dog, too?"

His father shrugged. "Eh, dogs aren't my thing. I'm honestly more of a turtle person, as you know." He looked up at Fort. "Hey. You can tell me if I'm rushing you, going back to school already. We've barely had any time together, between the army doing all their tests on me, and then them sending us home from wherever they were. I think it'll be good to get back to normal, but if you're not ready . . . ?"

"Oh, I'm fine," Fort said, figuring if he could handle a giant

Spirit magic monster, he could probably handle a new school, but mostly just not wanting his father to worry. "And you're right: Things going back to normal wouldn't be the worst thing. All I care about is that you're here, and safe."

"Ditto, kiddo," his father said with a small smile, then sighed. "I can't imagine how . . . unsettled you've been these past six months. And everything that's happened since I've been gone! It's all so unbelievable. Monsters in Washington, D.C., and now London? Some flying reptile in the skies over major cities around the world? I feel like I'm still asleep, still dreaming!"

"*Don't even joke,*" Fort said, a little more firmly than he'd intended. "You're awake now, and home, and you're not going anywhere. And any time you go to sleep, I'm going to be waking you up every hour just to make sure you're still with us."

His dad smiled at that. "That *might* be going a bit overboard, but I'm okay with it." His smile faded, and he gave Fort a serious look. "But you don't have to worry. I'm not leaving you, Fort, not again. You've got my word on that."

"I better have it," Fort said, forcing a smile.

His father crossed his heart, then shook his head. "I wish I knew more about what was going on. Cora's been telling me that the grocery stores basically empty out every time there's a new attack, like there's a huge blizzard coming or something. That's why she didn't have any food tonight, after everything that happened a few days ago in London. The whole city stocked up, and the stores have nothing left."

Fort nodded, not really knowing what to say. He could tell his father everything, from the Oppenheimer School to Damian summoning the Old Ones and causing the attack in D.C. to the part he played in it all, including the fact that it was him flying over all the cities in the world in the claw of D'hea, the Old One of Healing magic in the form of a dragon. Everything his father wanted to know, Fort could explain, probably in far too much detail.

But the military had told his father that they'd be checking in on him in a few weeks, just to be sure he was okay. And what would they do if suddenly Fort's father knew all about the books of magic? Colonel Charles would know that Fort had faked his memory erasure, and he and Rachel would both be caught. Not to mention that his father's memories would probably be erased too.

Besides, all in all, Fort was pretty sure his father wouldn't love hearing how he'd been turned into a giant monster, the same kind that had attacked D.C. in the first place. And once

Fort, Rachel, and Jia defeated the Timeless One, hopefully the Old Ones wouldn't be a threat anymore, and everything could go back to normal, at least relatively.

"I wish I knew too," Fort said finally as Ember hiccupped on the floor, then leaped up to the bed next to him and settled herself on his legs, glaring at his dad. He rubbed her head, both to calm her down, just in case, and because she really was a cute cat. She purred loudly in response, making his heart almost burst from how adorable she was.

"You're sure about school?" his father said. "I really don't mind telling them you've changed your mind and decided to wait a few weeks. We could take a trip, get out and see the sights before you're back behind a desk. Wherever you want to go, it's on me." He frowned. "Or it would be if I had any money. Did you know when you're assumed dead from a monster attack, they close all your bank accounts? Pretty rude, I say."

"So inconsiderate," Fort said, wishing Rachel really could create gold. But his father would figure something out. Aunt Cora had talked about maybe starting some sort of fundraiser for them, since there wasn't much money left over from Fort's inheritance when everyone thought his father *had* passed away.

"Cora said she'd been in touch with the people at my old

job, but they'd already rehired for my position," his dad said, shrugging. "I guess they couldn't wait for me to miraculously reappear. They just have no faith in your old man. But we'll soldier on. . . ." He paused, as if considering his own words. "By which I mean I *could* join the army and become a soldier. Pay them back for finding me, wherever I was, and bringing me home. They'd get me into shape, at least. Think I could jump in as, like, a major or a colonel or something?"

Fort's blood froze in his veins. "*Colonel?* Why did you say that? What about a colonel?" And then he realized what his father *had* said and turned bright red. "I mean, um, they'd just make you a joint chief or something!"

His father cracked all of his knuckles, then looked down at his hands sadly. "Maybe a joint apprentice, until I get better at that." He laughed at his own joke far too hard.

Fort groaned loudly, glad he'd been able to cover his outburst, and his father tousled his hair just like he'd always done. Even that small a gesture made Fort's chest tighten, and he had to stop himself from jumping up and hugging the man.

"I really am fine, Fort," his dad said. "Whatever happened to me, wherever the army found me, none of that matters now, because I'm home. And from here on, the two of us will always be together. You know, along with my sister-in-law, until we find a place to stay, and probably for the holidays. And that cat, too, of course." He glanced down at Ember. "Is it me, or does she look like she wants to eat me?"

"Volai hrana," Ember said, glaring at his dad.

Fort's heart immediately began to race again.

"Whoa, was that her stomach making that noise?" his father asked. "She must really have been hungry!"

"Yup!" Fort said, quickly standing up and pushing his dad toward the door before Ember could say anything else. "*Very* hungry. Which means I should feed her again! And don't worry about me, school will be fine, you'll find a new job, everything will be good, all good, nothing bad. Anyway, I'll feed her now and go to bed. Early morning with school, good night, Dad!"

And with that, he pushed his father out of the room, then closed the door hard, wishing it had a lock or something.

"What was *that*?" he whispered at Ember. "You can't just start talking whenever you want!"

"Sa, solip puv," the cat said, then nodded at the empty dish on the floor. "Volai hrana!"

- FOUR -

FORT DIDN'T GET ANY SLEEP THAT
night. In a normal world, knowing he'd be starting a
new school in the morning would have been enough
to keep him awake, but this time, it was the thought of leaving
a wild baby dragon—one who spoke an unknown language—
in an apartment alone with his father and aunt.

What if Ember tried talking to them? Or worse, straight-up
attacked one of the two?

"I left the cat in my room with a clean litter box and food,"
he told them both the next morning at breakfast. "I think she'll
be more comfortable there while I'm gone. You know, with my
scent on everything and all. So maybe don't go in there, just so
she can get used to things." He waited nervously, hoping they
wouldn't object.

Fortunately, neither his aunt nor his dad seemed to even give it much thought. "Makes sense," Aunt Cora said absently as she looked at a list the school had sent over. "Are you sure you have everything you need, Forsythe? Pens, notebooks, money for lunch?"

Fort patted his backpack behind him on the chair as he cut into his pancakes, just relieved that Ember's imprisonment wasn't going to be a problem. "All set," he said, shoving a bite in his mouth.

"You sure you don't want me to drive you?" his father asked, then turned red. "Ah, not that I have a car. I could ride to school with you on the bus, though! Sit next to you, share all the fun gossip, that kind of thing."

Fort almost choked on his pancakes before realizing his father wasn't serious, then rolled his eyes reflexively. As far as Fort was concerned, his dad could make all the terrible jokes he wanted, now that he was back, and Fort would enjoy every one of them. But he wasn't going to let his father know that. "No, I'm good, thanks. Those bus seats aren't that big."

"Your loss," his dad said, but grinned at him.

Good-byes took longer than Fort had expected on both sides. At first, his father wouldn't let him out of a hug, but when Fort was finally released, he found he wasn't ready to go yet either.

This would be the first time he'd be leaving his father—other than by teleporting—and part of him worried about what might happen if Fort wasn't there to watch over him.

Still, he had to let his dad go be free sometime, and going to regular, everyday nonmagic school was going to be weirdly relaxing after what he'd been through at the Oppenheimer School. Sure, it was still school, but at least he wouldn't be dealing with evil otherworldly horrors, hurrying to learn magic spells so he wasn't kicked out, or bargaining with faeries.

Homework and tests just didn't seem so bad in comparison.

Fort walked out the apartment door with one last look at his dad and aunt, then turned and almost ran down the stairs, 100 percent ready for some normalcy.

"Hey, you," someone said from his right. "Human kid. *Finally*. I've been waiting all morning!"

Fort froze and slowly turned to see who was speaking to him, only to almost teleport away instantly when he did.

A girl around his age stood tapping her foot in the middle of the sidewalk, which was all fine. The weird part was her green skin and bright yellow hair. And what was worse, he *recognized* her.

This was the faerie girl who'd tried to buy Damian from

them, back in Avalon, before disappearing with Ellora to meet the faerie queen.

"*You?*" he said, barely able to get the word out. He looked around quickly, but thankfully the sidewalk was empty for the moment. Still, it wouldn't be long before someone else showed up and saw this girl with green skin. "What are you *doing* here? You can't be here!"

"What do you *think* I'm doing here?" she asked, giving him an impatient look. "Do I really need to spell it out for you?"

"Yes!" Fort shouted, pushing her behind a nearby wall, his heart racing now. "You can't let anyone see you like this! They'll know you aren't human!" And as panicked as everyone was about London being destroyed, a girl with green skin was not going to get overlooked.

"What are you talking about?" she asked, a confused expression passing over her face. "I look completely human. See?" She lifted up her hair, revealing rounded ears. "Trust me, I did my research. I blend in completely."

"*We don't have green skin,*" Fort hissed at her.

"What, really?" she said, looking as surprised as he was about seeing her in the first place. "Why not?"

"Because we don't come in that color!" Fort whispered as a car turned onto the street, a few yards away. He quickly moved to stand in front of the faerie girl, pretending he was on his phone, barely breathing until the car passed by. As he finally took in some air, he turned back to find her staring at him weirdly.

"This is going to be harder than I thought, clearly," she said. "You people make no sense. Okay. So what colors *are* you?"

"I don't know—it depends on a lot of things," Fort said, then realized what he was saying. "Wait, that doesn't matter. You can't be here! Why *are* you even here?"

"I really thought you'd have figured it out," the girl said, raising an eyebrow. She stared at him for a moment, then her skin faded from green to a shade that matched Fort's. "There. Now no one will notice me."

He blinked a few times. "How did you do that?"

"Magic, obviously," she said. "I thought you people knew how to cast spells."

"We can," he told her. "But it usually has, I don't know, a glow."

She crinkled her nose. "Oh, seriously? You're using *their* kind?" She gave him a smug look. "Tylwyth Teg use *natural* magic. It's so much less involved."

Fort just stared at her for a moment, not understanding any

34

of this. "Can we get back to why you're here? Pretend I have no idea, and tell me slowly."

She sniffed. "It's not like I have to pretend. You made a bargain with my queen, and she's sent me to collect. Why *else* would I be here?" She seemed to consider this. "Though I'm sure the queen would have sent someone else if she weren't annoyed with *me* for trying to show your human companion the way to her. As if you wouldn't have found your way there on your own. But no, *I* get punished because 'humans cannot be trusted, only tricked.'" She rolled her eyes.

Fort felt his entire body go ice cold. "A bargain?" he whispered, backing away from her in horror. The faerie queen had given him a green jewel to make sure his father would be protected, which Fort had assumed would keep his dad safe when Ellora removed him from time.

Instead, it'd fixed his father so that the coming world war set off by his father's new ability to use magic wouldn't happen. And for that, Fort owed the faerie queen everything.

He just hadn't expected to be paying her back so soon. Or by way of a faerie showing up randomly on the street.

"Yes, a bargain," the faerie said, looking at him closely. "You're not too quick, are you?"

"What is it that she wants?" Fort asked, dreading the answer as a chill passed through him. "My firstborn child? My sense of sarcasm? My voice? Do I get to pick between options or something?"

The faerie's eyes lit up. "No, but I like where your head is at. Remember those things you just offered, and I'll make you a deal for them later. I have a piece of the North Wind that would be a great trade for your voice. Plus, you could swallow it and use it to howl, so it's not like you'd be *completely* speechless—"

"What does she want?" Fort practically screamed, then forced himself to quiet down as someone opened their door up the street, staring at them curiously. With the faerie girl no longer green, she didn't stick out as much, but either way, Fort needed her gone as soon as possible.

The girl moved in close, looking up and down the street to make sure no one was listening. "She wants your *dragon*," she whispered, then stepped back and clapped a hand on his shoulder. "Oh, by the way, my name is Xenea. Nice to meet you!"

- FIVE -

FORT SUDDENLY FOUND IT REALLY hard to breathe. "My . . . dragon?" he said, his voice just barely above a whisper.

Xenea nodded. "That's what I'm here for." She stuck out her hands and opened and closed them in a "gimme" gesture. "Any time now. I don't have all day."

Fort's mind raced as he stared at the girl, not trusting her or her queen in the slightest. Yes, he'd made a deal, but not for a living creature! What would the faeries do with a dragon? And how did the queen know he even had one?

Xenea started tapping her foot. "Is it . . . close by?" she said, glancing around. "Are we going to need to travel? What are we waiting for?"

"What . . . do you want the dragon for?" he asked, still trying to decide what to do. If the faeries loved dragons, and could raise Ember properly, maybe he *should* give her to Xenea, so she could take her away to safety.

"Oh, to use it as a hostage, I imagine," Xenea said, rolling her eyes. "There are a bunch of elder dragons on Avalon that refuse to give up their land to my queen, and it's always bothered her, so I'd guess she'd try to give them your dragon as a trade. And if they don't take it . . ." She gave him an evil grin. "Well, we wouldn't want the dragon to get hurt, now, would we?"

"Whoa!" Fort shouted, stepping backward with his hands up. "I'm not handing anything over to you so you can hurt it!" Okay, he hadn't known Ember that long, but even if she weren't incredibly cute and attached to him, there was no way he was giving her—or *anyone*—to the queen when Ember might be injured, or worse!

"I don't *know* that she's going to hurt it," Xenea said, sounding exasperated. "I said I'd *guess* that she would. There's a chance the dragons will take it in trade, too! They're all old, and I'm told there hasn't been a new one born in a few thousand years, so a young one would be worth a lot to them." She scrunched up her face. "Worth a lot to *me*, too, if you'd just let me have it earlier, like I asked."

Earlier? What was she . . . Wait, was she talking about

Damian right now? "You're saying you want that same dragon, then?" Fort said, suddenly feeling a lot less concerned. "The one that looked like a teenage boy?"

She gave him a strange look. "I assumed that, yes. She just said that you would be in contact with a dragon, and I should come to retrieve it. Why, how many dragons are you in possession of?" She leaned in closer, giving him a suspicious glare.

"Just the one!" Fort said quickly, blinking rapidly as he tried to figure out how to get rid of the faerie girl. "But I'm not in *possession* of him. He's his own person. I don't even know where he is. So you should probably go looking for him, maybe in the UK—"

"No, the queen was very clear that you'd have the dragon," Xenea said, still looking unconvinced. "Are you absolutely sure you don't have him in a cave somewhere?"

"I promise you, I do not have Damian at all, let alone in a cave," Fort said, breathing a sigh of relief. "But seriously, I'd look in Britain, where—"

"If he's not here now, then he'll probably come back," Xenea said, nodding to herself, before cringing. "Which means I'm stuck with you until he does. Ugh." She turned back to the street as if seeing it for the first time. "What sort of land *is* this, anyway? You live in stone houses when there's a perfectly good wooded area right over this path?" She pointed at the park across from Fort's aunt's apartment. "You people really *are* backward."

Before Fort could even respond, a rumble down the street told him that the school bus was almost here, and the panic set back in. "I have to go," he told Xenea, backing away from her. "But I'll be back later. You can wait for me in that wooded area, okay? I promise, I won't see any dragons while I'm gone."

She sighed, shaking her head as the bus turned the corner. "No, if you're going somewhere, I'm coming too. I have to at least confirm this dragon isn't there first." She paused. "Where exactly are we going?"

"To a school," Fort said, his nervousness increasing as the bus drew closer. "You wouldn't like it. It's a lot of learning about, I don't know, human stuff—"

Xenea's eyes lit up at that. "Really? That might actually come in handy, as the queen says we'll be taking back our la . . ." She trailed off and blinked. "I mean, so I can learn more about your people."

Fort had no idea what all of *that* meant, but now it was too late, and the school bus was pulling up. He couldn't let this

40

THE TIMELESS ONE

faerie girl come to school with him . . . but wouldn't it be more dangerous to leave her here, right outside his aunt's apartment where Ember was?

As much as he wanted to find a safe place for the baby dragon, that did *not* include handing her over to the faerie queen. He hadn't known the baby dragon for more than one night now, but the last thing he was going to do was let some stranger touch *his* cat-dragon. *That* was not going to happen!

At least now Fort knew that apparently there were dragons on Avalon, which meant that if he could figure out a way to do it, he could send Ember to *them* to be raised. All he'd need was his Reopen Portal spell, and she'd be safe. But he'd cast his last instance of that spell to get them to Avalon in the first place.

But right now, there were more important things to worry about, like how to get rid of Xenea. As the bus pulled up in front of them, a whirlwind of excuses passed through Fort's mind, but before he could even begin to say something, Xenea pushed past him and entered the school bus.

Oh *no*.

He quickly followed the faerie girl up the steps, his heart ready to explode out of his chest.

Everyone stared, but fortunately not in a panicked way, like

41

they should have been, considering a magical creature had just walked onto their bus. No, they were watching her more like she was just a new student, the same way they eyed Fort, with both suspicion and curiosity.

Before Fort could figure out a way to fix things, the door behind them closed, and the bus driver told them to take a seat.

Fort ducked into the first seat he came to, and Xenea followed him, touching the plastic seat cover with distaste. "What is this made of?" she asked, far too loudly. "It looks like leather, but this is no beast that I've ever seen. Do humans raise this green animal?"

"It's plastic—it's fake," he whispered. "You shouldn't be here, you know. We'll both get in trouble. They'll know you don't belong here!"

"Oh, it'll be fine," she said, waving a hand absently. "What's this vehicular conveyance we're on? What sort of magic does it use to move? Why do you look like you're going to be sick?"

"It's a school bus," he told her. "It's taking us to school, like I said, where they'll ask who you are and why you're there, since you aren't enrolled at the school, and then they'll probably hand us both over to the army or something."

"You didn't answer about what magic makes the school bus run," she reminded him, standing up to look around.

He quickly pulled her back down, his face glowing red. "The bus doesn't *use* magic," Fort hissed at her. "It's got an engine, and it runs on gasoline. And I probably look like I'm going to be sick because—"

"I've never seen you two before," interrupted a boy from across the aisle. "Are you new?"

Before Fort could stop her, Xenea turned to him and smiled. "New to your school bus? Yes. New to this world?" She gave Fort a quick wink. "Of course not! We've both been here our whole lives, fellow human."

- SIX -

FORT BLUSHED EVEN HARDER, HIS
face feeling like it was on fire, and he leaned
past Xenea to wave at the boy. "Sorry about her,"
he said. "She's just tired and likes to talk nonsense sometimes."

The boy gave Fort a questioning glance. "What do you
mean? She sounds normal to me."

"Yeah, what *are* you talking about?" Xenea asked, looking as
confused as their neighbor across the aisle.

"I just . . . oh, forget it," Fort said, not understanding the
other boy's confusion. He sank back into the plastic seat, trying
to pretend none of this was happening, that a faerie girl wasn't
following him to school and having a conversation where she
said things like "fellow human."

At least it couldn't get any worse than that—

"So what's your name, human boy?" Xenea asked the boy. "You may call me Xenea."

"Yejun," the boy said with a smile. "Where are you from, Xenea? It sounds like you've got an English accent, at least a bit."

"Oh, I'm from Earth, just as you are," she said, and Fort groaned loudly.

"She *is* from the UK, yeah," Fort told the boy. "That's why she's acting so strangely. It's a cultural thing."

"Okay, but she's *not* acting strangely," Yejun said. "Why do you keep saying she is?"

Fort opened his mouth to respond, then shook his head, not even knowing where to start. "You're right. I'm sorry."

"Excuse him," Xenea said. "He's in the middle of learning a life lesson about paying off his debts. Tell me, Yejun, about this place of learning we're traveling to, this *school*. Who runs it? Must we pay any fealty to them?"

Fealty? Fort waited for a reaction to that, knowing there was no way this kid could let that go.

"Oh, it's run by our principal, Mrs. MacNamara," Yejun said completely normally. "And you don't need to pay her any fealty. I'm not even sure what that means."

Fort's mouth dropped open as he just stared at Yejun, who gave him an odd look in return. How was he so calmly answering all of her ridiculous questions? He had to know that people from the UK didn't ask about paying fealty to school principals, not to mention probably didn't say they were from Earth, either.

And yet, here he was, acting like this was all completely ordinary. Was Yejun some kind of extradimensional creature too? Were there more of them at schools now? How many faeries were on this planet, anyway?

"Is there anything I should know about this MacNamara human?" Xenea asked. "For instance, the queen where I come from—by which I mean Earth, of course—does not react well to impoliteness, or if you break a covenant with her. Either one can lead to years in the dungeon."

Again, Yejun shrugged at this like Xenea hadn't just popped the word "dungeon" into the conversation. "Oh, sure, you should be polite, but she's not bad. She loves really bad jokes, so that's the only thing you have to watch out for. No dungeons. That might just be a UK thing."

Xenea nodded. "Bad jokes? I *shall* watch out for them. Can they be dangerous?"

"Only to anyone with a sense of humor," Yejun said with a smile.

"Hmm, that would include me," Xenea said. "Thanks for the warning, fellow human." Fort sighed loudly enough to make her pause, but she didn't wait long before continuing. "I might come to you later for more information. Please don't hold back if you think there are things my friend and I should know."

"Sure, and it's nice to meet you," Yejun said. "What's your friend's name, by the way?"

"Forsythe," she said, nodding at Fort.

"Forsythe, you should know that we don't judge other people's cultures here," Yejun said, giving him a sort of pitying look. "It's not okay. Everyone's from somewhere else, you know?"

That was it. "I *do* know that!" Fort shouted, as other kids turned to look. "And I don't care where other people are from. I just thought that *you* . . . and what she said . . . how she sounded . . ." He trailed off, noticing just how much of the bus was staring now.

"Sounded . . . what?" Yejun said. "Like she comes from a country that just went through something horrible less than a week ago? Wow, man."

Fort's mouth opened and closed as he had literally no idea where to even begin to explain. When Yejun finally turned away, Fort leaned in toward Xenea. "What did you do to him?" he hissed.

"What?" Xenea asked, looking confused, only to smile a second later as if she'd just realized what he was talking about. "*Oh*, do you mean the glamour? That's nothing." She paused, giving him a questioning look. "You really don't know about glamours?"

"No, I *don't*," Fort said, his irritation rising with his embarrassment over several kids still looking at him. "But you can't just use magic on random people!"

"Oh, it's *barely* even magic," Xenea said, shrugging. "It's just a bit of a gentle push, really, to make them see what they want to see. That's how I changed my skin color."

"That's still magic!" Fort said. "And people here are kind of freaked out by magic at the moment, so maybe don't use any more?"

She sighed. "I'm telling you, it's nothing. Watch. I'll cast a *real* spell, and you'll see the difference."

She stood up and started to wave her hand, only for Fort to yank her back to the seat. "I said no more magic!" he hissed as more people turned to glare at him.

Xenea smiled at him. "That would matter, I guess, if I had to do what you said. But you're the one who owes my queen, not the other way around. And since you're currently failing to keep your side of the bargain, you're basically useless to me." She patted him on the shoulder, then looked out the window. "Ah, I see we've arrived. This is your school?"

He followed her gaze, only to drop his head into his hands again. "No. That's the city dump."

She frowned. "Huh. The smell reminded me of humans, so I just figured . . . oh well. That means I have time to interrogate more of these children. Be right back!"

And with that, she jumped up from their seat before Fort could stop her.

"Fellow normal human beings!" she declared from the aisle. "I am Xenea, and I have come to learn from you about your culture and habits. Please educate me, that when my people rule yours . . ." She coughed awkwardly. "I mean, when my people *visit* yours, we shall exist in harmony. Now, who here has seen any signs of a dragon around?"

- SEVEN -

SOMEHOW, XENEA'S GLAMOUR HAD both charmed all the kids on the bus and convinced them that nothing was wrong with asking if they'd seen a dragon. In fact, they'd all been eager to talk about the one they'd seen flying over major cities on the news, which made Fort's heart start racing again, considering he'd been in that dragon's claws at the time. Fortunately, no one had been able to make out the features of the boy being held by the dragon, so he slumped back into the bus seat, agreeing with his dad that maybe he *wasn't* ready for a new school just yet.

The only good part of Xenea meeting the other students was that it gave him time to himself, which he desperately needed if he was going to figure out how to get rid of her. Xenea wanted a dragon? Well, he knew someone who could find one for her.

Sierra? Fort shouted out with his mind. *I need your help! Can you hear me?*

Only there was no answer. That was odd . . . what could she be doing? Sleeping? How did the time difference work, anyway? Was it nighttime in the UK right now? No, not when it was morning where Fort was.

But then what was she doing? He tried a few more times and still got no response. Great. Hopefully she was okay, but now he had that to worry about too.

By the time the school bus pulled in to the school, Xenea had managed to win over half the bus, while at least that many kids now gave Fort dirty looks. Yejun must have spread the news around. Fantastic.

When they finally got off the bus, Fort had a tiny hope that a teacher or the principal might point out that Xenea didn't belong, and she'd be kicked out of the place, but apparently her glamour power worked just as well on adults, as Fort's new teacher, Ms. Switzer, welcomed her with open arms.

For the first time since he'd been kicked out of it, Fort missed the Oppenheimer School and their protective mind amulets. Whatever Xenea's glamour was, it wouldn't work on Colonel

Charles. Though he'd love to lock them together in a room and see who annoyed who more.

For now, Xenea was sitting next to him at a group table, listening attentively as Ms. Switzer went over where the class had gotten to in American history. "Perhaps I should make notes," Xenea whispered, then turned to Fort. "May I borrow some sort of writing utensil? In exchange, I can make you two inches taller."

He took a deep breath, trying not to think about how much damage the faerie could do with the other students and her bargaining. "Here, just take it," he said, handing her a pen. "It's free. Keep it, *and* your deals."

"Did you have something to say, Forsythe?" Ms. Switzer asked from the front. "I didn't think I had to tell you not to talk during class."

For what felt like the thousandth time that day, Fort blushed. "Sorry, just giving Xenea a pen," he said, and instantly Ms. Switzer smiled.

"Oh, of course, I'm so sorry," she said, moving to her desk. "Xenea, do you need any other school supplies? I always end up having to buy extras for kids, so I've got plenty—"

Xenea was out of her seat in an instant and scooped up everything she was offered. "You humans are awfully free with your deal making," she said, making Fort groan. "Didn't you think about what you could get from me in exchange?"

This actually seemed to set Ms. Switzer back a bit. "Uh, no, actually. I do this for all my students. If someone doesn't have what they need, I'll make sure they get it."

"But what's in it for you?" Xenea said, sounding confused now. "Do your students become your minions, following your orders for all time? Do you use their youth to stay young? What's the advantage for you?"

"There *is* none," Ms. Switzer said, and from her reaction, Fort started to wonder if the glamour was wearing thin a bit. The harder Xenea pushed, the more their teacher seemed to react to what she was actually saying, rather than just see whatever Xenea wanted. "I'm doing it for *you*, all of you. That's what I care about, teaching kids what they need to know in life."

"That's so strange!" Xenea said, then seemed to notice the teacher's reaction, because she added, "But definitely good to know. Thank you." She moved back to her seat and began making notes in a notebook one of the other kids had given her (or at least Fort *hoped* they'd just given it, not traded for it). "I'm sorry, your teachership, you should go on with your lesson. I'm interested in hearing more about these thirteen rebellious human colonies, and what tactics the English king used to crush their insurrection as I imagine happened. This could come in handy."

The day only got more surreal as it went on. After history, an alarm started ringing, and all the kids immediately jumped up from their tables, everyone talking at once.

"This is just a drill, everyone!" Ms. Swizter said. "I warned you about this yesterday. Because of what happened in London, we'll be doing these all week, just to make sure you all know what to do."

The kids went silent and slowly ducked under the tables, bracing themselves there. "I should have told you this was coming," Ms. Switzer said to Fort and Xenea, who were both looking around in confusion.

"What's coming?" Fort asked, feeling his shoulders push up around his neck as the alarm sounded, making him feel like he was back at the Oppenheimer School.

"This is just a drill in case of an attack like the one that happened in Washing—" Before she even finished, she seemed to realize who she was talking to and immediately winced. "Oh, Forsythe, I'm so sorry!" she said. "It didn't even occur to me that . . . oh, I'm just making it worse."

But Fort barely heard her as he stared around at the other kids, all sitting silently under the tables, their hands covering their heads. He could suddenly feel his heart beating in his head, and his vision began to get darker.

All of this . . . because of the Oppenheimer School? There were kids all around the country who had to hide under their desks because Damian had summoned the Old Ones so many months ago?

But Damian wasn't the only one to blame. D'hea had come back because Fort had tried to rescue his father. And William wouldn't have been able to attack London if Fort, Rachel, and Jia hadn't retrieved the book of Spirit magic.

The enormity of it all hit him out of nowhere, in a way it never had before. Seeing the looks on the other students' faces, some bored but others wincing in fear, even though it was a drill . . . all of this was in part because of *him*.

Almost from a distance, he saw Ms. Switzer gently help him up from his seat and lead him to duck under the nearest table. Xenea joined him, but he barely noticed, his eyes on the boy next to him, someone whose name he hadn't learned yet. The boy was trying to look unconcerned, but he jumped at every little noise around the room.

This was too much. The alarm ringing, the other students all not knowing what was happening, it was just too much to take, and Fort began to feel dizzy, almost like he was going to faint—

"Are you ill, Forsythe?" said a voice, cutting through the terrible memories and pulling Fort's attention back to the faerie girl sitting in front of him. But unlike before, Xenea seemed to glow now, though not like she was using magic. It was more as if he couldn't look away and wanted to talk to her, to find out more about her—

And then the glow diminished, and the old Xenea was back, along with some of his fear and anxiousness. Still, whatever the glow had been, it'd calmed him down a lot and brought him out of his guilt, his realization of how much what he'd done had affected the world.

"What did you do?" he whispered to her, finally not meaning it in a bad way.

"You looked like you went somewhere bad," Xenea said. "The glamour's good for pulling people out of their heads."

He blinked. "Um, thank you. I . . . I actually really appreciate that."

"You can owe me," she said, and grinned far too evilly for Fort's liking.

Still, she *had* been nice to do that. And what was even more surprising, Fort now realized that other than changing her skin color, Xenea hadn't been using her glamour on *him* at all.

That was probably because she didn't need to: He didn't have a choice and had to help her, to fulfill his favor to the queen. The last thing he was going to do was put his father at risk again for not following through on his bargain.

But still, wouldn't Xenea's job have been easier if she'd charmed him like everyone else? And she still hadn't done so. Huh.

The piercing alarm went silent before he could ask her about it, and everyone climbed out from under the tables.

"We'll have another drill each day this week," Ms. Switzer said, giving Fort a pitying look. "But maybe I'll speak to Mrs. MacNamara about you, Forsythe. You shouldn't have to, you know . . ."

"It's okay—I'm fine," he said, forcing a smile. The last thing he needed was the other students thinking he was getting special treatment, not after many of them already had a bad opinion of him from the bus. Four more drills like that one sounded pretty terrible, yes, but he'd have to get used to it. This was how normal life was.

It wasn't until lunch that he finally had a chance to talk more to Xenea about things. But after following him through the cafeteria line, she got pulled away to a table full of their classmates, taking the last seat.

Fort sighed, far too aware that only a few hours earlier, he'd been walking out the door to his normal school in his normal life. Sure, a cat-dragon was waiting for him back home, and they still had to find Merlin and defeat an Old One, but for just one day, Fort had been a bit excited to have things back like they were supposed to be.

But instead, there was Xenea and drills in case of monster attacks. The latter he could handle, assuming he could get his panic under control.

Xenea, though? He glanced over to where she was sitting, as all the other students stared in wonder at her.

Xenea was going to be a *problem*.

Sierra? Fort tried again, but still received no response. He began to worry even more about his friend. The only times she hadn't responded in the past were when she was in trouble, or asleep. He hoped it was the latter, because at the moment, there wasn't much he could do if she was in danger, not without knowing exactly where she was.

He sighed, dropping his head into his hands. He'd keep trying Sierra when he got home from school, when Xenea would go back to wherever she came from, hopefully, and he'd have more time to think of how to handle all of this.

And then a horrible thought occurred to him: What if Xenea *didn't* go back to Avalon? What if she really meant it when she said she had to stick by Fort until she found a dragon? What if she barged into his aunt's apartment, too?

No, there was no way, not with Ember there. He'd just have to find some reason that she couldn't come in.

- EIGHT -

I T'S NICE TO MEET YOU, XENEA," FORT'S aunt said as she welcomed the faerie girl into the apartment. "I'm so glad Fort's already making friends at his new school!"

"He is?" Xenea said, frowning as she sat down at their dinner table. "It didn't look like that to me. He mostly seemed worried the whole time. Thank you for offering me sustenance for the evening, though, especially without asking for anything in return. You . . . I mean, *we* humans seem extremely gullible in that way!"

Fort clenched his jaw, wanting to punch something. After school, Xenea had followed him to the bus, then straight up the stairs to his apartment. "Well, this was a fun day," he lied to her, then reached out to shake her hand. "See you here tomorrow? Hopefully, I'll be able to find Damian for you then, and you can go home."

She just laughed. "Ah, no. Where you go, I go. Imagine how much trouble I'd be in if the dragon turned out to be hiding in your domicile here! So let's go in, Forsythe. Unless you're not planning to pay my queen back for her favor?"

He quickly shook his head, not even willing to consider that. If the queen had given him his father back, she could take him away just as easily . . . or even just restore his ability to do magic, and who knew where that would lead. He couldn't risk a world war just because this faerie girl wanted to follow him home after school.

And now here he was, his aunt showing Xenea to the kitchen table, with his baby dragon just down the hall. Fortunately, Ember hadn't made any noises yet, but Fort knew that would only be a matter of time: He had to find a way to sneak away from the table and get her somewhere safe, at least as long as Xenea was here.

Though if he knew of a safe place to send her, then he wouldn't be having this problem in the first place.

"I'm afraid it's just pizza for dinner," his aunt told them, back at the dinner table. "What do you like on it, Xenea?"

"What is pizza?" she asked, tilting her head. "Is it some sort of plate? If so, I'll have food on it, please."

Fort blinked, then leaned in closer. "Do you eat meat? Are you a vegetarian?"

She leaned in as well, looking horrified. "What kind of beast kills and eats another living thing? Of course I don't eat meat!"

"Just cheese, please," Fort told his aunt, pulling away again as Xenea stared at him in disgust. His aunt nodded with a smile, then left to get her phone and call in the order.

"Tell me that this cheese you mention isn't some sort of thinking, feeling creature," Xenea said to Fort.

"No, it's just a mold made from the milk of a cow," he whispered back, then enjoyed her reaction.

"What is *wrong* with you humans?" Xenea said, looking sick. "Tell me I didn't eat a mold today at the school."

"No, those were tater tots," he told her. "Just potatoes, fried in oil."

She narrowed her eyes suspiciously. "And the white drink in the box?"

He couldn't stop his grin. "That'd be the milk of the cow again."

She gagged and shook her head. "Perhaps I'll skip this meal. I don't know how you people grow so large, eating such things."

Before Fort could encourage that, maybe suggesting she just

find somewhere else to go for the night, the front door opened, and he heard footsteps coming toward them.

"My boy returns victoriously from his first day at school!" Fort's father yelled as he stepped into the kitchen. "Did they give you medals yet, or will that come later?"

Fort turned his usual red, then stood up to introduce the faerie girl to his father. "Dad, this is Xenea, a friend of mine. Um, from school."

His father took one look at Xenea, and his smile disappeared. An odd, surprised look passed over his face, but he quickly covered it by replacing his smile. "Xenea, welcome!" he said. "Any friend of Fort's is a friend of Fort's, as I always say. I hope you like pizza, because the grocery stores are still out of everything except anchovies and olives." He winked at Fort. "Don't worry—I got you enough of both for your usual lunch."

"Yes, we already resolved the pizza issue," Xenea said, her eyes on Fort's father. Fort hadn't known the faerie girl long, and for most of that time he'd been incredibly embarrassed by everything she'd done, but one thing he'd never seen was her looking like she was now. It was almost like she had been surprised by something as well, just like his father had been. What was going on?

"Fort, why don't you give Xenea a tour?" his aunt said, returning from placing the pizza order just in time to suggest the worst possible thing. "I'll call you two when dinner's here. I'm guessing you're going to want to play with Ember?"

Fort's blood went cold. "Ember's my cat," he told Xenea. "My perfectly normal house cat. Nothing weird about her at all. We don't even need to see her if you don't want."

Xenea shrugged, barely even looking at him. "Yes, let us see your cat, if you want." She walked into the hallway and stopped just out of earshot of the kitchen, giving Fort a strange look. "What is going on here? Why do I smell magic?"

"What do you mean?" Fort asked, his eyes widening. "No magic here. Just completely normal, everyday nonmagic here!"

Her eyes narrowed, and she turned to look back in the direction of the kitchen. "Your father reeks of my kind. Is he involved in the bargain you made with the queen?"

Fort let out an explosive breath in relief. "Yes!" he shouted, then lowered his voice as Xenea raised an eyebrow. *"Yes,"* he repeated more quietly. "She fixed him a bit, that's all. I'm sure that's all you smell, magic-wise." And definitely not the trans-formed dragon down the hall.

Xenea shrugged. "My queen didn't specify, only that two of

you had made individual bargains with her. Come, let us tour your domicile."

Fort frowned and stopped her before she continued on down the hall. "What do you mean, two of us made bargains? Are you talking about the deal for Excalibur?" That hadn't seemed like an "individual" bargain, since he, Rachel, and Jia had all been involved.

She opened her mouth to say something, then paused, sniffing at the air. "And now I smell some sort of animal, only . . . unnatural. What is happening in here?"

Fort's panic returned with a vengeance. "Just my cat!" he said quickly, trying to pull her back to the kitchen. "Nothing important. She doesn't like strangers. Hates them. Will probably attack you, claw you up."

A loud meow came from his bedroom, followed by scratching on the door, and he winced. Ember must have heard him and was ready to be fed. But he couldn't let Xenea see her, no matter what. As the faerie girl looked down the hall, Fort readied his teleportation spell. He could send Ember to the cave beneath the old Oppenheimer School for a few minutes at least, but he'd definitely be caught doing magic, considering Xenea seemed to be able to smell it.

But what else could he do?

The scratching grew louder, and Xenea seemed to pale a bit. "Claws, you say?" she said, turning away from the sound. "Well, she doesn't smell like the dragon you had with you, back at the door to Avalon, so I don't know that there's any need to check her out."

Again, Fort almost fainted in relief. "You're totally right!" he said, turning her gently the rest of the way from his room. "She's no dragon, just a cat, an evil cat who will scratch you and probably give you diseases."

"Diseases?" Xenea said, looking even more sick.

"All kinds," Fort said. "There's even one named after cat scratches. Cat-scratch fever. It makes you explode in a huge pile of pus. Just horrible."

Xenea nodded, swallowing hard. "I never knew there were such dangerous animals in this world. And that you would keep them as pets!"

"Well, they're cute," Fort said. "But speaking of diseases, you should probably wash your hands before dinner. Wouldn't want you to eat any germs. Those are little animals too small for you to even see, by the way, and they're covering you at all times while you're here."

She dry heaved. "The queen said nothing about tiny animals! This assignment gets worse every minute." She gave Fort an appreciative look. "Where can I wash my hands free of these animals?"

With Xenea safely in the bathroom, Fort closed the door behind her and ran to his bedroom, where the scratching was getting louder. He worried that if he left Ember alone for even another minute or two, she might decide to just set fire to the door, which would sort of attract Xenea's attention no matter how afraid she was of the cat.

In between scratches, Fort slipped into his dark bedroom and quickly shut the door behind him before Ember could sneak out. He flipped the light switch and looked around, only to find an empty room.

"Ember?" he said, taking a tentative step in.

Out of nowhere, a blur of black fur and needle-sharp claws came flying at him, and he shrieked in surprise. Ember slammed into his chest and knocked him to the floor, then began licking his face with a tongue like sandpaper.

"Pare pala," she said in between licks. *"Volai hrana!"*

He slowly looked up at her in surprise. When he'd left this morning, she'd been the size of a kitten.

Now a full-grown cat stood on his chest.

- NINE -

FORT IMMEDIATELY LIFTED EMBER OFF, cringing at the cuts she'd left in his skin from her claws, then stood back up. "How did you get so *big*?" he whispered, staring at her in disbelief. "You were, like, the size of my hand when Jia turned you into a kitten yesterday!"

She just stared at him, looking irritated. "Volai. *Hrana*." She tapped one of her empty bowls, sending it skidding to his feet.

"You're hungry, I get it, but please don't attack me again," he said, and quickly grabbed her bowl as she threaded in and out of his legs, constantly threatening to trip him. As soon as he opened a new can of cat food and filled her bowl, though, she turned her attention to that, and he was able to slip back out, closing the door softly behind him.

"Did I hear your cat speaking to you?" Xenea said from directly behind him, making Fort leap in the air in surprise.

"I hadn't realized you had animals capable of human speech."

Fort just stared at her for a second, hoping his heart rate would slow down enough to keep him from having a heart attack. "Yes, they do," he said. "*All* our cats speak. You're thinking of dogs. They're the ones who don't know words."

"Hmm," she said, narrowing her eyes. "Are you sure—"

"Oh, completely sure," Fort said, pushing her down the hall. "I'll prove it. Let me show you something we call the internet, where cats are always speaking through the magic of these things known as memes."

A half hour later, when the pizza arrived, Fort ended up having to yank Xenea off his aunt's laptop. "It is full of nonsense and hate, yet I cannot stop looking at it!" she said to him, reaching back toward the laptop in desperation. "Please, for my sake, don't curse me with such magic again!"

"We're all cursed with the internet, and we have to learn to live with it," he told her, walking her into the kitchen, thrilled that he'd made her forget completely about Ember. "It's part of being human."

His aunt and father carried two pizzas in from the front door and set them down on the table. Cora opened the first and showed it to Xenea. "Cheese, as ordered."

Xenea's eyes widened as she stared at the pizza. "The mold smells strangely appetizing."

"Oh, it's great, as molds go," Fort told her, grabbing a piece of pepperoni from the other box and taking a bite.

Xenea gave him a disgusted look, but she mimicked how he held the pizza in his hands and took a tentative bite, as Fort's father and aunt each grabbed a piece, and his aunt poured some sodas for them. As Xenea tasted the pizza, her entire face lit up, and she excitedly took another bite, then began talking with her mouth full, completely incomprehensibly.

Fort just frowned at her. "What did you say? Swallow first."

She did, then took another bite before speaking. "I said it's fantastic. What sort of wizardry *is* this?"

His aunt laughed, while his father smiled gently, watching the faerie girl closely. "Just the magic of Italy," his dad said. "Brought right to our door. Speaking of, I can hear an accent in your voice, Xenea. It sounds British. What brings you here to the U.S.?"

"I've come to find something, and learn what I can in the meantime," she said, taking another huge bite, almost finished with her first piece. She looked at Cora expectantly. "May I have more? I can pay, if you'd like. I would offer you—"

70

"Have all you want!" Fort shouted, pushing the box at her. "No need to offer anything, trust me!"

Xenea nodded happily and pulled half of the remaining pieces onto her plate. "You have my thanks!" she said to them all.

"Of course," his father said. "But back to why you're here. You said to find something, and learn about us? I thought schools in England were pretty good."

She shrugged as she stuffed more pizza in her face. "I don't know that *any* human schools are that good," she said. "Mostly I'm here to find—"

"The differences between America and the United Kingdom," Fort said quickly. "It's like an exchange-student thing. To bring our countries closer."

"Did you have any family in London?" his aunt asked, sending a chill through Fort. He quickly took a bite of his own pizza. "I hope they're okay if you did."

"No, my family was all exiled over a thousand years ago," Xenea said, making Fort almost choke on his pizza. "That's why I'm learning about you, since they're thinking of returning."

Of course, Xenea's glamour covered for her, and Fort's aunt just nodded. "That's fascinating. What happened, if you don't mind me asking? Was it a political matter?"

"Humans didn't like us stealing their children," Xenea answered, and this time, Fort *did* choke. He quickly stood up, his face turning red from lack of oxygen, and pointed at his throat.

"Fort!" his father shouted, and jumped up from his seat. But Xenea was faster. She slapped Fort hard on the back, and he felt a strange energy pass through him. Whatever it was immediately cleared his throat, and he could breathe again. He thankfully took in a huge breath, then dropped back into his seat, feeling faint.

"Sorry," he said, his voice sounding a bit raspy. "Took too big a bite."

"That was careless of you," Xenea said as she shoved half a slice of pizza into her mouth.

All in all, this was going about as badly as Fort could have imagined. If not for Xenea's glamour, both his dad and aunt would be completely losing it right now over basically everything she said. Not to mention that Ember was going to be finishing her food soon, which would probably lead to more scratching at the door, if not worse. But what could he do? With Sierra not answering him, Fort had no way of finding Damian, and therefore getting rid of Xenea.

With one last attempt, he sent his mind out, shouting as loudly as he could: *SIERRA! I need your*—

"Whoa!" shouted a voice from the other side of the kitchen, surprising Fort to the point he almost fell off his chair. He looked up behind his aunt to find a glowing yellow image of Sierra, shimmering with the light of Mind magic. "There's no need to yell! Sorry I was out of touch today, but I had some things going on. Anyway, I was on my way here to tell you that Jia and Rachel both have decided to go find Merlin *tonight*, that this can't wait, and frankly, I agree with them. So are you ready or . . ."

She paused, her eyes turning to the faerie girl sitting at Fort's side, slowly pushing another slice of pizza into her face.

"Um," Sierra said, tilting her head with a curious look. "Who's the girl?"

- TEN -

N*O,"* SIERRA SAID, PACING AROUND his room as Fort sat on his bed, Ember on his lap. "You are not handing Damian over to that girl. You said yourself the faerie queen might hurt him!" She paused. "Plus, she's creepy. She kept sniffing in my direction, and I wasn't even there!"

"She can smell magic," Fort said, shaking his head as he petted Ember, the cat purring loudly. "And Damian can take care of himself! That was pretty obvious when he tried to kill me, Rachel, and Jia. Or did you need to see my memories of what he did again?"

She sighed. "You don't know how hard this has all been on him. He just found out he wasn't human, and then you were all accusing him of destroying London. Which he only did under that William kid's control, by the way."

"No one was controlling him when he attacked us," Fort growled, and Ember hissed at Sierra's image in unity. He petted her even more for that, thinking what a wonderful little dragon she was. "How do you know he won't want to go, anyway? There are other dragons there. He'd probably enjoy meeting them!" He looked down at his cat, and then covered her ears. "And if he goes, and comes back, maybe he can take . . . other little ones too. Make sure they're safe."

"No, it's too dangerous," Sierra repeated. "Besides, he'd never go. He's obsessed with finding the book of Time magic, and the Spirit book, wherever that one went."

Fort's eyes widened, and he sat up so suddenly that Ember leaped from his lap. "Wait, you've talked to him? I thought you didn't know where he was."

Sierra blushed, even in the yellow light of her Mind magic. "Yes, I know where he is. But I didn't want to tell you because I know how you three feel about him. And he's just as upset with all of you." She winced. "I wish I'd been there. None of you know how to have a conversation. Instead you just leap in and throw magic at each other. Not the most mature."

He tried to kill us!" Fort hissed, keeping his voice down in spite of himself. The last thing he needed was his dad or aunt hearing him, not after he'd told them he wasn't feeling well so was going to bed early. Not to mention that that he hated lying to his father in the first place and would much rather have been spending time with his dad than arguing with Sierra.

In her defense, Sierra *had* tried to fix everything by using her Mind magic on Xenea, to make her decide to return home to the faerie queen and say she couldn't find the dragon. But whatever magical defense Xenea had, it was far more powerful than Sierra was used to, so the suggestion hadn't worked.

And then things had gotten worse after dinner, when Xenea had declared she found the apartment satisfactory and planned on living there throughout her stay, mostly so she could use the internet. Fort had told her that wasn't possible, and Xenea had threatened to go to the queen and say he wasn't cooperating, until Sierra had tried her Mind magic again, to convince the faerie that the apartment smelled too much like humans to stay in.

But even that little of a suggestion had been hard for Sierra, almost sending her to her knees with the effort. And it still hadn't completely clicked until Fort handed over his aunt's laptop and told Xenea she could use the internet as much as she wanted if she stayed somewhere else. Thankfully, that had done it, though the faerie girl had promised to see Fort bright and early for school the next day, at which point Xenea had finally left, though she hadn't gone far—she had picked a spot in the park across the street to stay, close enough to see any dragons that might show up, but hopefully far enough away not to notice if Fort teleported out.

"You know, I was there," Sierra said, her words pulling him out of his memory. "You don't need to start remembering it for my sake." She rolled her eyes. "Anyway, we don't have time to argue about Damian. *You* need to teleport Jia and Rachel to that cottage where you met Merlin. They don't have a lot of time, and I promised I'd make you take them tonight."

He glared at her, hating that they disagreed about this, but not able to understand why she couldn't see how bad a guy Damian was. She'd witnessed everything that Damian had done and yet still wouldn't give an inch on him. "Fine," he said, picking Ember up in his arms. "But only because I want to ask Merlin about Avalon, and see if there's a way to sneak this little fire-breather to the dragons there."

Sierra sighed and reached out to pet Ember, only to yank her hand away as the cat-dragon hissed at her again.

Fort quickly grabbed the two presents he'd made for Jia and Rachel after Xenea had left, then opened a portal for himself, and a portal for each of the others, to the spot where they'd first met Merlin in the UK.

The forest clearing was dark, lit only by the moon through the dense trees and the three green teleportation portals Fort had just made. Sierra came with him in Mind magic form, which Fort now realized was probably because she was with Damian and didn't want Fort to know where the older dragon was. Great. That was probably why she hadn't answered him earlier in the day too, when he'd really needed her.

"I can hear what you're thinking, you know," she whispered from his side.

He blushed again. Usually it wasn't a problem, but now that they had something between them . . .

Most of the clearing was covered by the wreckage of Merlin's cottage, with wood and ash spread out like it'd exploded. Fort hadn't seen the actual destruction of the cottage, as he'd been visiting a potential future at the time with Cyrus, but that there wasn't more left from Damian's attack said a lot about the dragon's power.

Before he could get a closer look, though, Rachel and Jia both stepped through their respective portals. He waved at them, then winced as Ember climbed up his chest to his shoulder and turned to face the two new arrivals, hissing.

"You sure you want to bring her along?" Rachel asked. "And is it my imagination, or did she get bigger overnight?"

"You're not imagining it," Fort said, cringing in pain as Ember dug her nails into him. "And that's why she's here. I took enough of a risk leaving her at home today, and you should see what she did to my bedroom door with her claws. But I think I might have somewhere to send her where she'll be safe."

Sierra quickly caught the other two up on Xenea and her mission, while Fort remembered something the faerie girl had said. "You know, she mentioned that I wasn't the only one who made a bargain with the faerie queen. I assumed she meant our deal for Excalibur, but maybe not. Did either of you ask for anything?"

Rachel shook her head. Jia paused, then looked away. "She probably did just mean the sword," Jia said.

"Only you would end up with a faerie girl following you home, trying to steal your baby dragon, New Kid," Rachel said, staring at Ember. "But you're right. Getting her to the Avalon dragons might be our best bet. And Merlin would know if there was another way there."

"Assuming he's still around," Fort said, nodding at the destroyed cottage. "But before we start here, I wanted to give you both something." He held up two neon strips of plastic, one green and one red. "There's one for each of you."

Rachel raised an eyebrow, while Jia took the green strip and slapped it against her wrist. As it hit her, the strip curled over, making a sort of bracelet. "A slap bracelet?" she said. "Um, okay?"

"I put a bunch of teleportation spells in each of them," Fort said, and immediately Rachel grabbed hers, much more excited now. "They should be able to get you around if I can't."

"Ooh!" Rachel shouted, and slapped the bracelet on her own wrist, then punched out with her hand. Instantly a green portal opened into what looked like a dark movie theater. "Oh, *yeah*. I'm going to enjoy this."

"Don't use the spells too soon," Fort said, and she sighed, then punched it closed again. "And you probably don't need to actually punch out like that."

"I think I do, actually," Rachel said. "It's a lot cooler this way."

Jia smiled, then whispered something in her ear. Rachel turned red, then grinned.

Fort didn't want to know what they were talking about. "Anyway, let's get back to what we're doing here, like you said, Rachel?" He pointed in the direction of the cottage's debris. "It might take us a while to find anything in all the wreckage."

"He only destroyed it because he was possessed by Spirit magic," Sierra told him. "Damian didn't have a choice."

Fort gritted his teeth. "What about when he tried to kill us the other times? No Spirit magic then."

"I'm with Fort, Sierra," Jia said. "Whatever Damian used to be, he's completely lost it. You should have seen him."

Sierra sighed and turned away, blocking off her thoughts from Fort, which was probably for the best. But she was right that Damian wasn't their concern right now, not if she wouldn't tell him about the Avalon dragons. They really needed to search through whatever was left of the cottage to see if they could find a way to contact Merlin.

In spite of how spread around the remnants of the cottage were, it actually looked like Damian's dragon fire had been carefully targeted, as the trees around the cottage appeared untouched. The spot where the cottage had stood, though, was mostly just ashes and an occasional leftover piece of wood or charred metal.

"This is odd," Rachel said after a few minutes of sifting through the ash with her hands. "The cottage was so much bigger on the inside, but I'm not seeing nearly enough wreckage here. Even if it was all burned up."

"Plus it was mostly made of high-tech plastic," Jia pointed out. "That might have melted, but it wouldn't have turned to ash. I'm not seeing anything like that here."

They had a point. Fort frowned, running his eyes over what was left. There really *should* have been more remains here, even the cottage had been destroyed. From what he could tell, there looked like enough debris to account for the outer cottage, but nothing inside.

Which meant maybe the cottage hadn't been as destroyed as it looked.

Near the front of the wreckage, a larger piece of wood had survived, if singed on all sides. It looked familiar enough that he began to wonder, and he stepped over to it, then picked it up.

"Hey!" something shouted, and he immediately dropped the piece of wood. Whoever it was that had spoken let out a groan of pain. "A little warning would have been nice!"

Fort gently turned the board over this time and found a

metal imp staring back at him, attached to the wood.

Right. These were the remains of the front door and its magical door knocker.

"Oh, it's *you* lot," the imp said, glaring at him. "Haven't you all done enough?"

Ember hissed at the imp, and it hissed back.

"Where's Merlin?" Fort asked as his friends all came around to see what was going on.

"Inside, as usual," the imp said, rolling its eyes.

"Inside?" Jia said. "But the cottage is gone."

"The outside is, maybe," the imp said with a sigh. "Do you truly not understand? I shouldn't be shocked by human ignorance anymore, I suppose."

Fort stared at it for a moment, then lifted the piece of door with one hand until it stood vertically in the dirt. Then he knocked on it.

The door pulled out of his hand almost instantly, flying open. A wave of warm air flooded over Fort.

"Finally!" said an old man wearing a tattered brown robe, with a long white beard tossed over his shoulder, ducking out of the door-sized hole in the air. Behind him, Fort could make out a cozy-looking light but not much else.

"Merlin?" Rachel said, a huge smile spreading over her face. "We're here for training!"

"Good, because we don't have much time," the magician said, waving them inside. "You're due to face the Timeless One in just under a year, and if you're not ready by that point, humanity is doomed." He waited as they all stared at him in shock. "Well? In or out, children. We have to start your training *now*, or you'll never be ready in time!"

- ELEVEN -

YOU JUST SAID WE HAVE A YEAR," Fort said. "Is that really not enough time to train?"

Merlin looked at Fort with a raised eyebrow. "Oh, did you gain the power of time in the last few days, boy? I must not have noticed. Those who believe they have enough time will find they always come up short. What you think will be around forever will someday disappear, leaving you with nothing but regrets." He frowned, then looked at his wrist, where a hologram appeared, showing a bunch of strange numbers. "Or maybe my watch is broken?"

Fort, Jia, and Rachel all looked at each other, while Sierra snorted. Merlin quickly looked up at her image, glowing with Mind magic. "And *you*, young lady, don't belong here. Don't you have somewhere else to be?"

85

Sierra looked at him in surprise, then flashed a sad, guilty look at Fort. "Yeah, I guess I do," she said. And then she disappeared.

"Wait, where is she going?" Fort asked Merlin. "What just happened?"

"She's got other things to do now," Merlin said. "Just as important as me training my new apprentice, if you'd get out of her way."

Confused over what had just happened, Fort looked back at Rachel, who shrugged. Sierra had something else to do? She clearly had known what the old man was talking about, but why hadn't she told Fort about it before?

Did this have something to do with Damian? It must, since there wasn't anything else that Sierra would need to hide from him. He began to regret their argument even more now, realizing that Sierra felt like she had to keep a whole side of her life from him. Maybe if he'd been more open-minded, she would have told him what was going on.

"Or maybe she didn't tell you because you don't need to know," Merlin said, doing that annoying thing that Cyrus used to do, using his Time magic to see what Fort was going to ask, and then answering it before he could. "Now can we get started?"

"Okay, fine," Fort said, gritting his teeth. "But before we

start training, I have a question about Avalon, and the dragons there." He patted Ember, who was looking at Merlin with curiosity. "We think the faerie queen is trying to capture Ember, and I want to send her somewhere safe, which would probably be to her own kind on Avalon. But I don't have the spell to—"

"Wait, am I getting mixed up here?" Merlin asked him. "Did *you* pick up Excalibur? I thought my apprentice was the girl with the fire inside." He pointed at Rachel.

Fort looked back to find Rachel beaming, though she blushed when she saw his glance. "I didn't pick it up, at least not at *that* moment," Fort said. "It sort of burned me. But later—"

"That's what I thought," Merlin said, and turned to Rachel. "What are you waiting around for, apprentice? Get in here. We have work to do!" He beckoned her through, and she quickly passed by Fort, wincing at him as she went.

"I'm *not* letting Rachel fight an Old One by herself," Jia said, pushing past Fort as well. "If you're training her, you're training *me*, too."

Rachel squeezed Jia in a side-hug, while Jia gave Merlin a defiant look.

"Of course I'll be training you, Jia," Merlin said, looking confused now. "No one said you couldn't help Rachel."

"Okay, so then I'm helping her too!" Fort said, and moved toward the door as well.

Merlin put up a hand. "I'm afraid not, boy."

This stopped Fort dead in his tracks, and he stared at Merlin in shock. "What? But why not?"

Merlin gave him a pitying look. "You don't have the power to fight an Old One, not directly. If you attempted to battle the Timeless One, you would not only fail, but you'd doom your friends as well. I'm sorry, but I will not train you."

Fort's mouth dropped open, not believing what he was hearing. "I . . . I faced the Old Ones twice, though."

"No, you fought a possessed teenage dragon, the first time," Merlin corrected him, his tone gentler now. "And the second time, you wisely chose to run after D'hea was destroyed. You aren't without your talents, boy, but you are sadly bereft of the power needed." He nodded over his shoulder at the others. "Even these two, born on the day magic returned, might not have what it takes. But at least there's a chance with them."

"Wait, Merlin, uh, *sir*," Rachel said, coming around to stand in front of a now-speechless Fort. "If Fort wants to help, he can! He's gotten really good at his teleportation spell—"

"Does everyone now think they can see the future as well as

I?" Merlin said, his bushy eyebrows rising. "Why must apprentices always think they know so much? I have *seen* it, child. And perhaps what I do, I do for the boy's sake as well? Would you see him get hurt, or worse?"

Rachel quickly shook her head. "Of course not! I just—"

"If Merlin's seen it, we should listen to him," Jia said to Rachel, grabbing her arm and softly pulling her away. She gave Fort a sad look, but he could barely process it.

After infiltrating the Dracsi world and fighting William in London, he'd almost forgotten that he wasn't as powerful as the others. Not being born on Discovery Day had sort of faded from his mind, what with everything else going on. But now, here was an ancient wizard to bring it all back up, and Fort couldn't think of a thing to say to argue.

There wasn't any denying it. He just wasn't as powerful as the others and knew only two spells by heart. Really, he should have realized he'd just get in the way if they actually had to fight an Old One. Merlin wasn't wrong: Damian was just possessed by one the first time he'd faced the eternal creatures, and Fort had barely lived through his actual encounter with them in the Dracsi dimension.

"Okay," he said quietly, nodding his head. "You're right,

and I understand. Maybe you could help me with my dragon, then?"

Rachel sighed, but Merlin just smiled at him. "Of course, boy. I offered to do just that the last time you were here, if you remember."

Fort didn't, given what had occurred in between, but now that Merlin mentioned it, he could recall the old man saying something about dragon problems. Fort had assumed at the time that Merlin had meant Damian, but this was just more proof that the old wizard knew what was to come, and if he said Fort shouldn't fight the Old One, then Fort should listen.

"I just need to get her to safety," he said miserably. "I've heard there are other dragons on Avalon, and if you can tell me where there's a door or portal or something—"

"There *were* a dozen different ways," Merlin said, nodding. "Unfortunately, they all require Space magic, and from what I recall, that book's been destroyed now, hasn't it? Still, I do have a way to help." He glanced back at Jia and Rachel. "Are you two still here? Why haven't you gotten started?"

Rachel and Jia shared a look. "Because you haven't told us what to do," Rachel said.

"Do I have to tell you to breathe as well?" Merlin said, pointing inside the cottage. "Go, apprentices! We have little time as it is!"

Rachel and Jia both slunk through the doorway, looking guiltily at each other. Fort took a deep breath, glad at least that Merlin was willing to help him with Ember. The last thing he'd expected was to be sidelined in the upcoming fight so harshly, but now that it'd happened, Fort felt like he should have known. Who was *he* to think he could face the Timeless One? Excalibur had known, back when he first held it and the sword lit on fire, rejecting him. Why hadn't he himself seen it?

Ember meowed sadly and began rubbing her face against his cheek. In spite of himself, he smiled and reached up to rub her head. It was almost like she'd sensed his sadness and was trying to console him.

"Thanks, little girl," he said to her, and she purred, then relaxed back to his shoulder as he followed the others inside.

Lost in his thoughts, Fort almost bumped into Jia, who'd stopped a few feet into the cottage. "Whoa," she was saying, looking all around. "How is this possible?"

Fort followed her gaze and gasped. He'd expected at least *some* damage to the place, given the utter destruction outside, but instead, everything looked exactly like it had the last time he'd been here, utterly untouched.

"*Welcome* to my sanctuary," Merlin said, gesturing grandly to them. "Try not to make a mess, eh?"

- TWELVE -

HOW COULD THIS BE? IT WAS AS IF nothing had changed from the last time Fort had visited the cottage, that time with Cyrus present. A long table filled the dining room, while a pot of something bubbled over the fire in the fireplace, filling the cottage with an aroma that made Fort's stomach rumble.

But Damian had completely destroyed the cottage. What sort of magic had protected it? And where *was* the cottage, if not connected back to the outer shell? Fort had definitely noticed it being larger on the inside than outside when last he was here, but this was something else entirely.

"Where are we, exactly?" Jia said, asking Fort's question for him. "This can't be connected to the cottage we saw in the clearing."

"Oh, this is just the space between moments," Merlin said,

waving his hand absently. "Time doesn't pass here, so you won't be missed while you're training, or babysitting exotic pets." He nodded at Ember, who didn't seem to notice.

That was something, at least. The last thing Fort needed was for his father to come looking for him and discover his empty bedroom. If time really didn't move here, then he'd arrive back just minutes after he left. Not to mention he felt far less guilty about not spending that time with his dad.

But still, the whole thing made Fort's head hurt. "How are you doing it, though?" he said, looking around. "If this is Time magic, how can it be connected to a doorway back in the clearing? That seems more like Space magic if anything. But then you couldn't freeze time here."

Merlin grinned. "Look who's an expert now. If you must know, boy, Time and Space magic are closely related. You'll find quite a bit of overlap between the two."

"Closely related?" Fort asked, feeling even more lost. "What do you mean?"

Merlin winked as two other versions of the old man appeared next to Rachel and Jia, who both jumped in surprise. "When it comes down to it, space and time both describe where something is. And just because I'm here now . . ."

"Doesn't mean I won't be over here in a minute," the Merlin near Rachel said.

"Or here in two minutes," the third Merlin added.

For a second Fort thought this was it, the moment his brain just gave up on all of this magical stuff and went on vacation. Instead, he forced himself to try to figure it out, whether this was some of the hidden technology at work or Time magic. Or both, maybe. But how could—

The Merlin near Rachel looked down at her. "As I said, we have to get started, or you'll never be prepared for the Timeless One." He paused, looking at the original Merlin. "I did say that already, didn't I?"

"Yes, just a bit ago," the first Merlin said.

"Well it bears repeating," the third Merlin said. "We've trained six Artorigios to defeat the Timeless One, and every one failed to defeat him. And they had a *lifetime* to prepare! So we're going to have our work cut out for us."

"Indeed," the second Merlin said. "You're quite wise, my friend."

"Ah, you're too gracious, and likewise," the third Merlin said, bowing low.

Fort rolled his eyes at this, suddenly more annoyed than

confused, while the second Merlin turned back to Rachel. "Now, young lady, where is your sword, may I ask?"

"Um, about that," Rachel said, cringing. "I sort of lost Excalibur, so we probably need to find that first."

All three Merlins stared at her for a moment, then began to laugh. "Well, that's the first time I've heard *that* excuse," the one closest to her said. "Points for originality, my dear."

"You're misremembering," the original Merlin said. "Didn't that Roman legionnaire lose it against the Saxon invaders once?"

"Oh, that was temporary at best," the second Merlin said, waving his hand dismissively. "A matter of moments, all told." He glanced at Rachel. "How exactly did *you* lose it? And don't say Saxon invaders—that excuse has apparently already been used."

"Ellora sent it through time so that Colonel Charles wouldn't get it," Rachel said, blushing and staring at her feet, which surprised Fort more than anything. Rachel hadn't been this intimidated by *anyone*, even the colonel. "It was the right call, but she went with it, and we have no idea where they went or when she'll be back."

"Oh, *that's* what you meant by losing it?" her Merlin asked, shaking his head with a laugh. "I thought you were referring to something else. I knew about *that*, child!"

"Of course I did," the third Merlin said, laughing as well.

"From the start," the original Merlin told her.

"The sword and Ellora will return in five days, and you three will retrieve it," Rachel's Merlin told her. "Simple as that."

The *three* of them would retrieve it? So Fort was going to be allowed to help with that? That made him feel a little better, at least.

"Retrieve it?" Rachel asked. "But won't it just show up where she was at the time? So in the medical bay at the Oppenheimer School?"

"Of course," the Merlin closest to her said. "Why? Is that a problem?"

"A *bit* of one," Rachel said, sounding almost apologetic. "We, I mean Fort and I, were kicked out of the school. Jia's still there, but she's under guard, and I'm not sure—"

The Merlins all laughed again. "You children need some perspective," Rachel's Merlin said.

"Indeed," Fort's Merlin said. "You're going to face the Timeless One, Old One of Time magic, and enemy to your entire species. He has the power to ensure you never existed, and here you're worried about getting in trouble at school?"

"It's not that simple," Rachel said. "They think we lost our memories. If they find out that we kept them, they'll come after us and wipe our minds for real this time."

"Then I suppose you shouldn't get caught, eh?" the third Merlin suggested.

"It won't be difficult," the second one said. "At worst, truly the most difficult scenario, you'll be facing maybe, *maybe* a dozen or so soldiers."

A dozen soldiers? That didn't actually sound *that* bad. Fort could teleport the three of them into the medical bay, Jia could put the soldiers to sleep, and the sword would be Rachel's—

"Oh, and twenty to thirty students as well, don't forget," the third Merlin corrected himself.

"Of course, I misspoke," the second one said. "Thank you for the reminder. There will also be twenty to thirty students guarding it, as they know when the sword is due back as well."

Twenty to *thirty* students? And they knew when Excalibur was reappearing too? Fort's eyes widened, but the Merlins hadn't stopped yet.

"That may sound like a lot, but don't worry—only half of

them are as powerful as you two are," the original Merlin said, pointing at Jia and Rachel.

"Yes, but the other half will be a *challenge*," the third Merlin said.

"Obviously," the first Merlin said with a laugh. "And then there are the magical weapons the soldiers have."

"That, and they'll know you're coming," the third Merlin said, and this time, Fort, Rachel, and Jia all gasped in surprise. "What? Hadn't I mentioned that? Simply unavoidable, I'm afraid, as they have one of the Carmarthen Academy students supplying them with the immediate future." He shrugged at Rachel and Jia, who were now both in various stages of panic. "Now then, shall we get started on the training?"

- THIRTEEN -

THEY HAVE A STUDENT FROM THE Carmarthen Academy?" Rachel said, looking shocked. "But we used Excalibur on all of them, so they wouldn't have their magic anymore!"

"Well, not all of them," Jia said, giving her a worried glance. "What if Ellora arrived back before the sword does, and Colonel Charles has her locked up? Even if she tried not to tell them when Excalibur was going to reappear, they might have used magic on her to get it anyway."

Fort rubbed his temples, trying to work this all out in his head. Merlin had dropped way too much information at once on them, but something was still bothering him about it all: Merlin's own magic. "Wait," he said. "Since you can use Time magic, Merlin, why don't you just bring Excalibur back to us right now, from the future?"

"First of all, because I'm not considered 'worthy' and therefore can't touch it myself," the Merlin closest to Fort said with a small grin. "Second of all, I have very strict rules that I have to follow. I can train you, help guide you, but I *can't* face the Timeless One, or win Excalibur for you in any way. These are your tasks, your challenges, and we'll all lose if you can't perform them."

"Is this one of those time travel things where you can't change the past too much, or it'll mess everything up?" Rachel asked.

"But aren't you *from* the past, so this is your future?" Jia said. "Or am I wrong about that? I still haven't read any of the King Arthur stories."

"Oh, you really should!" the Merlin nearest her said. "I come off quite well in most of them."

"That's why they're fiction," said the Merlin next to Rachel, and winked at her.

Fort frowned, not sure Merlin had actually answered Rachel's question about changing the past. But it wasn't like they could force the magician, and he *was* giving them all kinds of information they didn't have, not to mention training Rachel and Jia—

"Fort's right, back to the training," his Merlin said, then

gestured at the other two Merlins. "We only need one of you. Choose among yourselves who's going back to our present time."

The two Merlins glanced at each other, and one shrugged. "I have a stew on, so I'm happy to leave it to you." He waved at Jia and Rachel, then disappeared, leaving just two Merlins now, the one by Fort and the one standing near Rachel.

"Now," said Rachel's Merlin, "this is where the hard part begins." He shook his head dismissively. "Honestly, considering how little magic you've picked up so far, I'm a bit ashamed of your teachers. It's like they had no idea what they were doing."

"They didn't, actually," Jia pointed out. "They couldn't use magic themselves, after all."

Their Merlin harrumphed. "That's no excuse. And why haven't you read the more advanced books of magic, the ones detailing the *mixing* of magical types? Where are *those* books?"

Fort, Jia, and Rachel all shared a look. "Um, there are more powerful books of magic?" Rachel said. "I don't think anyone's found those—"

"That's because they didn't survive when magic left this world," the other Merlin said, shaking his head at his counterpart. "You should remember that, old man."

"I remember *everything*!" the first Merlin roared. "Even things that contradict each other! Fine, if that's the case, then I know where we'll start."

"So we've just been using *beginner* books?" Jia asked, looking back and forth between the two Merlins. "But there have been some pretty powerful spells in there. . . ."

"Oh, you've got no idea how powerful magic can get," her Merlin said with a grin. "Those books were created for apprentices, solely so they couldn't jump ahead into stronger magic until they were ready, or share the spells they'd learned with others. If you'd found an advanced copy of, say, Space magic, the entire book would have been readable from the beginning, and you could have told anyone else the words to the spell Change Orbit, if you'd like. And that's not a spell you want to play around with."

Fort's eyes widened. Change Orbit? Like, of the planet? That wasn't possible . . . was it?

"That's a real spell?" Jia said, her voice as soft as a whisper. "But that could—"

"Send the planet hurtling into the sun, or too far away for its heat to reach us, killing all life," her Merlin confirmed. "You see why the beginner books are a good way to start. But we've got no time for that anymore. Rachel, Jia, together we're going to delve into advanced magics, combining types to create more powerful spells. There's no way you could master any one magic enough to stand against the Timeless One, so this might be your only chance."

Rachel's eyes lit up. "Um, yes, please. I'm in."

"Me too," Jia said, looking as excited as Rachel. "If you can teach us magic that we can remember and share, then we won't even need the books of magic that everyone's fighting over! We could make our own, or share whatever we decide is safe with every country in the world. Everyone could actually get along again!"

Her words reminded Fort of a vision she'd had of the future, where her parents had been killed in a war between China and America over the books of magic, and he wasn't surprised how strongly she felt about it. And if they could find a way to share magic with *every* country, that would definitely level the playing field.

But it would also completely change the world, even more than it had already been changed by the attacks in D.C. and London. What would that mean for everyday life? How would it change if *everyone*—or at least the kids of every country, to begin with—could do magic?

"Why don't you wait to see if you three can defeat the Timeless One before worrying about the future," the Merlin closest to him said. "Now, say good-bye to your friends, Forsythe. You won't be seeing them for a while."

"A while?" Rachel said. "What do you mean? How long will we—"

And then she, Jia, and the other Merlin disappeared in a burst of black light.

"Ah, and now for you and your dragon, boy," the remaining Merlin said, giving Ember an appraising glance.

"Wait, where did they go?" Fort said, moving over to the spot they'd disappeared from. "Where did you—the other you—take them?"

"Oh, into the past, I assume," Merlin said, waving a hand absently. "Who really knows what that man is thinking. But that's none of your concern. *You* are here to get your dragon to safety, aren't you? Or was I mistaken about that?"

"We need a way to get back to Avalon," Fort said, still eyeing the spot his friends had just been standing in. "Or maybe to talk to the dragons there, if they could open a portal. That might solve everything?"

"That would require magic beyond your ability," Merlin said.

"No, we'll have to rely on *this* little one to do all the work." He reached out to scratch Ember's chin, and strangely, she let him, purring loudly.

"Her?" Fort said. "But she's a baby!"

"Oh, do dragons also fall within your expertise?" Merlin said, raising a bushy eyebrow. "Why don't you tell me how you found this one."

Fort sighed. If King Arthur had to deal with this sarcasm, then Fort could too. "Fine. When I met the Old One of Healing, or Corporeal magic, whatever it is—"

"Corporeal is more accurate," Merlin said, "but you'll be surprised how deep each type of magic truly extends."

"Sure, okay," Fort said, trying to get to his point. "He was going to attack a bunch of humans because he was mad at us for killing all the dragons, even though we didn't, so I told him he could just make a new one. And here she is." He gently put Ember down on the dining room table before them. "Now the faerie queen wants her to use as a bargaining chip with the Avalon dragons, not to mention that I can't keep her here . . . people would flip out, including my dad and aunt. So even if the faeries weren't after her, I couldn't keep her in my bedroom."

"Oh, of course not," Merlin told him. "She'd be too large for it in less than a week. Dragons mature extremely quickly. But you neglected to mention one thing about dragons, the most important thing, in fact. Do you recall how D'hea created them?"

Fort frowned, the image of a D'hea-sized dragon exploding out of his apartment distracting him. "Um, I think he said they were made out of magic—"

"Precisely!" Merlin shouted, startling Ember. "Which means that if you learn to communicate clearly with the little one here, *she* has the power to open a portal to Avalon, or anywhere, really. There's a reason the Old Ones feared dragons and went to war against humanity once dragons taught humans magic. D'hea unleashed a power that rivals that of the Old Ones themselves."

Fort looked down at Ember, who was currently trying to attack her tail. Could she really already have access to magic like that? If Merlin was telling the truth, then that was all the more reason he had to get her to others of her own kind, if just so she didn't hurt herself with that kind of power.

"Unfortunately," Merlin continued, "so many dragons were lost to the war that the remaining ones fled to Avalon to ensure their survival. There aren't more than five or six left, all told, and each is extremely old." He petted Ember's head. "The queen of the Tylwyth Teg is right to think those dragons would be willing to do almost anything for this child."

"You said communicate clearly with her?" Fort said. "What do you mean by that? She seems to understand her name, but—"

"But you don't know *her* language," Merlin finished. "I have just the thing for that." He snapped his fingers, and a loud crash came from the other room, like several books falling from a shelf. A moment later, an enormous book at least three feet tall came soaring through the doorway to land gently on the table in front of Fort. "There," the old man said, his eyes shining. "Some light reading for you."

Fort cautiously reached down to pick up the book, only to almost drop it instantly, it was so heavy. This thing had to be at least fifteen pounds and more pages than he could count! "What *is* this?"

"A way to communicate," Merlin said. "Think of it as a dragon dictionary, in a sense."

"A dictionary?" Fort said, not able to believe it. "I have to learn all of *this* to talk to her?"

"Of course not!" Merlin said. "No more than half, I'd imagine. Now you see why you won't have time to train. Still, better get cracking, my boy . . . the longer you wait, the more chance the faerie queen will capture her. The dragon is your responsibility now. Good luck, and I'll be back soon with your friends. Or the other me will be, but that shouldn't matter to you. See you soon!"

And he disappeared, just like the other Merlin had with Rachel and Jia.

Fort stared into space for a moment, then looked down at the enormous tome in front of him, alone but for this cat-dragon, who had now leaped from the table to explore whatever was bubbling in the pot over the fire.

"Are you really that powerful, Ember?" Fort said to his cat-dragon as she sniffed at the pot. "Are you some kind of little genius, ready to cast spells that we can't even understand?"

Apparently liking what she smelled, Ember let out a joyous meow, then leaped face-first toward the pot. Fort shouted in surprise, but just before she hit the scalding-hot contents, a floating serving ladle scooped her up and deposited her into a bowl, which floated over to Fort. He just stared at her for a moment, then burst out laughing, then petted her lovingly.

"Okay, maybe not a genius, but you're just perfect the way you are," he said to the now-annoyed cat in front of him, just before she let out a huge burst of flame straight at the offending ladle.

- FOURTEEN -

WHATEVER THIS DICTIONARY OF dragon language was, it didn't work like any of the books of magic. Instead of spell names and descriptions, each page contained exactly one word in a language that could very well have been the one Ember was speaking, followed by an English equivalent.

But whatever the dragon words were, Fort couldn't even begin to know, because they weren't written in an alphabet he recognized. Instead, Ember's language looked like it was written in runes, which meant that even if he found the right word in English, he'd have no idea how to pronounce the dragon equivalent, or even read it.

But maybe there was a way around that? After all, the book could tell he spoke English instead of French or German or something, so maybe he just needed to figure out the right way to access the dragon language, have it turn into an alphabet he recognized, even if it just had to spell out how to pronounce it in English.

He pulled the heavy cover back over to close the book, hoping the book's title would help him with things. But whatever it said was entirely in the dragon runes and therefore completely unreadable.

"Fantastic," he said to Ember, who was back to sniffing at the food in the pot over the fireplace, in spite of the dishes already carrying her away twice now. "I'm never going to learn your language, you realize. You'll probably learn to speak English faster."

Ember eyed him, then reached a paw up to grab for the pot.

"Ember, no, that's hot!" Fort shouted, and bolted up from his seat to grab the cat. He reached her before the ladle could this time and gathered her up into his arms. "You're going to hurt yourself if you keep doing that. Can't you feel the heat?"

Ember pushed indignantly against his grip, and he released her onto the table, glaring at her. "Listen to me," he told her. "Fire will *burn* you. Just like the flames that come out of your mouth burn, well, everything they touch. Do you understand me?" This whole raising a dragon child was going to be the death of him if she kept putting her life in danger like that!

Ember stared at him for a moment. "Solip sefen fio," she said, then began to lick a paw.

Fort started to respond, then paused. Maybe he could use that? "Sole lip say fen fee oh," he repeated to himself, then reopened the book, hoping by sounding it out, maybe he could find something recognizable in the runes. "Sole lip say fen fee oh. Sole lip say fen fee oh."

But no, the runes weren't even close to the alphabet he knew, and they could have represented any type of sound. He sighed, then turned to Ember.

"I don't suppose *you* can help me read this, can you?" he asked. "I'd really like to keep Xenea from stealing you, if possible, so anything you can do to speed this along would be appreciated."

His cat-dragon paused in her paw cleaning to stare at him again, then walked over to the book, used her claws to turn a few pages, and stepped right into the middle of the page she'd chosen, as if ready to say something of great importance.

Then she began to lick her paw again.

Fort groaned, banging his head lightly against the table.

"This is *pointless*! What am I even doing here? I can't talk to a dragon. It's impossible!"

Except it couldn't be impossible, since Damian had learned to speak English at some point. But how? Had he picked it up just like a human baby, learning at a natural speed? Considering Damian hadn't even remembered he was a dragon, that did sort of imply that he'd been human from a pretty young age.

"You don't know how to turn human, do you?" he asked Ember, almost pleading.

She meowed at him for being bothered, then glowed with such a strong blue light that he had to look away. And when Fort turned back, he found himself staring at a very cranky human toddler girl.

"Ember?" he said slowly.

"Solip ertum," human Ember said, glaring at him. She banged her little hand down on the page she was sitting on. "Lesa kniha."

"That's not really helping, actually," he told her, still amazed that she'd been able to turn herself human. Merlin was right, the dragon really *was* incredibly powerful. If Fort could just learn how to get her to open a portal, he could get her to safety and still have time to train.

As she stared up at him, a look of both love and trust in her eyes—if also a little annoyance that he wasn't understanding her—Fort began to realize something: This little girl, no matter what species she actually was, saw him as her dad. Or if not a father, at least a guardian, a caretaker.

Just like he'd been for so long, Ember was basically an orphan. And the way she looked at Fort almost broke his heart. He imagined that was how he'd looked at his own father, when his dad had first awoken after everything in London.

"I'll do my best for you, okay?" he said, and smiled gently at her.

She smiled back, then banged the book again, so hard it almost shook the whole cottage. Fort's eyes widened at her strength, even in human form, but there was no time to think about it, as the force of her hit knocked Ember off-balance, sending her dangerously close to the edge of the table.

Fortunately, Fort leaped forward and caught her before she could fall. "Whoa!" he shouted. "Can you turn yourself back into a cat? At least then you'll be able to jump off things."

Human Ember pouted a bit, then glowed again and emerged as her cat self. He set her back down on the table, where she pawed at the page below her again. "Lesa *kniha*."

"Less a kinney ha?" he said.

She pawed the page one last time, then stepped off into his lap and curled up, purring happily. He sighed, then turned to look at the book. "I don't know what you want from me. It's all complete gibberish, and I can't—"

Hrana, the page said now. *Hrana—Food.*

The runes were gone, and he could read it! Not that he knew what language "hrana" was, but at least he could see the words in letters he recognized. What had changed?

He stared at the book in shock, then looked down at Ember, who yawned widely, then gave him a *I know—I was the one who told you to look at it!* sort of look.

"How did you do that?" he asked, turning the pages to find even more legible dragon words on the next few. "Was that magic?"

She grabbed his hand and gnawed at his knuckles, forcing him to yank his arm away. "Okay, okay, I'll read the book! I'm sorry!"

He turned back to the original page.

Hrana—Food.

Food. Okay. Ember obviously knew what she was doing, opening the book to that page. He'd been joking before about her not being very smart, but that wasn't true at all. Not only could his little dragon already cast spells, but she could read as well! Granted, she also liked to jump into boiling-hot stew, but not everyone was perfect.

"Hrana?" he said to Ember, and her purring grew twice as loud. She hopped down to the floor and went to sit next to the bubbling pot by the fire, waiting expectantly for him.

"Volai hrana," she said, and he leaped up from his seat again, this time in victory. He *understood* that now! Well, part of it anyway. She'd been asking for *food* this whole time!

. . . Okay, yes, he probably should have been able to figure that out from the fact that she was so hungry she ate everything in sight, but still!

"No time for 'hrana' right now," he said, quickly turning back to the book. "I'm getting the hang of this! What was the other word? Vole lei?"

She began to growl, low and angry, and he realized maybe he shouldn't leave the dragon hungry. He quickly moved to the pot, grabbed a nearby bowl, and started to fill it, only for the bowl to pull out of his hand and float through the air back to the pot by itself, where a ladle poured stew in instead. Apparently Fort wasn't allowed to serve himself any more than Ember was.

After the bowl filled itself, it floated to the floor just in front of Ember, and she began to lap up the stew happily, her purrs now filling the room. Good. That meant Fort had a chance to figure out the other word she was using. "Vole lei," he repeated. Probably something along the lines of "Give me what I want or I'll claw you to death."

He flipped through the pages, looking for "vole lei," or something that resembled it at least, but as it turned out, the pages seemed to be in no particular order, and none of the dragon words around "hrana" matched the second word she'd said. Not finding what he needed, he began to randomly page through the book, finding the word for "fire" ("fio," which he thought Ember had used earlier when talking about the pot . . . maybe she *did* understand it was hot?) and the word for "I or me" ("solip").

But the book was just too large to track down "vole lei" just yet.

Still, he'd found a word she'd said, and that was a *huge* victory, considering the size of the book.

"Ember, I can actually do this!" he told the cat as she ignored him, concentrating on her stew as more bowls floated toward the pot, ready to replace her dwindling supply. "I can learn your language and talk to you. As soon as I figure out more words, we can talk about Avalon, and where you need to go, and then you can go join the other dragons and be safe. Isn't that great?"

She glanced up at him, then went back to her stew.

"That's fine—*don't* be excited," he told her, shrugging. "I don't even care. 'Cause I'm on *fire* right now!" He paused. "Or in words you'll understand, um, solip fio!"

Ember reared back in surprise as soon as the words left his mouth, hissing wildly. But before Fort could figure out why, his entire body burst into flame.

FIFTEEN

AAAH!" FORT SCREAMED, IMMEDI-ately dropping to the floor and rolling, trying to smother the flames like he'd been taught so many times in school. But for some reason, the fire *didn't* go out, and he managed to spread it to the cottage's curtains, which immediately went up as well.

It took a moment through his panic, but gradually, as Fort slapped his burning clothes, he finally realized something: He couldn't feel the heat, in spite of his skin literally burning. His clothes were fully aflame now, yes, but the fire wasn't hurting him. What was going on?

He stood up, still on fire, and looked down at himself in confusion.

Ember, meanwhile, hadn't moved from her stew, though she was staring at him with a fairly condescending look.

"Tolsp marnequ frenoir?" she said, tilting her head.

"I don't know what you're saying, but *I'm on fire!*" he screamed at her. "Why isn't it burning me?"

She blinked. "Tolsp tefen fio," she said.

Fort just groaned. Whatever she was telling him, it wasn't helping. And the fire was spreading from the curtains to the walls now, so he had to do something *quick*.

He started to run for the sink, before remembering what the situation was here. "Cottage!" he yelled. "Use the sink to put out the fire, *please!*"

Instead of the sink, though, jets of ice-cold water began shooting out of the ceiling throughout the room, making Ember screech in surprise and rage as they soaked both her and Fort to the bone. And yet, somehow, in spite of now being completely wet, he was *still* on fire, as were the curtains and the walls.

So instead of helping, he'd just managed to drown the cottage as well. *Perfect.*

"What is going *on* here?" shouted a voice, and Fort whirled around to find Merlin, Jia, and Rachel standing in the middle of the room, Merlin glaring at Fort with his mouth wide open. "You did all of this in *that* short a time?"

"You have *no idea* what he's like," Rachel said, stepping forward. She raised her hands, and they instantly glowed a deep red as the fire and water all shot toward her, like she was vacuuming them up. Even the flames from Fort's skin disappeared into her palms, along with all the water from his clothes and Ember's fur.

And just like that, the cottage was out of danger.

"Are you *okay*, Fort?" Jia said, moving quickly to his side now that the fire was out, her hands glowing blue with Healing magic. "You must have at least second-degree . . . Um, how are you not burned at all?"

"I don't know," he told her. "I just said 'solip fio' to Ember, and—"

Just like that, he immediately burst into flames again.

"*Seriously?*" Rachel shouted, and yanked the fire off him once more. "Maybe don't keep repeating it!"

"It's not hurting you," Jia said, inspecting him closely. "How is that possible? I mean, don't get me wrong, I'm really glad you're okay, but how did you do it? You only know the one Healing spell."

"I have no idea," he said. "I didn't even use Heal Minor Wounds."

Ember hissed. *"Tolsp tefen fio,"* she said, glaring at Fort. "Solip toloa frenoir tolsi!"

Rachel looked from Fort to the cat, shocked. *"Whoa.* Did you hear what she just said?"

"I only knew the one word," Fort said. "I think 'fio' is 'fire.'"

"Of *course* it is," Rachel said. "It's one of the words in the fireball spell. But how does *she* know spell words?"

Fort frowned, not sure what she was talking about. "She's speaking dragon. That's . . ."

And then it hit him. Both the Old One of Healing magic and Merlin had said dragons were made out of magic and were inherently connected to it. So maybe it made sense that their language would actually *be* magic!

Fort glanced down at the book on the table, his sense of wonder from his discovery quickly turning to horror as he realized what he'd been doing, randomly saying various magical words without knowing it. He looked back up at Merlin, barely able to speak. "You told me that book was a dragon dictionary!"

"And it is," Merlin said. "I didn't think I'd have to spell it out for you." He chuckled low. *"Spell* it out. Where do I come up with these?"

Fort's eyes widened. "But I was just yelling random spells

then. I could have killed someone. Or myself! *I set myself on fire!*"

Merlin raised an eyebrow. "Well, what exactly did you say? In English, please. My cottage can't take much more of your magic."

Fort angrily opened his mouth to explain, only to realize how bad this was going to sound, and his anger disappeared, replaced by embarrassment. "I was, um, happy that I'd figured out how to read the book," he said so quietly that the others all had to lean in to hear him. "I was celebrating by saying I was on fire, like a *metaphor*."

Rachel snorted loudly, while Jia just stared at him sadly, shaking her head.

"Ah," Merlin said. "Well, you're far from my first apprentice to regret words spoken without thinking. Let this be a lesson to you about being careful what you say. Still, all in all, you're unscathed, and it all worked out fine in the end."

"That doesn't . . . that's not . . . it's *not* fine!" Fort shouted. "Does that mean *everything* Ember is saying is a magical spell?"

Merlin laughed. "Of course not! Not *every* word has power, Forsythe. Just . . . most of them."

Fort fell backward into one of the chairs, which was still a bit wet in spite of Rachel's mopping-up spell. This was going to be *so* bad. He had to learn the actual *language* of magic just to speak to his baby dragon?

"Wait, shouldn't we be studying *this* book then?" Jia said, reaching for the dictionary. "If we knew every word of magic, we'd have a much easier time fighting the Timeless One." Her eyes seemed to light up as she spoke. "And if we've got *this* book, we can share it with the world, so there's no reason for anyone to go to war over the other books of magic!"

"I'm afraid it wouldn't help you much at all," Merlin told her. "Imagine trying to build a house without any blueprints, just some wood or nails. The words to the spell are merely the foundation. To command the universe to obey you requires an exact phrasing, something magicians have been studying and experimenting with for thousands of years, and longer. The books of magic you've been training with in the past, and the ones that your school has, contain the blueprints. *This* book has the nails and wood." He paused. "Not to mention Forsythe managed to set himself on fire in five minutes with it."

Training, in the past? With all the craziness over being on fire, Fort had barely noticed that Jia and Rachel both looked different. They'd been wearing regular clothes before, but now

Jia had some kind of cloak on, with intricate sewing around the edges, covering what looked like some kind of medieval tunic. And Rachel was wearing pieces of leather armor, strapped into place over her arms, legs and torso, in just enough places not to restrict her movement.

They also both looked exhausted, like they hadn't eaten or slept in days. How long had they actually been gone, in the thirty or so minutes since they'd left?

He also might have been imagining it, but Jia and Rachel both seemed a bit uncomfortable with one another, something he hadn't seen since Rachel had first tagged along to try to find Sierra in the depths of the original Oppenheimer School. They'd gotten so close since then, but now there was a distance between them, both literally and figuratively.

But whatever was going on would have to wait for a bit, as Rachel had more questions.

"So Fort might accidentally cast a spell when trying to ask Ember what she wants for breakfast?" she asked Merlin, raising an eyebrow. "Are you sure *he* should be studying this book?"

"Trust me, apprentice," Merlin said with a small smile. "I hope by now I'd know what I was doing."

At Merlin's words, Fort caught Jia throwing a glance at

Rachel, but Rachel turned away, leaving Jia to sigh and look away herself. Something had happened during their training, something that changed things.

But he still didn't even really understand where they'd been.

"Can we back up please?" Fort asked. "You all just show up here a half hour after you left wearing different clothing, talking about training. Where did you take them, Merlin? Why are they wearing these costumes? And what did you show them about the Timeless One?"

"Don't worry about such things," Merlin said to him. "You won't be facing him, and the less you know about the Old Ones, the better."

Fort just stared at him as his cheeks slowly flushed, all the embarrassment from their arrival at the cottage returning in a wave. Right. He'd gotten so wrapped up in the dragon diction-ary that he'd forgotten he wasn't good enough to stand by his friends.

"Okay," Fort said softly. "But if there's anything I *can* do to help, please tell me. I'm already figuring out the dictionary, and I'll have Ember gone soon enough. Then I could—"

Ember hissed at him, then sent a small plume of fire into his face. He jerked back so quickly he almost toppled over, but the flame struck him anyway . . . yet didn't cause any more damage than the previous magical fire had.

"Hey!" he shouted at her. "What was *that* for?"

"Tols'unt sol pare!" Ember shouted, followed by more fire. "Solip volai nen plat tolsi!"

"She's saying she wants to stay with you, Forsythe," Merlin said quietly. "Because you're her father."

Fort looked at the cat in surprise, and she shot another burst of fire at his face. "Hey, Ember, *no!*" he shouted, then turned to Merlin. "And it sounds like *you* can speak her language. Why don't you convince her to go to Avalon before I accidentally set fire to the world?"

"You think a dragon would do what I say?" Merlin asked, his voice rising in surprise. "She's made from magic, the opposite of natural laws. You believe a creature formed from pure chaos would listen to *anyone*, except maybe the one she sees as her parent, her guardian?" His face clouded over with irritation. "Besides, this child is *your* responsibility, Forsythe. You were the one who suggested D'hea create it. I cannot clean up all of your messes for you."

Fort winced at that, knowing Merlin wasn't wrong. Fort *had* convinced the Old One of Healing to create Ember, back at the La Brea Tar Pits, when they'd found the shell of the last dragon's egg—Damian's shell.

"Okay," he said. "But if I destroy the cottage, that's not my fault."

"Wouldn't be the first time this week," Merlin said, just as Ember shot Fort with more flames.

- SIXTEEN -

YOU KNOW WHAT YOU'RE GOING TO face," Merlin told Rachel and Jia after they'd returned from changing back into their normal clothes in one of the cottage's bedrooms, preparing to go home for the night. "The more you train, the better chance you'll have, so I want you two back here as often, and for as long, as you can manage. No excuses, my apprentices."

Rachel and Jia both nodded, still not looking at each other. "We'll be here," Rachel said, sounding a lot less excited than she had before the training had begun. She opened the door to lead the others out, only to stop. "Um, something's off, I think?"

Fort looked past her out the open door, only to find that the clearing had disappeared. Instead, the door now opened onto the treetops and sky, as if it were lying on the ground.

"Oh, the door must have fallen over when we closed it," Rachel said, leaning outside to look. "We should be fine if we just jump." She illustrated by leaping forward through the open door, only to immediately fall right back into the cottage, where she skidded to a halt on the floor.

"Or maybe we could climb," Jia said, giving Rachel a smile, which Rachel didn't return. Jia's face fell again, but she knelt down to the floor, grabbed the bottom of the door, then slowly pushed herself forward, crawling out of the door when gravity shifted on the other side. It hurt Fort's brain to watch, but Jia managed pretty easily, then stood over the door and waved for them to follow her out, as if she was standing on the outside wall of the cottage.

"Climbing it is," Rachel said, and followed Jia's example, with Fort right behind her, Ember on his shoulder. Passing through the door to regular gravity was an odd shift, especially when half his body was still inside the cottage, but he quickly kicked himself the rest of the way through and picked himself up from the clearing floor to look back down into the cottage.

"Next time, prop me up good and well!" the imp door knocker shouted, its voice muffled with the front of the door now on the ground. Fort quickly turned the door over to close it, the imp giving him a dirty look as he did. Ember hissed at it, which at least helped a bit.

"Fort?" Jia said, grabbing his arm to turn him around, as Rachel moved toward the center of the clearing. She looked nervous now, combined with whatever was going on with her and Rachel. "There's . . . something we have to tell you. About the Timeless One—"

"Jia, *no*," Rachel said, shaking her head a few feet away. That had to be the first time in a while that Rachel hadn't used Jia's nickname. "We can't—we *promised*. Besides, I figured you'd be all about not sharing secrets."

Jia flinched at this, almost as if Rachel had slapped her. "You know why I couldn't tell you that," she said quietly.

"No, I don't," Rachel said, looking away. "But I *do* know why we can't tell Fort about . . . everything. I don't know how much I trust Merlin, but he made sense about this."

"Tell me what?" Fort asked. "Is this about the training or something? Because if there's a way I can help, I *want* to!" Ember meowed loudly in support, which he absently petted her for in thanks.

Jia stared at the ground. "He deserves to know," she said. "I don't care what we promised."

Rachel snorted. "It's weird how these promises of yours come and go, isn't it?" She turned to Fort. "Hey, remember when you asked if either of us made a deal with the faerie queen, because that girl said something about it? Well—"

"Rachel, *no!*" Jia shouted, stepping in front of Fort and holding up her hands.

"Why not?" Rachel asked, looking miserable but not backing down. "Do you really think Fort doesn't need to know? Or is this why you want to tell him what we found out in the past, because you feel guilty about keeping this from us?"

"What is going *on?*" Fort shouted. "What happened between you two?" *And did Jia make some kind of deal with the faerie queen that she hadn't mentioned? Why would she hide it?*

Jia gave Rachel a pleading look, and the other girl just rubbed her eyes. "I'm sorry—I'm tired. I haven't slept in days, and—"

"Days?" Fort said, his eyebrows rising. "What are you talking about?"

And then it hit him: wearing different outfits, traveling through time, training for as long as they could. They hadn't been gone for just a half hour.

"How long?" he asked. "How long were you training for?"

"Two weeks," Rachel said, hugging herself with her arms.

"Two *weeks*?" Fort said, his voice rising an octave. "You're joking. There's no way!"

But Jia nodded in confirmation. "Merlin had a lot to show us. About the Old Ones, and—"

"And more that we're not allowed to *talk* about," Rachel said, interrupting Jia. "So that's all we can say." She looked down at Ember, who was batting her paws at Fort's earlobe now. "Are you going to be okay with this murderous cat while you figure out her language?"

"I'd be a lot more okay if I wasn't maybe going to cast a random spell every time I said something to her," Fort said, deciding to let whatever their secret was go, since Rachel was obviously trying to change the subject. Not to mention he knew he'd never get anything out of Rachel that she didn't want to tell.

Jia, though, definitely seemed to be feeling guilty about something, and for good reason if she'd been hiding a deal with the faerie queen. Granted, Fort hadn't initially told either of them about his own deal with the queen, the one that had ended up saving his father, but he hadn't believed it would actually work. Now that they'd seen what the queen could do, it seemed like a pretty good time to share any other deals.

Rachel smiled slightly. "I'd avoid the word 'fio' if I were you. Now I'm heading home to sleep for as long as my parents let me." She turned without another word, or even a look at Jia, while Jia just watched her go. Rachel opened a portal with her slap bracelet and, a moment later, was gone.

"Jia, if there's anything you want to tell me now that she's not here . . . ," Fort said, trailing off, but Jia just shook her head.

"I don't know, I . . . I have to think about it all," she said, and the expression on her face made his heart break for her. Whatever had happened, it'd hurt them both a lot.

Still, Fort couldn't help but be a little annoyed himself. What had Jia kept from them? Whatever it was had to be worse for Rachel, too. As close as they were, Fort couldn't imagine what Rachel must have felt if she'd found out about Jia keeping something from her. It would be as if Sierra hadn't told *him* something, which he already was way too familiar with, considering she'd been hiding Damian from him.

But it wasn't going to help anyone to go over all of that with Jia now. It looked like she and Rachel had already had it out, and Jia looked like she could use a friend at the moment.

"Try to get some sleep, okay?" Fort told her, but she was

already opening a portal. She gave him a wave, then disappeared inside, taking the teleportation circle with her.

Weirdly, standing alone in the clearing with Ember on his shoulder, Fort felt more alone than at any time since the original attack in Washington, D.C. He, Rachel, and Jia had been a team for so many weeks now, it felt odd to be left out of secrets, to know they were hiding things from him, even if there were good reasons.

Once again, he was reminded of what it felt like to be the only student at the Oppenheimer School not born on Discovery Day. Just like then, he seemed to be left out of everything, like he didn't belong.

At least he had Cyrus in those days, someone who didn't care when Fort was born, or how talented at magic he was. Hopefully, Cyrus was somewhere okay and would be back soon, because right now, Fort could have used a friend.

"*You* want to know what's going on, don't you?" he asked his cat-dragon.

Ember briefly opened her eyes, yawned, then closed them again.

"Yeah, me too," he said sadly. Speaking of the original Oppenheimer School, he suddenly missed having access to

Sierra's Mind magic, even if it was all by accident on her part. If he could read minds like she could now, he wouldn't need Jia to tell him what they'd found out, whatever it was that Rachel was so insistent he couldn't know.

But they'd destroyed the book of Mind magic, back when they'd stolen it and the book of Summoning from Colonel Charles, so there was no way to . . .

Wait. Of course there was a way.

The dragon dictionary had every possible spell word in existence!

All he had to do was find the right words, something like See What Jia and Rachel Were Hiding That They'd Learned from Merlin During Their Training—or maybe a bit simpler than that—and he'd figure out whatever this secret was, without Merlin even knowing or Jia and Rachel getting in trouble. It'd be *easy*, and wouldn't be dangerous at all, considering there was no fire involved this time. And while he was looking for this new spell, he'd still be learning Ember's language, so doing exactly what he was supposed to!

And hey, once he knew Merlin's secret, maybe that'd help Fort find a way to actually help against the Timeless One, as soon as he got Ember to Avalon. This was starting to feel like a plan!

"C'mon, little girl," Fort told Ember, rubbing her head. "We're going to have a lot of studying to do tomorrow night, so we need to rest up tonight!"

"Volai hrana," Ember hissed at him, then went back to sleep.

- SEVENTEEN -

UNFORTUNATELY, BEFORE FORT COULD get back to Merlin's cottage the next night, he had to spend a full day with a certain faerie girl.

Xenea was waiting for him the next morning as soon as Fort stepped outside the apartment complex. "I didn't see any dragons last night," she told him without even a hello. "And I was watching."

"Fantastic," Fort said. "I didn't see any either." Considering Ember had stayed in cat form, that at least wasn't a lie. "Xenea, you mentioned that one of my friends might have made a deal with your queen. Do you know what that deal was?"

Xenea slowly smiled. "Maybe. Why? What's it worth to you?"

Fort sighed deeply. "Forget it. I don't want to know."

"I think you do," she said, staring at him suspiciously. "You better watch out, or I'll use my glamour on you to find out what's actually going on here."

Thankfully, the school bus pulled up just then, and Xenea was distracted away from Fort's eyes widening at her threat. He hadn't even *considered* that she might use her magic to force him to reveal things. He might tell her everything about Ember, and that'd be it for the baby dragon!

Fortunately, Xenea seemed to forget what had just happened as soon as she stepped aboard the bus, surrounded as she was by other students. And once at school, she seemed even more distracted, which was perfect, since Fort had a lot of thinking to do.

Unfortunately, instead of the faerie girl sitting with her new friends at lunch, she brought them all to Fort's table, where they crowded in, giving Fort a bunch of side-eye while fawning over her. Perfect.

"So explain this one more time," Xenea said to Fort as she stared at the chicken tender in his hand with distaste. "*What* part of that strange white feathered bird you showed me is that again?"

"No one really knows," Fort admitted, putting the chicken back down on his plate, suddenly not very hungry.

"And the 'money' they wanted for this?" she asked, picking up a pudding cup and happily spooning its contents into her mouth. "Food should be free for all. But if they *have* to make a deal for it, why not just let me bargain with this so-called 'lunch lady'? I could have gotten all our meals, plus the net she wears in her hair, for a pittance!"

"We use money instead of making deals," Yejun told her. "It's like saying 'I gave someone a dollar's worth of something, and they gave me this piece of paper to prove it.' Now I can trade that piece of paper to someone else for the same amount of stuff."

Xenea sniffed disdainfully. "Seems overly complicated. Why not just negotiate directly? That way you can *outwit* your opponent."

The rest of the table all nodded in agreement, while Fort rolled his eyes. "Because not every deal has to be about *beating* someone," he said. "Wouldn't it be nicer if both sides were happy with what they got?"

Xenea's eyes flashed dangerously, and she slowly stood up from her seat. The entire lunchroom went silent as she turned to Fort, her face flushed with righteous anger. "Because that is how you get *tricked*, Forsythe!" she roared. "Do you remember what the Timeless One did to my people?!"

"That's what she calls someone who makes clocks where she's from," Fort said quickly to the lunchroom, but no one seemed to even hear him, as they were all watching Xenea with an almost reverent gaze.

"Why do you think I was changed back into a child, and stuck at this age for a thousand years?" she kept right on going, though none of it was affecting the students through their glamoured minds. "I was an *adult* once! But he reversed us all back in time to when we were kids, and now I'm here with you sad little humans who don't understand that *everyone* is out to get you, unless you get them first!"

"*We're* not out to get you!" Yejun shouted, and the rest of the lunchroom loudly agreed.

"If I agree with you, would you turn down your glamour a little?" Fort asked, getting extremely uncomfortable with how much his schoolmates were worshiping Xenea. It reminded him way too much of Spirit magic and how he'd felt while under William's spell.

Xenea rolled her eyes at him but dropped back into her seat, then snapped her fingers. All around them, kids began talking to each other instead of focusing on every word she said. Even

Yejun turned to the girl sitting next to him and began chatting quietly. "There," Xenea said to Fort. *"Better?"*

"Yes," Fort said, breathing a sigh of relief as he leaned in closer so the other students couldn't hear. "It just makes me nervous when you use it that much on them. I mean, you don't like it when other faeries use a glamour on you, do you?"

Maybe if he could convince her to stop using it, she'd keep her magic away from *him* and not force him to tell the truth about the dragon in his room.

"First of all," Xenea said, "our glamours don't work on each other, only on *lower* life-forms." She paused, giving him a long look. "Second, you have to quit being so naive, Forsythe. Life is about taking what you can get before someone else takes it from you. If you can't admit that, you're already losing."

He sighed. "Even glamoured, Yejun was right: Not everyone is like that. Don't you have any friends, or family? People who watch out for you? People who *don't* want to take advantage of you?"

"Of course I do!" Xenea said indignantly. "Who do you think teaches us our first lesson in making deals? My family made a point to cheat me out of anything I ever got, just to show me how it's done. I still haven't bargained back any of my toys." She sniffed loudly. "Not even Mr. Uni-Bear. I miss him the most."

Fort had no idea where to even begin with *that*, but he did have an idea to keep her distracted from all things dragon. "That's not what humans are like. And since you said you wanted to learn about us, I have a plan for this afternoon. Maybe there's something we can teach *you*."

She snorted. "Really? Because so far, all I'm seeing is greed." She pointed at the cash register at the end of the lunch line. "You make children *pay* to eat. Food in Avalon is free for everyone, no bargaining required. Just like everything else you need to live. What happens if a child can't pay for their food? Would you kind, nice people who don't bargain for anything just let them starve?"

Fort sighed. "I hope not, but that's a fair point. Still, where I'm taking you isn't about food."

"Is there a price to visit this place you speak of?" Xenea asked suspiciously. "Because if so, if you wish me to go, I will need you to pay for it."

"Yes, and I was planning on doing that anyway," Fort said, shaking his head.

She snorted. "You're so truly bad at this, Forsythe. You wouldn't last two minutes on Avalon." She paused to consider. "That's about as long as you *did* last, wasn't it?"

After school, Fort texted his dad to let him know he'd be home for dinner, in case his dad got back earlier (being able to text his father still seemed like the most amazing thing ever), and took a bus to the mall with Xenea. When they walked inside, she stopped dead, staring at all the things for sale in the storefronts, but Fort dragged her on. "We're not going shopping," he told her. "Come on. The movie theater is just around the corner."

"But I could *own* this market!" she shouted, people staring to look at her. "Own it *all*!"

He eventually got her to the movies and handed over cash for two tickets, then popcorn and sodas (which she finally consented to trying after making sure there were no hidden animals or molds within either one). Finally, they grabbed some seats in the theater, which was thankfully empty.

"What is this?" Xenea asked as she sat down in a chair, then looked down at her feet, which were sticking to the floor. "Some kind of punishment? Is this for all the glamouring I was doing?"

"Just wait," he told her as the lights began to dim. "You need to see that we're not all out for ourselves."

Two hours later, Fort walked out of the theater with a wide-eyed Xenea just behind him. He wanted to ask how she'd enjoyed the movie, but the look of sheer awe on her face stopped him from saying anything. In fact, she ended up staying quiet all the way back to his apartment.

"We don't have anything like *that*," she said finally, when they got off the bus. "Those humans on the lighted wall were so *big*!"

"It's definitely a kind of magic," Fort told her. "But what did you think about the story?"

"What do you mean, the story?" she asked, her eyes widening farther. "Wait, that wasn't a magical window into something happening right at that moment?"

"No, that was actors, people pretending to be someone else to tell a story," Fort said, realizing he probably should have made that clear before going into the theater. "We don't actually *have* space aliens here. Magical monsters, sure, but no aliens."

Her face fell a bit. "Oh, really? I was going to ask to see some later."

"What? Did you not see the moment the aliens ate almost the entire crew?"

"Sure, but they were so good at it!" she said, then bared her teeth and swiped at him in an imitation of the aliens. "So that was all made up? How disappointing. What was the point of it, then?"

"The *point* was that the hero tried to save everyone!" Fort said. "Even though she could have died herself, and almost did. She went back into danger, and got nothing out of it, all because she wanted to help the others!"

Xenea wrinkled her nose. "Yeah, that part was the most confusing. Why would she do that? Isn't her life worth more to her than someone else's? And if she got eaten, then they'd both be gone." She snorted. "Just seems illogical."

"Okay, maybe it *is* illogical," Fort said. "But that's the point! Sometimes people *do* illogical things because they're the right thing to do. We try to help other people, even if we suffer for it, because we don't want *them* to suffer too."

And then sometimes, even when you wanted to help, you weren't allowed to because some old man who could see the future told you that you'd mess everything up if you tried. But that wasn't anything he was going to share with the faerie girl.

Besides, he was still working to keep Ember out of the faerie queen's hands. That counted for something.

Xenea snorted. "Then how do you win, if you suffer too?"

Her question made Fort pause. "I don't know," he said honestly. "I guess you win by doing the thing you wish other people would do for you, if they were in your situation. Because then everyone wins."

"Or everyone loses," Xenea said, making a disgusted face. "Why take the chance? If I'd been her, I'd have taken that ship and gotten out of there the moment the aliens started turning your people into chicken tenders." She paused. "So you're saying you'd help *me even* if it meant you might get eaten by an alien, Forsythe?" She raised an eyebrow questioningly. "Even if I didn't promise you any treasure or make a bargain with you to save me?"

Fort started to make a joke about how if it was *her*, he'd leave her to her fate, but somehow he didn't find it as funny as he'd thought it'd be. "I hope I would," he said quietly.

"This makes no sense," Xenea said. "And it doesn't track with everything else I've seen. No wonder you come up with stories like that, to make yourselves feel better for all the greedy things you do." She shook her head. "You humans might want to think you're good, but deep down, you're just like we are, Forsythe. And that's smart, because it will keep you safe."

"Maybe you're right," Fort said, thinking about the Timeless One and his friends again. "Maybe there are times where we want to help, but can't, because it'll just make things worse. But we still *wish* we could."

"What do you mean, wish you could?" Xenea said. "It's always a choice. You're just trying to comfort yourself, saying you wanted to help but couldn't."

Her words made Fort's heart begin to race as his embarrassment grew once more. "Or maybe we really do want to help, even if it *is* dangerous, but are told no because we're not *good* enough! Did you ever think of that?"

She just stared at him for a moment. "Of *course* I didn't think of that. What are you even talking about? Who isn't good enough?"

He just shrugged, his mind immediately going back to his dragon back home. He had to be careful with Xenea, not reveal anything he shouldn't. If she found out he had teleported to Merlin's cottage, she might wonder what else he was hiding. "It . . . it doesn't matter. I just meant, what's the point of being safe if we let people get hurt? How could we live with ourselves if we just ignored what they were going through? That sounds awful."

"But at least you'd *be* living with yourself, instead of in some alien's stomach!" She growled in frustration. "You humans are so . . . *human*! You think you're all so great, but you're not, Forsythe. So go home! Feast upon your moldy cow milk and bread. You've made my mind hurt, and I will speak no more of humanity tonight." She turned away, then paused. "Instead, I will go back to the marketplace, and make it *mine*."

And then she disappeared, leaving Fort with a very uncomfortable feeling about what was about to happen at the mall.

- EIGHTEEN -

AS PROMISED, XENEA DIDN'T SHOW for dinner that night, which Fort was thankful for. He was sure her glamour would probably convince his dad and aunt that it wasn't strange having her there for a second night in a row, but he didn't want to worry about her seeing through Ember's magical disguise, or forcing Fort to reveal his dragon's whereabouts.

Not to mention after the day he'd had, he just really wanted some regular, normal family time.

As he sat down, Aunt Cora had the television on, and the news wasn't great. "Tensions between the United States and China reached an all-time high today as the Chinese fleet moved to—" the anchor said, only for Cora to shut the TV off.

"Like that's what we need now," she said, angrily shaking her head. "With everything that's happening, why can't our countries just work together?"

Fort nodded without saying anything, running his fork around in his mashed potatoes. He knew why they weren't working together. China wanted their book of Healing magic back to protect themselves from the Old Ones, and Colonel Charles was refusing to hand it over.

At least things weren't at the level they would have been if the faerie queen hadn't saved his father. Then they'd be heading for a world war fought by magic-using soldiers. He had to remember that was why Xenea was here. Even hiding Ember from the faerie girl was still nothing in comparison to stopping a war.

Sometimes he really hated knowing what was actually happening. It had to be so nice, just to have no idea that magic existed, or why the world's governments were on edge.

"At least there haven't been any more attacks since London," his father said, looking tired. "That's something, right? And I talked to my old boss today. He said there was a slim chance they could find some consulting work for me, since my old job is gone. See? Good news is everywhere if you just look for it!"

Fort forced a smile at him, just to make his dad happy. Fort couldn't imagine how hard it would be to come back to a life with no memory of where you'd been for six months, only to find the rest of the world had moved on without you.

"I can't *stand* what those people said about you on TV," his aunt said, attacking her chicken so hard her fork clanked against the plate. "Who do they think they are? They have no idea what we've all been through."

Fort looked up at her, confused. "What people?" he asked. "What are they saying?"

This time, his father and his aunt shared a look. "It's nothing, Forsythe," his father said. "Just filling the time on the news."

"They're saying he was never taken by . . . whatever that monster was," his aunt said, stabbing her fork against the plate again. "That your father faked his disappearance in the attack for . . . what? Publicity? It doesn't even make sense! The military should put out a statement! They know the truth, and the fact that they won't say so—"

"They're the military," his father said with a small smile. "They never tell *anything*. And I'm just happy they found me, wherever I was. I really don't care what anyone says, Cora. That's their problem, not mine."

Fort felt the blood drain from his face. People were accusing his father of lying? But how could they even think someone would make that kind of thing up? And just to get some attention?

"It'll be your problem *and* mine if people believe it," his aunt said, not looking at her brother-in-law. "That could be why O'Connoll won't hire you back full-time, you know. These horrible rumors!"

"But there were *witnesses*," Fort said, still not able to believe what he was hearing. "I mean, besides me! There were people there who saw it all, two girls and their mom. And you saved that old woman who couldn't get down the stairs at the memorial. We have to tell them, Dad. This isn't right!"

His father put up his hands in surrender. "No, it's not, but that doesn't mean we'd make things any better by coming out and talking about it," he said, giving Fort a sad smile. "I don't remember anything of that day, not even what you just mentioned, Forsythe. So I couldn't really say anything that'd help my story, unfortunately."

"Then Aunt Cora is right: We need to talk to the military!" Fort said, pushing to his feet. "I'm not going to let someone accuse you—"

"The military's job is keeping us safe, not arguing on the

news," his father said, motioning for Fort to take his seat again. "Really, it's fine! This will all blow over in a few days, and no one will care. There are a lot more important things going on to worry about than whatever happened to me."

"That's another part of the problem," Aunt Cora said, shaking her head. "If they'd just *tell* us what's happening, where all these monsters are coming from, then there'd be something to focus on. But since they just keep ignoring all the questions, no one knows anything. They won't even say what that giant orange creature was in London, and that destroyed the entire city!"

"I saw someone interviewed on the BBC claim to have been absorbed into the monster somehow," his father said, his face showing he didn't believe it. "This is just what people do, make up stories when they don't know any better. Once the government figures out what these things are and where they're coming from, they'll tell us."

"If we're even still around," Cora muttered.

"Hey!" his father said, now sounding angry. "What did I say about that, Cora? Not in front of Forsythe."

Fort looked between his father and his aunt, suddenly realizing that everything *hadn't* just gone back to normal now that his father was back. "What can't she say in front of me, Dad?" he asked quietly.

Cora rubbed her eyes. "He's right, Fort. I'm sorry. I never should have said that."

"What can't she say in front of me?" Fort repeated.

His father sighed. "These attacks have everyone on edge, Forsythe. And no one knows when the next one might come, so understandably, your aunt sometimes fears the worst. And I do too. But I asked her to not talk about that in front of you, because I don't want you to have to worry about it, kiddo." He reached out and squeezed Fort's arm. "You deserve to have a normal childhood, if that's possible anymore. And I don't want you panicking about something you can't control."

Fort just stared at his father, his mouth hanging open. "Panicking about something that *I* can't control?" he repeated back, barely sure where to even start with that. "But I . . ."

"Everything's going to be fine, Fort," Cora said. She gave him a smile, though it didn't feel natural. "Really. It's easy to give in to the fear and all, but we have to have faith that things will be okay. Whatever these creatures are, the authorities will figure out how to deal with them. That's their whole job, right?"

Fort swallowed, thinking about how useless both the military and even the students had been when the Old Ones had attacked the original Oppenheimer School. And they hadn't fared any better against D'hea's rampage, or William in London. "I guess," he said.

"No guessing," his father said. "Everything's going to be just fine, you'll see. Now, no more talk about monsters, only regular, normal things. How's that kitten of yours doing?"

- NINETEEN -

A S IT TURNED OUT, EMBER WAS hungry—and nowhere close to a kitten anymore. After dinner with his dad and Aunt Cora, he brought Ember in dragon form to Merlin's cottage. There, he sat with her at the long dining room table as she lapped up her third bowl of stew, her scales glistening in the light of the fire. She'd grown again and now was about the size of a golden retriever.

Soon, she'd be bigger than Fort, and there'd be no way he could keep her in the apartment. He'd have to hurry and study, or she might get discovered by someone, or worse, Xenea.

Across the room, Jia and Rachel prepared for their next trip into the past for training, as Merlin waited impatiently. Part of Fort wanted to ask one last time if he could go, promise them he really could help with the Timeless One, but the rest of him knew the answer would still be no. Not when they believed Merlin that Fort might get hurt, or lose the battle for them.

Not to mention that they had their own stuff to deal with. Whatever had happened between them hadn't been worked out, or at least Fort assumed it hadn't, since Jia and Rachel weren't looking at each other. He could feel the tension in the silent air and almost considered saying something random just to lighten things up. But whatever problem they were having wouldn't be fixed by him interfering, so he turned back to Ember and smiled as she slopped some stew on the floor.

In spite of having to hide the dragon from Xenea, not to mention his father and aunt, there was something about her that made Fort feel better when Ember was around. Everything was either a threat (mostly) or a friend (rarely) to Ember, and with all his worries, he almost found that comforting. If nothing else, she wasn't going to leave him behind and go off to fight an Old One.

She finished her dinner and made her way over to Fort, then dropped her stew-covered face into his lap, beaming up at him. "Hey!" he said, pushing her off to try to clean his pants, but it was a losing battle, and Ember just replaced her head anyway before he could accomplish much. He rolled his eyes. "Happy?"

"Sa," she said, and closed her eyes. "Sa."

He shook his head, but smiled again and petted her head as she started to snore. At least there were some advantages to not going with Merlin for training, he had to admit. Whatever Jia and Rachel were doing, it seemed both physically and mentally exhausting, over who knew how many days or weeks. All Fort had to do was study in a cozy little cottage while being served by high-tech devices.

If only he could bring his father here and let his dad relax in front of the fire with him. He knew his dad could use it.

He sighed, trying not to think about his father's troubles right now. He was here to study, and he couldn't let himself be distracted.

Especially not since he had a very specific plan in mind for tonight: find a spell that would let him learn the secret Merlin didn't want him to know.

Fort absently turned the book's pages as he waited for Merlin, Rachel, and Jia to leave, not wanting them to accidentally discover what he was planning.

"For the next six weeks," Merlin told the two girls, who were standing much farther apart than they usually did, "we're going to concentrate on perfecting the new types of magic you've learned, while also training on how to defeat Time magic with your own specialties."

New types of magic? Ways to defeat Time magic? Fort started listening closer, just in case, while pretending he was lost in the book of dragon language.

Jia sounded confused. "I don't really see how Healing or golem building—"

"Puppetry," Rachel said, sounding almost mocking.

"—could offset what Time magic can do," Jia finished, ignoring Rachel. "Anything I try, the Old One can just speed himself up or freeze me completely in time."

"Every type of magic has its strengths and weaknesses in relation to the others," Merlin told her. "To use your example, Jia, if the Timeless One were to speed up his own personal time, a Corporeal magician might use their own magic upon themselves, changing their body so their reaction times were quicker, while evolving their mind to think and interpret their senses faster, so they could see, move, and think as quickly as the Timeless One."

"And as an Elemental magician," Rachel asked, lighting up, "I could move as fast as lightning or something?"

"Oh, no, I'm afraid that's impossible," Merlin said, patting her shoulder. "That would be one of the weaknesses I mentioned. Elemental magic is particularly vulnerable to Time magic. Which is why, my apprentice, you'll need as much training time as you can get."

Rachel's excitement faded, and she nodded. "Okay, fine, let's get to it."

The three of them disappeared, and for a moment, Fort looked up to where they'd been standing and couldn't even believe how different things were with Merlin here, someone who *knew* about magic, instead of adults who couldn't use it themselves. They'd spent so many months trying to learn without knowing what they were doing that in spite of the upcoming battle against the Timeless One, it was pretty nice to have a knowledgeable teacher on their side.

But now that he was alone, he could get to the important stuff. Ember's snoring had grown louder, and not wanting to wake her, Fort flipped slowly through the book before him, hoping he could find the words he needed.

As he turned the pages, some of what he found honestly terrified him with what they could do: "explode," "destroy," "disease" . . . okay, that last one he'd learned briefly when he'd first been studying Healing magic, but still. Mixed in with those were much more normal words, like "speak," "learn," and "home," which were less scary on the surface.

And then there were the ones that could go either way, like "cook," "knot," and "grow." He didn't want to think about the giant, cooked knot he could make out of someone if he combined those three.

These words were just so *dangerous*. Any one of them could be used wrongly and set off a whole chain of magic he never intended, if he wasn't careful. The fact that Merlin hadn't even mentioned that they were words of magic before letting Fort loose on the book made him wonder what the magician thought would happen. Couldn't Merlin see the future? If so, he shouldn't have been surprised that Fort had set himself on fire.

But the one word he was looking for didn't have any negative drawbacks that he could think of. It was one of the pretty normal ones, but it also had its uses, if he could just find it. . . .

Thankfully, it wasn't much longer before he actually managed to stumble upon it randomly. It helped that he wasn't pausing to learn any of the other words, but instead was just searching as fast as possible, hoping to find it before the others returned. Even so, he was beginning to worry when he turned the page and found the following:

Vede—See

That was *it*, the spell he'd been looking for! Sure, he'd hoped to find some other related words in the process, just to help pin things down, but this one should do the trick—*if* he was careful. He would just have to picture clearly what he wanted to "see," and things should be fine.

Gently he lifted Ember's head off his lap, getting growled at in return, then prepared himself. Whatever was going to happen, he knew he shouldn't be in any danger, not if the See spell worked as it should. But what it would do was show him what Merlin's secret was, whatever the old man hadn't allowed Jia or Rachel to tell Fort.

Taking a deep breath, he slowly let it out, then said the words to the spell.

"Vede Timeless One."

See the Timeless One, wherever he is, Fort thought as he said the words, repeating the idea over and over. . . .

Of course, Fort had no idea what the Timeless One looked like, but in his mind, he pictured a creepy, cloaked creature like the other Old Ones he'd seen. Maybe his body was a huge hourglass, filled with running sand. And he'd be old, like the Father Time cartoon they showed around New Year's Eve.

But hopefully none of that mattered, since the magic *should* take care of it, just like when he'd cast Cause Disease and just pictured whatever sickness he'd wanted to cause in his mind. It wasn't like he knew which virus or bacteria caused a cold, but he was still able to cast it. And if this didn't work, then probably nothing would happen, and—

Out of nowhere, a deserted, barren landscape appeared, right over the top of the cottage's dining room, as if someone was projecting it. This new land looked like it'd been destroyed by something apocalyptic, though from what Fort could see, there were still buildings . . . or at least one large tower in the background, black as night. The sky was a dark red, and there was nothing living as far as he could see.

Something fluttered above him, and he looked up to find a cloaked figure floating in the air, just like he'd imagined. Instantly his blood ran cold, and Fort had to remind himself that he was seeing the Old One from afar, and the monster couldn't see him in return. Slightly reassured, he stepped closer, hoping to see whatever it was Merlin wanted to keep from him.

One of the creature's hands was just bone, like the hand of a human skeleton, while the other seemed to be a spiked, armored glove of some kind. Inside the cloak, the being seemed to have no body, just shimmering images that made Fort's head hurt. And where the face should have been was what looked like an infinity symbol, only melting, making it even more horrific.

This *had* to be the Timeless One. But other than how terrifying he looked, what was it that Jia and Rachel couldn't tell him about? What was the secret Merlin had sworn them to secrecy over? What—

"FORSYTHE?" the Old One said, pointing straight at him with a finger. "YOU CANNOT BE HERE. WHERE DID YOU GET THAT POWER? MERLIN MUST BE *CHEATING!*"

And before Fort could even begin to understand what was happening, black light surrounded him, and the cottage faded the rest of the way from view around him, leaving him fully, physically in the apocalyptic land of the Timeless One.

- TWENTY -

FORT JUST STARED UP IN HORROR AT the Old One, his limbs all frozen with fear. How had the spell gone so wrong? All he'd wanted to do was *see* the Timeless One, not talk to him, not let him know he was being watched!

The Old One must have felt it somehow and brought him to . . . wherever, or *whenever*, this was.

But maybe it wasn't too late. Maybe he could still teleport away—

"WE ARE *FAR* FROM YOUR TIME, FORSYTHE," the Timeless One said, slowly descending toward him. "YOU WOULD HAVE NOWHERE TO GO. BUT HOW DID YOU GAIN THIS POWER, THE MAGIC TO FIND ME? YOU SHOULDN'T HAVE MORE THAN A TELEPORTATION AND A HEALING SPELL!"

Now confusion competed with fear in Fort's mind. What had he said? How could an Old One know that much about him? "I know a lot more magic than that!" he shouted, trying to act brave, even while he backed away from the monster on trembling legs. "Stay back, or I'll . . . knock this world from orbit!"

"THIS WORLD IS *YOUR* WORLD, HUMAN," the Timeless One said, advancing slowly toward Fort. "JUST IN THE FUTURE. BUT *ENOUGH* OF THIS. I WILL SEE FOR MYSELF HOW YOU LEARNED THIS MAGIC."

Black light filled Fort's eyes, and he was blinded for a moment, only for the light to disappear as quickly as it'd appeared.

"HE GAVE YOU THE *BOOK*?" the Timeless One roared, and all around Fort, black light infused the surface of the ground, causing rocks to crumble into dust and dirt to fade away into nothingness. "MERLIN CHEATS AT OUR GAME. *THIS WILL NOT STAND!*"

Even the ground beneath Fort began to shake now, losing any cohesion as the dirt and stone withered into nothingness, and Fort scrambled out of the beginnings of a sinkhole to what he hoped would be solid ground . . . if anything could escape the Old One's rage.

If this was Time magic, Fort couldn't even begin to wrap his head around how powerful it must be to dissolve earth and rock. For the first time, he realized just how right Merlin had been: There was no way Fort would have stood a chance against the Timeless One. At best, he'd have only gotten in Rachel's way, and then, only if she had Excalibur. Without the sword, how could *any* of them face this creature?

Just as Fort's feet began to sink into the ground, the Old One's anger seemed to lessen, and the light of Time magic disappeared as the Timeless One floated closer once more. "HE HAS BROKEN THE *RULES*, FORSYTHE," the creature said. "YOU WERE MEANT TO BE KEPT OUT OF THIS BATTLE. MERLIN AGREED TO THOSE TERMS, AND YET, NOW HE WOULD ARM YOU AGAINST ME. I SHALL NOT ALLOW IT!"

The Old One's rage returned as he spoke, and again, black light seemed to appear all around Fort, but this time, he knew he had to try to calm the Timeless One down, or he'd tumble into whatever lay below the ground beneath him. "I don't know what this deal you're talking about is, but Merlin didn't arm me *or* train me. He said I wasn't allowed to face you, because I was useless!" Saying it out loud would have embarrassed him in any other situation, but right now, the terror was too real to worry about that. "Whatever this thing is, I promise you, Merlin didn't break any rules!"

Or at least Fort desperately hoped Merlin hadn't, or else there was no telling what the Old One might do.

"OH, I KNOW WHAT HIS EXCUSES WERE," the Timeless One said, floating toward Fort so quickly that Fort couldn't help but leap backward in surprise. The creature's infinity-sign face came within inches of him, and Fort could smell an awful sort of decay, like the monster's cloak had been rotting away for centuries. "HE TOLD YOU IT WAS TO LEARN THAT DRAGON'S LANGUAGE, BUT THAT WAS ALL A FACADE. HE *MEANT* FOR YOU TO FACE ME, BATTLE ME!"

"No!" Fort shouted, flinching away from the creature. "I swear, he never—"

"AND NOW THAT HE'S BROKEN THE RULES, I NO LONGER NEED TO ABIDE BY THE AGREEMENT!" The Timeless One whipped around, almost knocking Fort over with his cloak. "I SEARCHED FOR THAT BOOK FOR MILLENNIA, BUT HE'D HIDDEN IT WELL. NOW I WILL TAKE IT, WHEN I BEAT THE FINAL

ARTORIGIOS AND DOOM THE OLD MAN!"

Fort's heart raced so fast he could hear it in his ears, but still he couldn't help but wonder about the Old One's words. A game, rules, an agreement . . . what was going on between Merlin and the Timeless One? Fort knew that Merlin had been training Artorigios against the Old One for centuries, but why? What sort of person was Merlin to make deals with an Old One?

And why would the Timeless One want a book of dragon language?

"I promise you, he wasn't letting me do anything!" Fort shouted, raising his shaking hands to try to calm the creature down before the Timeless One wiped him from existence. "It really was just about learning to speak to Em . . . to my dragon. That was *it*!"

"YOU CANNOT KNOW HIM LIKE I DO, HUMAN," the Old One said with disgust. "HE *ALWAYS* CHEATS, BUT NOW I KNOW HIS METHOD AND CAN PLAY HIS GAME. THE AGREEMENT WAS THAT I GAVE HIM A YEAR TO TRAIN HIS NEWEST ARTORIGIOS, BUT THERE ARE WAYS AROUND THAT. ALL SHE TRULY NEEDS IS THE SWORD, AND ONCE SHE REGAINS

THAT, THEN I SHALL END THIS RIDICULOUS GAME ONCE AND FOR ALL!"

What? Rachel wouldn't have a year to train? This was all going to happen as soon as she got Excalibur back? He had to warn her, warn Merlin! He—

"YOU WILL *NOT* WARN ANYONE, FORSYTHE," the Timeless One declared, and the black light intensified, pushing in on Fort from all sides. "AS FAR AS YOU'RE CONCERNED, NONE OF THIS WILL HAVE HAPPENED, SO YOU WILL NOT REMEMBER ANYTHING TO TELL MERLIN OR YOUR FRIENDS. BUT I SHALL BE SEEING THEM ALL SOON, AND FOR ONE, FINAL TIME!"

Before Fort could respond or react, the ground dropped away beneath him, and he tumbled into darkness, screaming in surprise and horror. The blackness of the Time magic grew as he fell, blinding him with its light, and then . . .

Fort flipped through the book in front of him, Ember's head in his lap as she gently snored. These words were just so *dangerous*. Any one of them could be used wrongly and set off a whole chain of magic he never intended, if he wasn't careful. The fact that Merlin hadn't even mentioned that they were words of magic before letting Fort loose on the book made him wonder what the magician thought would happen. Couldn't Merlin see the future? If so, he shouldn't have been surprised that Fort had set himself on fire.

But the one word he was looking for didn't have any negative drawbacks that he could think of. It was one of the pretty normal ones, but it also had its uses, if he could just find it. . . .

He flipped past the remnants of a page, looking like someone had ripped it out, and absently he hoped that wasn't the one word he was looking for. But what would the odds be?

But as the night progressed, Fort got more and more frustrated. No matter how quickly he searched, he just couldn't find the word for "see" in Ember's language, the one spell he'd need to find out whatever it was Merlin was hiding from him.

And it was getting late. Well, okay, time wasn't actually moving, not here in Merlin's cottage, but Rachel and Jia would be back soon, and he'd have completely missed his chance.

"I don't suppose you know the word for 'see' in your language, do you?" he asked Ember.

She glared at him as she woke up, then yawned widely. "Ve—" she said, right as black light filled the cottage, and Rachel, Jia, and Merlin returned.

- TWENTY-ONE -

"HEY," RACHEL SAID, LOOKING EXHAUSTED as she dropped into the seat next to him. "Got anything to eat?"

She was covered in dirt and dust now, and back to wearing her leather armor. Jia had the same cloak on she'd been wearing after her last training, though now it had several slices out of it, as if she'd been dodging swords, though maybe not very well. She sat down as well, though far enough from Rachel that Fort could tell they hadn't fixed their problem while they were gone. He wondered again if he should try to help.

"Um, there's stew," Fort said, nodding at the dishes that were already floating over to them. "Are you both okay?"

Ember sniffed at Rachel, then turned up her nose and settled her head back into Fort's lap and closed her eyes.

"Not even a little bit," Rachel said, greedily reaching for

the bowl before it landed, then immediately starting in on the food. On the other side of the table, Jia was doing the same without even saying a word. "I think I made a rock so heavy it will mess with time, so that's fun," Rachel continued through spoonfuls. "Never thought I'd say *that* sentence."

"Um, what?" Fort said, briefly thrown out of his own thoughts about his two friends. "Does that mean you're basically making a black hole?"

"Is that what I'm doing?" Rachel asked Merlin.

The old man just shrugged. "Don't try to make science out of magic. The two fundamentally are the same thing, but neither particularly likes the other. You should see how they fight when you lock them together in a room."

"He's always like this," Rachel said to Fort, when he gave her an odd look. "Don't question it."

"Fair enough," Fort said. "Jia, were you really learning puppetry?"

Jia slowly looked up from her stew, some of which was now dripping from her chin. She held out a hand and opened it, revealing a tiny wooden sculpture of a person, complete with a face, clothes, everything. She set it on the table, then went back to eating.

"Jia says she's too hungry to talk," the sculpture said, making Fort leap out of his seat in surprise. "Whoa there, giant human. You need to calm down!"

"Is that Jia talking through the puppet?" Fort said, pointing at the tiny wooden sculpture. "That's amazing!"

"Who are you calling a puppet?" the sculpture said, stalking toward Fort. It gestured, and the seat Fort had just been sitting in reared back like a horse, then slammed its legs into Fort's chest, knocking him to the floor. He looked up in shock to find the sculpture standing over him on the table, a satisfied expression on its face, as Fort's chair began to buck around wildly. "That's what I thought, big man!" it shouted down.

"Your golem's getting out of control again," Rachel said to Jia, not looking at her. "You should probably fix that."

Jia sighed as Fort stood back up and snapped her fingers. The puppet froze in place, right in the middle of giving Rachel a dirty look, and Fort's chair immediately froze as well. "Sorry about that," Jia said to Fort. "I think she might have developed sentience at some point along the way, because I used to be able to control her. Now she's a little tyrant and has figured out how to use the magic that infuses her on *other* things. If I leave her alone for even a minute, I come back to a small army."

Fort just stared at her. "You learned all of this in a month and a half?"

"Actually, I kept them a bit longer than I originally thought," Merlin said. "After all, Excalibur is due to return soon."

Right, Fort had almost forgotten it was so soon. At least *that* he was allowed to help with—though he wasn't exactly excited about how many soldiers and students they were going to be up against. They'd definitely need a plan.

Once they had Excalibur, Rachel would still have the rest of the year to train with it, so that was something.

"How long were you gone, then?" Fort asked.

Rachel winced. "Four months."

"*Four* months? You can't keep going like this!" Fort shouted. "You need rest, and apparently food. Aren't you feeding them, Merlin?"

"I'm trying," Merlin said, shrugging. "Food is available, but both are just too engrossed in their studies and practice."

"Engrossed is the right word," Rachel whispered. "The food is *disgusting* in medieval times. No one washes their hands, and everything smells like horse and cow manure. And the water? *Yikes.*"

"Jia had diarrhea for *weeks*," the little puppet said, only for

Jia to snap her fingers, freezing it again, turning red as she did.

"How do *your* studies progress, Forsythe?" Merlin asked him, nodding at Ember, who climbed up to sit in the middle of the book, covering it with her body, she was so large now. "Soon she'll be too big to hide effectively from the faerie."

"Oh, it's going okay," Fort said, cringing a bit. "Ember knows how to ask me for food and water, and I can tell her 'My name is Fort' and ask her where *la biblioteca* is. So, you know."

"Two very important first steps," Merlin said, his eyes twinkling in the light of the fire. "So nothing out of the ordinary happened while we were gone, then?"

Fort blinked, wondering if the magician knew what word he'd been trying to find. "Nope, everything's fine!" he said. "Just reading over vocabulary words and trying to memorize them. Having a great time with it all." He winced. "Though it'd help if the words were in alphabetical order. It does take forever to find anything."

"They *are* organized alphabetically," Merlin said. "Only it's by the word of power, not your language, so I understand the issue."

"Hey, Fort," Jia said. "I meant to ask you before we left, but I got caught up in everything. Do you know what's going on with Sierra? I couldn't reach her last time I was here . . . so, um, yesterday." She threw a look at Rachel, who was avoiding her gaze. "I wanted to have a talk about something."

"Yeah, I couldn't get ahold of her either. What's she doing?" Rachel asked.

"Ask him," Fort said, nodding at Merlin, not liking the reminder that Sierra was off somewhere with Damian, the Worst Dragon of All Time. "He's the one who's hiding everything."

The old man smiled gently at them. "We all have our parts to play in this game, and she's busy with hers. You can chat in your heads later. I swear, you teenagers always need a phone, or magical equivalent. I never had this problem with Wart when he was your age."

Rachel almost choked on her bite of stew.

After eating, Rachel and Jia both used their slap bracelets to return home, saying good-bye to Fort, but not to each other or Merlin. Fort decided that next time he saw them, he really *did* need to say something, if just to see if he could help. Maybe he'd try Rachel alone first, then Jia, in case either was more comfortable sharing with him.

But for now, it felt like he'd been studying for hours, and

he could barely keep his eyes open. "I guess I should get going too," Fort said to Merlin, who was staring into the fire. "I could use some sleep."

Merlin nodded, turning back to look at him. "Sleep *is* important. But perhaps you haven't learned enough for tonight. Trouble will follow at the same rate your dragon grows later, Forsythe. The sooner you get her to safety the better, I would imagine."

Fort stared at him for a moment, then sighed and dropped back into his seat. "Good point," he said, trying to pull the book out from under Ember and failing miserably until the dragon indignantly picked herself up off it. "I'll stick around awhile longer now and see if I can't figure out how to teach her the phrase 'please make a portal to another dimension so that the creepy faerie queen doesn't use you against your own kind.'"

"Poetry in any language," Merlin said, his hands glowing black. "I bid you good luck and a good night, Forsythe. Learn all you can."

Ember looked up at him with a strange look, and he winked at her, then glitched out of sight, leaving Fort alone.

"I wonder if he was always weird, or if it took a few thousand years to make him that way," Fort said to Ember. The dragon ignored him. Instead, she reached out and yanked the book closer to herself, digging her dragon claws into it as she flipped several pages over. "Hey, I need to read that," Fort told her, and tried to retrieve the book, but she batted at him with her other claws as his hands got close. "Hey!"

She just stared at him for a moment, then closed her eyes and made herself comfortable, her dragon paw now lying right in the middle of the page. He leaned closer to her, thinking he could quickly pick her paw up and yank the book away before she noticed, only to stop as he saw what page she was on:

K'paen—Learn.

"You're never going to k'paen to behave, are you," Fort told her, scratching her behind her triangular, scaly ears. She began to purr, sounding strangely like she did in cat form, then opened her eyes and stared up at him again.

"K'paen," she said, tapping the book with one claw.

He stared down at her in confusion. "You want to learn the book? It sounds like you know all the words already. Really, I'm the one who . . ." He trailed off as the dragon's meaning finally occurred to him. "No, you want *me* to use it, don't you?"

She purred again, then turned over to her back, releasing the book, and stretched to about twice her length, making the table creak below her.

"K'paen," he said quietly, staring at the book. Was it possible that he could just use that magic word to *learn* everything in its pages, instead of doing it word by word? It'd certainly be a lot faster.

For a moment, he almost considered using it then and there. It'd be so easy, just cast the spell and see what happened. But even though this wasn't a spell like "fio," it still wasn't just some straightforward word. "Learn" could end up meaning a lot of things, and he'd have to make sure he knew how it worked before taking in an entire language at once.

On one hand, if it worked, he wouldn't need Ember's magic to send her to safety. He'd have all the spells he needed to get her into the care of the Avalonian dragons. Not to mention he'd have the power to help his friends against the Timeless One, and not mess everything up.

On the other hand, who knew what kind of side effects the spell might have? After setting himself on fire, maybe some experimenting was in order. The spell might not even work the way he needed. He'd have to test it first, before figuring out what he wanted to do.

"You really *are* smart, aren't you?" he said to Ember, grinning at her.

"Sa," she told him, giving him a knowing nod. "*Rexe* sa."

- TWENTY-TWO -

GIVING UP FOR THE NIGHT AFTER learning his Learn spell, Fort brought Ember home—making sure she was back in her cat form—and spent as much time as he could with his father, watching some television. He hated not having more moments like this, what with everything that was going on, but maybe once Ember was safe, he could spend more time with his dad, before everything happened with the Timeless One. After all, that was still so many months away.

Finally, his father forced him to go to sleep, since it was still a school night, not to mention that Fort had passed out a few times whenever there was a moment of silence, given how exhausted he was. He reluctantly agreed and stumbled into bed, where Ember curled up around him protectively, which was nice, considering how warm she was.

• • •

Fort woke up the next morning with Ember sleeping at his feet, only instead of a furry cat, she had reverted to her dragon form and was now even larger than she had been the night before. The bed was tilting in her direction, she was getting so heavy.

"Hey!" he said to her, and she looked up at him lazily, then yawned, showing him far too many razor-sharp teeth for his comfort. "What are you doing? Ember, *ma'cae* in the house!"

Fortunately, one word he *had* learned was the one for cat, and she obediently changed back into her cat form, now easily the size of a tiger. Merlin had been right . . . even when she was in cat form, Fort couldn't let his dad or aunt see Ember now. And worse, Ember was probably too big to even live in the room anymore by herself, though he wasn't sure what other choice he had. What if Xenea came back for dinner again, and Ember knocked down the door? The faerie girl would see through Ember's magic in seconds, and that'd be it.

But maybe this Learn spell would solve all of his problems. He could learn Ember's language and send her to Avalon, while also locating Damian for Xenea, and let those two fight it out. That'd solve his biggest issues, and Merlin might even change his mind about letting Fort help with the Timeless One, if he had actual magic to back Rachel and Jia up.

Thankfully, he'd already thought of the perfect way to practice it today: He'd just use it on one of his textbooks at school, and he'd be able to test it instantly by checking what he now knew against the book. What could go wrong with *that*?

For the first time ever, Fort wished he'd had homework the night before, just so he'd have taken one of his schoolbooks home to begin with. He did have some fiction books, but he wasn't quite sure what learning one of them would do. Besides, using the spell on a textbook would help with his grades anyway.

After Fort took a quick shower and got dressed, he found a strange sight in the kitchen: *Xenea* was sitting at the table. And even worse, she was speaking softly with his father, and neither looked happy. But when Fort walked in, his heart now racing from terror, his father smiled widely, even as Xenea continued looking annoyed. "Good morning, Mr. Future President," his dad said. "What can I get you for breakfast? Today's special is some farm-fresh, organic cornflakes, along with my own personal recommendation, toast."

"Cereal's fine," Fort said, too worried about Xenea's presence to even roll his eyes at his dad. He poured out a bowl, followed by the milk, as he watched Xenea closely. What had she been talking to his father about? She must have been using her glamour on him, which explained why his mood had matched hers. Did this have something to do with their first meeting, when both had been all awkward?

"What are you doing here so early?" he asked her, trying to sound casual.

"Waiting for you," she said, fiddling with some half-eaten toast. "By the way, *my* recommendation would be the flakes of corn. This toast stuff tastes like grilled bread."

Fort just stared at her. "That's . . . what it is."

She held up the toast on her plate, giving it a close look. "Oh, really? Hmm." She poked at it, her finger going right through the bread, then dropped it back to her plate. "I was offered some sort of translucent red glob to put on top of it, apparently to make it sweeter?" Her face showed exactly what she thought of *that*. "Needless to say, I passed."

"That's called jelly," Fort told her. "And you should try it. It's made of fruit."

She raised an eyebrow, then reached for the jar of jelly and sniffed at it tentatively. "Lies," she said. "I don't smell real fruit *anywhere* in there."

Fort sighed, but at least that explained her mood. "Fair enough," he told her as he spooned cereal into his mouth as quickly as he could. "We should get going, so we're not late."

"Agreed," she said, "if just to get out of this smell."

Fort had never been so happy to be insulted in his life. He ended up almost choking on his breakfast, he ate it so fast, but at least managed to get Xenea out of the apartment before she said anything too odd to his father, or worse, gave Ember any reason to come out.

"Listen, I'm not sure how effective I'm being about finding your dragon, spending all day in this school place," Xenea said as they waited for the bus. "I think maybe we should try another one of those 'move vee' things, just in case it shows up there."

Fort just blinked at her, wondering if she really thought she was tricking him. "Was there a movie in particular that you thought the dragon might show up to?"

She stared off in space as if to think about it. "Yes, I believe we should try the one where the aliens eat everyone again. It seems like a natural temptation for any dragon, given how much they like to eat things."

This time, Fort couldn't help but laugh. "Just admit that you want to see it again. You don't have to *lie* to me."

"Lie?" she said indignantly. "I would never! Though I do admit the alien story *has* made me think about a great many things, Forsythe. What would *I* do if those monsters attacked me or my queen? Would I attempt to 'flame throw' them like the hero lady? Or would I run? I don't know, and it disturbs me!" She grabbed him by the shirt and pulled him closer. "Now take me back so I can figure out what to do!"

Fort stared at her in disbelief. "You just like watching the lady kill all the aliens, don't you."

"*Yes!*" Xenea screamed at him, a fire in her eyes. "It makes my heart race, and I want *more!* More explosions, more chases, more thrills!" She shook him by the shirt now, getting a little too violent.

"Whoa," Fort said, backing off. "If we don't go to school, we'll get in trouble, and then there won't be any movies for anyone, okay? I'll take you again, but not tonight. I've got something I have to do." Just use magic to learn an entire book of dragon language, if the spell worked. Nothing big.

The fire in her eyes turned into a wild, raging stare, and she looked like she might take a swing at him. "Tell me you're joking. Tell me that the bargain you made with my queen isn't less important than some . . . *human* task. Because if we don't go to the move vees, I *will* march right back to my queen, and—"

"Fine!" Fort said, as the bus pulled down the street. "I'll take you, but I can't stay for the whole thing. And don't try to make this about the queen's bargain. This is all *you* wanting to see the movie again."

She looked away, crossing her arms. "I can neither confirm nor deny that."

Fort closed his eyes, sighing deeply. "Anyway, I may have a way to fulfill the queen's bargain. I can't really tell you everything yet, but I have a spell that might help you find Damian. And then you can leave this world, take him back to your queen, and I'll be done with all of this!"

She gave him a suspicious glance but tentatively backed off, allowing him to climb up into the bus. It wasn't full today, which meant they had a little room to themselves at the back, so Fort was able to explain his plan to use the Learn spell, to help her learn Damian's location. "You'd find him immediately!" he told her, only to pause at her horrified look. "What?"

"Have you lost your mind?" she shouted, loud enough for

the entire bus to look at them. Fort turned bright red as he slipped down behind the seat, but Xenea didn't seem to even notice. "Do you know what that spell could *do* to you?"

"Help me learn?" he whispered. "And you have to be quieter! They don't know about magic, remember?"

"Oh, it'd help you learn, that's for certain," she said, sounding a lot less positive about it than he had. "It could also wipe out your mind if you learn too much! You people don't have that much room in there." She rapped her knuckles on his skull, which hurt, frankly, but was insulting to boot. "Do you know what kind of damage you could do?"

"I'm not going to just use it randomly," Fort said, still blushing, but now more from her comments. "I'm going to try it out on one of my textbooks at school!"

She groaned loudly. "Like you could even take in *that* much information. Just watch: You're going to forget your own name, but more importantly, you'll forget who *I* am, and then I'm going to have to explain it to you all over, but all you'll know is what an egg-naceous rock is—"

"I think it's igneous," Fort told her.

"I'm surprised you already know that much!" she said, throwing her hands up in frustration. "*Fine.* Do your experiments. But if you forget about taking me to see the move vees, I'm going to tell the faerie queen that you humans want to invade Avalon, and see what she does."

Fort laughed again, then trailed off as she glared back. "You're not actually serious, are you?"

"You want to test me?" she asked, and he really, really didn't.

Still, all of her worry about the spell seemed to come from the fact that she thought humans weren't the sharpest knives in the drawer, so Fort didn't let her warnings bother him *too* much. Besides, the whole point of school was to learn everything in a textbook, so his brain *had* to be able to hold that much knowledge . . . right?

- TWENTY-THREE -

AS IT TURNED OUT, THERE WASN'T any time during school that Fort could sneak away to try his Learn spell experiment. Lunch was another nightmare, with Xenea holding court over everyone, only this time getting movie suggestions from the other kids, which didn't bode well. She ended up with a list of films that would take days to watch.

After lunch came another monster-attack drill during class, which set Fort's anxiety racing. He found himself staring at his classmates with guilt, unable to stop himself from thinking about how so much of this was his fault. Not Damian summoning the Old Ones the first time, no, but too much of the rest of it. In a normal world, these kids wouldn't be doing safety drills, and Fort knew he was at least in part to blame.

But more than that, he kept coming back to not being good

enough to help. Merlin, Rachel, Jia . . . they all had made clear what Fort kept trying to forget, that he'd never have the talent, the power to really fix things, to stop the Old Ones, to help the world.

"I just wish I could do something," he whispered to Xenea as the alarm blared, not really sure why he was telling her, maybe just because he couldn't tell anyone else.

But instead of sympathy, her eyes grew wide from anger, and she turned on him. "Was that a joke? Is this some poor human attempt at humor? You *wish* you could do something?"

"Quiet!" their teacher yelled, but Xenea ignored her.

"Are you powerless here?" she continued, getting more and more angry as Fort got just as confused. "Are you chained up so that you can't act? Because I don't see any chains!" She glared at him, her eyes burning with rage. "This is just like you humans, complaining you can't help, when the reality is you *choose* not to. Especially *you*, who actually *can* do something!"

Fort just blinked in surprise. What was she talking about? What had he said that set her off like this?

As she kept yelling, more faculty members came into the room, thinking it was an emergency, since they were supposed to be silent for the drill. Somehow, Fort had worked Xenea up so much she'd completely forgotten to use her glamour and ended up almost getting them detention for her outburst.

Ironically, the only thing that saved them was that their teacher assumed this was all due to Fort being present for the D.C. attack. But she made it *very* clear there wouldn't be talking during the next drill, no matter what.

Xenea went quiet after that and didn't talk to Fort for most of the rest of the day. And while he normally would have welcomed that, considering the faerie girl wouldn't be saying anything too alien to the other kids, for some reason, he felt like he'd done something wrong and wanted to make it right. Even for someone trying to steal his dragon.

It took until he and Xenea went to the movies later that Fort finally had some time. He pulled out his textbook as they sat almost alone in the theater, Xenea watching the screen impatiently.

"Enough with these product descriptions!" she shouted, waving at the front of the theater. "I want to see the woman destroying aliens again!"

"They're just ads," Fort said, opening the textbook and placing it on his lap. "The movie's going to start soon enough. What was with you earlier, anyway?"

She glanced over at him. "You're a fool."

He immediately looked up from his book. "I'm a what now?"

"You're a fool," she repeated. "This is what I was trying to calmly explain to you that—"

"You screamed so loudly that the principal came in!"

"I was *calmly* explaining to you that you're out of your mind if you feel helpless when you have so much power!" she said, her voice getting louder again. Though the movie hadn't started, Fort could still feel the eyes of the couple of teenagers in the seats a few rows back, and he sank down in his seat, just like he had on the bus.

He should have just let it go there. But with everything happening between Rachel and Jia, and Sierra being off somewhere out of reach with Damian, somehow Xenea was the only person he could actually talk to about this.

"I *don't* have any power," he said to her, trying to keep his voice down. "I wasn't born on some specific date, so I'm not as good at magic as others. I'm just like those other kids at school, except I know how bad I am at magic. I've got two spells— that's it! I'm not even allowed to fight an Old—to be with my friends when they're facing something bad. How sad is that?"

"Oh, it's incredibly sad," Xenea said, narrowing her eyes.

"Sad that you're letting someone else tell you all of this. 'You're bad at magic; you're useless; you're weird-looking.' Is that what they say?"

Fort blinked. "Not that last one—"

"Who *cares*!" she shouted, and Fort ducked down even farther. "I'd never let anyone tell me if I was good enough. Of course there will be people with more magic than you, but why would you ever let that stop you? My queen has more power than *anyone*, and we break her rules constantly when we want!"

Fort raised an eyebrow. "You do? I thought the whole reason you were here is because you were afraid of her."

"I'm being *punished* for breaking her rules!" Xenea hissed. "Yes, when we get caught, we do what she says, but only so we can be free to do as we choose later. How is this hard to understand, Forsythe? You have *magic*, the ability to change things in your world. Why would you care if it wasn't as good as others'? Use what you've got the best way you can!" She growled in frustration and shook her head. "*Humans!* You amaze me every day with how wrong you can be!"

Fort started to respond, then stopped, his mouth hanging open. Was she right? He'd let everyone from Dr. Opps to Colonel Charles to Merlin tell him he wasn't good enough because he was born on the wrong day. But that hadn't stopped him from rescuing his father or facing down William, not when he was needed.

Maybe things could have gone better if he'd been more powerful. But he and his friends had gotten his father back, safe and sound, and prevented a world war, not to mention helped create a new dragon! If he were going to judge himself so harshly for all the mistakes, shouldn't he take into account the *good* things that had happened too?

"Okay, you could have a point," he whispered to her as the lights began to dim for the trailers. "I should help when I think I'm needed, do what I think is right, even if other people disagree."

"Oh, I didn't say *that*," Xenea told him as she turned back to the screen. "I don't know that you're smart enough to figure out the best thing to do. Just ask me—I'll tell you." And she patted his hand, and then went silent as the trailers started, her face lighting up with joy.

Well, *that* was irritating. But it didn't keep Fort from thinking about what she'd said all through the trailers, and even the first half of the movie. Even with the little magic he had, he'd managed to fix some pretty big problems. And there were hundreds of millions of kids just like him, not born on Discovery

Day, all of whom could learn magic too. Who cared if they weren't as good as the millions born on the right day? Did that mean they couldn't accomplish as much good?

For a moment, Fort imagined what the world would be like if all the kids hiding under their desks had their own books of magic, if every one of those kids could heal wounds or teleport or do all kinds of other stuff. How much better would the world be? Did it matter at all that there would be others stronger at magic, if those kids were healing diseases or teleporting food to starving people?

And yes, that wasn't fighting an Old One. But that didn't mean Fort couldn't help, no matter what Merlin said. Maybe he'd be hurt in the battle, or worse. But Fort also knew what it felt like, losing his father when he was powerless to stop the Dracsi. Now he at least had *some* power, and if he didn't use it to help his friends, he knew he'd regret it just as much as when his dad went missing.

Xenea clapped beside him in excitement as something or other happened onscreen. Fort couldn't pay attention now, his mind completely elsewhere. But as he shifted in his seat anxiously, the textbook on his lap moved, and he remembered what he had brought it for.

This was his moment to experiment. He'd gotten so distracted in his thoughts that the movie was already half over, and he still had to try out the spell before going to Merlin's tonight.

His train of thought had been interesting, and he knew he'd have to get back to it soon. But for right now, he had some studying to do.

He couldn't see the American history textbook in his lap, not in the dark of the theater, but he shouldn't need to. Instead, he brought to mind the word for Learn in the language of magic and put both hands on the book, concentrating on it.

"K'paen," he whispered, too softly for even Xenea to hear. Hopefully, he didn't need the word for "book," since he didn't know that yet, but other spells worked by thinking of what you wanted to—

Pain erupted in his skull, which felt like it might split in two. He groaned loudly and pushed back in his seat so hard it squeaked.

"Shush!" Xenea said, barely looking at him as she watched the movie with a huge grin.

Fortunately, as quickly as it'd come on, the pain lessened, then disappeared entirely, and Fort was able to think again. He looked down at the textbook in his lap and suddenly realized he knew everything about it. And not just about American history.

Yes, he knew that the Constitution was signed in 1789; that the War of 1812 was between the Americans and the British, and the British soldiers burned down the White House; and that the Civil War started in 1861 and ended in 1865.

But Fort *also* knew now that this particular copy of the book was a thirty-second printing, and the publisher had offices in New York, London, Paris, and New Delhi. Not to mention that fourteen students had used this copy before, and five of them had killed bugs with it. Three of those bugs were spiders; two were mosquitoes. And this book had been chosen by the Texas School Board because—

"Whoa," he said, his eyes wide as he stared at it. The spell had not only worked, but it had gone beyond even his wildest expectations—

And then pain shot through his skull again as Xenea slapped his head. "Stop talking!" she whispered. "People are *trying* to watch a move vee here!"

- TWENTY-FOUR -

ORT KEPT HIS EXCITEMENT TO HIM-
self as he left the movie early, telling Xenea he had to
hit the restroom but walking out instead. Xenea barely
heard him anyway, as caught up in the movie as she was, and he
wondered if she'd end up sitting through another showing, or even
two. He felt a little bad for leaving her there, but he'd warned her
he had things to do tonight, and he really didn't want to wait to see
how the Learn spell worked on the dragon dictionary.

Sure, the spell had told him some useless stuff: The last thing
he needed to know was who had checked out the book before,
or where the publisher had offices.

But who cared, when he now knew when the Smoot-Hawley
Tariff Act was signed, and who had signed their name the larg-
est on the U.S. Constitution. School was going to be *so easy*
now. Tests would be a breeze!

But that was all just frosting on the cake, because the important thing was he could learn to speak to Ember in minutes instead of days, or longer. He could get her to safety tonight, and then show Merlin all of the magic he knew. All that thinking about making the world a better place could start with helping his friends fight an Old One!

Weirdly, Ember leaving gave him a heavy feeling in his chest, which was odd. He'd known ever since she was born that she couldn't stay there, not in his aunt's apartment. But even thinking about sending her to Avalon made him strangely sad, like he was losing a friend.

Except she wasn't his friend, not really. She was a dragon who mistakenly thought he was her father. And she'd realize her mistake when she met others of her kind and they helped her grow into the amazing dragon she was always meant to be, and Fort would be incredibly proud of her if he ever saw her again.

But he wouldn't see her again. And there was that same empty feeling inside.

"Stop it!" he yelled at himself, punching his chest. "Quit feeling things!"

Someone coughed, and Fort looked up to find several people

staring at him in the mall. He blushed and quickly ran into the nearest store, finding a place to hide. When no one seemed to be looking, he teleported home, completely embarrassed.

He quickly opened the apartment door, only to find Cora and his father sitting at the kitchen table, talking in low voices. Both seemed anxious, so Fort stopped before going to grab Ember from his room.

"Is everything okay?" Fort asked after saying hello.

"Nothing to worry over," his dad said, winking at him. "Just having a bit more trouble getting any leads on a job than I'd have hoped. Too bad I can't remember anything about the D.C. situation, or I'd write a book!"

"I'd be happy if the news people stopped calling," his aunt said quietly.

Fort cringed. "Are they still accusing you of making it all up?" he asked.

"They're just doing their jobs," his father said, shrugging it off, but Fort could see how much it bothered him. "You know how it is. But the last thing we need to do is keep rehashing history. All I care about is getting back to work and taking care of my son." He glanced at Fort's aunt. "And maybe paying Cora back for taking care of you while I was away, too."

"Oh, don't worry about that," Fort's aunt said, but he could tell the subject wasn't comfortable for her. That was understandable, since she hadn't had much money even before needing to put Fort up when his father disappeared.

"What about the insurance money, the money Dad had saved?" Fort asked. "I thought that helped."

His aunt dropped her fork loudly, and they all turned to look at her as she blushed. "Sorry," she said, then looked at Fort's father.

"It, ah, seems that the insurance company wants its money back," his father said, not looking at him. "Since, you know, I did not, in fact, visit the great beyond. So, um, we're figuring it out." He looked up at Fort, and for the first time that Fort could remember, there was fear in his dad's eyes. "But again, nothing for you to worry about, kiddo! Your old man has this all under control."

"Right, under control," his aunt said. "Excuse me." She stood up and walked over to the sink, where she turned on the water but just stood staring at it, lost in thought. Fort's dad watched her for a moment, then sighed, rubbing his forehead.

"Is there any way I can help?" Fort asked quietly, thinking maybe it wasn't just his dragon that could use some gold.

"You just concentrate on your schoolwork, so you can grow up and become president," his father said, his smile returning, though the fear was still in his eyes. "Then I can write a thousand books all about how great you were as a kid, and make millions. Deal?"

Fort nodded, a large lump in his throat. He leaned over and gave his dad a quick hug. "Don't worry. If we can make it through D.C., we can handle this, too."

"Oh, are you *my* dad now?" his father said, squeezing him tightly in the hug. "When did you get to be such a grown-up?"

"I learned from the best," Fort said quietly, then patted his father's arm and left him in the kitchen, hating that he couldn't spend more time with him. But they'd have all the time in the world once Fort memorized the dragon language. Maybe he'd even use magic to make some money for his dad, to take some of these worries away. Not exactly doing what he thought was right, like he'd been thinking about back during the movie, but his father didn't deserve any of what he was going through either.

Ember greeted him at his bedroom doorway, not even waiting until he was inside before meowing loudly. Somehow she'd grown, even since that morning, and now was almost big enough for him to ride, *far* too large for his bedroom.

Not to mention that Aunt Cora's exercise equipment was now strewn about the floor, with the metal dumbbells half-eaten. Apparently even in her cat form, the dragon craved metal. *Yikes.*

At this rate, she wouldn't last another night. But hopefully that wouldn't matter, now that he could learn the language of magic and get her to a better place.

Again, that emptiness returned, but he ignored it. There were far more important things to worry about right now.

"Volai hrana," she said, nudging him with her head hard enough to knock him into the wall. *"Volai hrana!"*

"I get it, you want food," Fort told her, and quickly closed the door behind him before opening a can of cat food. She attacked the bowl as soon as he put the food on it, finishing it in one bite, then waited impatiently for him to open another can.

If nothing else, he had to get her to Avalon, or she was going to bankrupt his meager funds and go hungry.

As soon as Ember had finished her dinner—which included every can of food Fort had left—he opened a teleportation circle into Merlin's cottage. He wasn't sure if Rachel or Jia would be there, or if they would have already left to go back to the past for their training. But when he arrived, Rachel was waiting.

And she looked like something was *very* wrong.

"Good, you're here," she said, jumping up from her seat. "We have a problem."

Fort sighed. Of course they had a problem. "What's going on?"

"The sword showed up *today*," Rachel said, her forehead creased with anxiety. "It's at the school, right now, Fort. I thought we had more time. Merlin told us two days ago that it'd come back five days from then, but it's there now, and we've got to get it!"

"But . . . how?" Fort said. "I thought he could see the future! What went wrong?"

"I don't know, and he's not here!" Rachel said, pacing around. "And what's worse is that as soon as the sword arrived, Agent Cole grabbed Jia from her room, took her down to the cafeteria, and locked her in there, surrounded by guards. They *suspect* her, Fort. Which means they suspect us. They don't know for sure, they *can't* know, but Merlin said they do know someone's coming, and we're pretty obvious suspects."

"Okay, we can figure this out," he said, not really sure he was right, but wanting Rachel to calm down. "Is Sierra back? Is that how you found out about Jia?"

"No, she's still gone," Rachel said, rubbing her temples with her thumbs.

Fort frowned. *Sierra?* he shouted in his mind, hoping she'd hear him and respond, unlike the last two days. *Hey, can you hear me? We need your help!*

But again, there was no response. Great.

"So if not Sierra, how did you find out about Jia?" Fort asked.

Rachel pointed down at the table, and Fort's eyes widened. There, right next to where Rachel had been sitting, was a familiar-looking wooden sculpture of a person.

He gasped and leaped away from it. "That thing's still here?" he said, cringing.

"It's *me*, Fort," it said, sounding like Jia instead of whatever creature had been speaking to Fort the day before. "I left it there in case of emergencies, which was good, because otherwise I wouldn't have been able to communicate. There are more there in the other room, too. Rachel, can you grab them?"

Rachel nodded and picked the puppet up, sliding it into a pocket on her shirt, leaving just the puppet's face peeking out. "Are you ready for this, Fort?" she asked. "Even with Jia's puppet, we're going to need all the help we can get. If you're not up for it, tell me now—"

"I'm up for it," he said, nodding at her in what he hoped was a confident way. He glanced down at the book of dragon language on the table, then looked back up at Rachel. "Go get her golems. I'll be ready."

Rachel nodded. "Thank you, New Kid. And don't worry. We've got this."

Fort wasn't sure about that, especially considering how worried *she* looked. But he saluted her with a grin and waited for her to leave.

Then he moved to the table and sat down in front of the dragon dictionary. Ember distracted herself with the same stew as usual, bubbling over the fire, so he was free to do what he had to.

The school knew they were coming. The time for tests and experiments was over.

"K'paen," he said, his hands over the book.

And then his entire world exploded.

- TWENTY-FIVE -

THE COTTAGE, THE SURROUNDING clearing, *all* of it just disappeared.

So did Fort. His body, his mind, both gone.

All that was left was . . . a presence. Something that *knew*.

Knew that everything he'd left behind wasn't real, not the way he'd thought. It existed, yes, but it was all so . . . temporary. It wouldn't last; it never did.

The oldest trees, the tallest mountains, all would disappear, replaced by new saplings, new canyons, new everything.

And for once, the presence didn't feel like something he wished could stop, could stay still, could be like it'd always been.

Now, instead, he saw it as a whole and was amazed that he'd ever been so afraid.

Everything fit together. *Everything.* The human beings, the tiniest bacteria, the Old Ones, the blades of grass. It all had its place.

And binding it all together was magic.

A spark, an energy, something that created the dimensions humanity lived in, the space where they thrived, the time for change to take place, the elements they built with, and the life that birthed them into the world.

It was *all* magic. And it had never gone away.

Even though humanity had forgotten, lost access to it, magic still existed in the tiniest of moments, bringing change to a world that no longer understood why it couldn't stay as it was.

And that confusion, that anger, came from forgetting.

The presence didn't want to forget, not anymore. He remembered it all, a body he once had, a name.

Forsythe. A name that had once been an ancestor's, passed down to him in order to remember. And to honor the idea that the young would come after the old and take their place.

Just as it had always been, and would always be.

Magic.

Somewhere, a great distance away, Fort could feel tears on his face, a face he still felt connected to, in spite of seeing *everything* now, feeling everything, knowing how it—

Wait. No. Something was pulling on him, yanking him back to his body.

He screamed, both in his present form and in his body, trying desperately to hold on to what he'd learned.

But something was drawing him back, returning his mind to an earlier state. Healing magic. No, *Corporeal* magic. That was the only thing that could do this, yank him back from what he was seeing, force him back to normal.

Everything he'd learned, everything he'd seen left him, as if he'd been trying to hold a cloud in his hands. And then the presence and the body were one again, and both were screaming.

"Fort!" shouted a voice, as blue light covered him. "It's okay! You're going to be okay!"

Back in his body, Fort let the scream die, then glanced down at his chest, where a tiny, doll-like wooden puppet was staring at him worriedly, her hands glowing blue. "Jia?" he said, his voice cracking from all the screaming.

"Yes!" she said. "What happened? Are you okay?"

That's when Fort's head began to split apart.

He shouted in agony, in *sap'a, douleur, smarta, bolest bol mina dor PAIN!* His mind felt like it was exploding into his skull, too much information filling it. Words he'd never heard before now leaped out at him in a hundred different languages, and he couldn't separate them from each other.

Nen, he thought. The book: It'd translated every word of magic into other languages.

And now he had *all* of them, every word of every language, within his head.

"What's happening to him?" he heard someone shout, Rachel this time.

"Father!" said another voice, this one growly and rough. *"You are in pain? Shall I help?"*

"I don't know what it is," the Jia golem said. "I'm going to use more powerful Healing spells."

"Irora!" Fort shouted, holding his head as if that would help. *"Xanuun!"*

Jia shook her head, not understanding his different words for pain, but her Healing was gradually helping, though not quickly; she didn't know where he was hurt so was concentrating on his whole body instead of his mind.

He tried to do his own magic, fight through a wave of words that washed over him at the thought of healing and grasp for the ones he knew best.

214

"Mon d'cor," he shouted, and the cooling magic of Heal Minor Wounds flowed into his head. But it wasn't anywhere close to enough and only succeeded in clearing his mind a bit, allowing him to think through the eternal pounding that still hammered against his head.

"It must be in his skull," the Jia puppet said, and put her little wooden hands on his chin. Blue light much more intense than Fort's had been passed through them into his head, instantly relieving the pain. Fort let out a cry of relief, letting himself settle back to the floor of the cottage.

Except it wasn't wood beneath him. It was grass.

"Where am I?" Fort asked. He tried to remember what had happened, but that just resulted in a weird mix of pain and something . . . comforting, something much bigger than he was.

"You're outside," Rachel said. "You blew right through the front door. The dining room is a mess, but Ember's okay. She's right here."

Fort felt a warm head nuzzle his hand. *"Father is okay?"* the dragon said, and he looked over at her in amazement.

"I can understand you?" he said to her, a grin slowly spreading over his face. *"It worked, Ember. I can speak your language!"*

The dragon glared at him. *"You took on too much, for such a*

215

beginner. You are too new for such magic, Father! I would not have shown you the spell if I had known what you intended to do with it. This is what I get for listening to the Merlin creature." She gave him a sad look. *"I mostly wished you would stop reading, and take me hunting."*

He smiled at her in spite of the situation. *"I didn't realize. I'll . . . figure out a way to do that, okay?"*

Instantly the dragon smiled. *"Father promises? Then I have great happiness."* And she rubbed the top of her head against his hand.

"Um, what are you doing?" Rachel asked.

"What?" Fort said. "I was talking to Ember."

"It sounded like you were speaking in magic," Jia told him. "When did you learn so much of her language?"

Fort winced, not looking forward to telling them.

"I . . . used a spell on the dragon dictionary," he said, slowly sitting up. A new wave of pain passed through his head as he did, and he quickly braced himself, but this one was thankfully just temporary. Apparently even Jia's Healing magic couldn't fix everything. "A Learn spell. I thought I could just take in the entire language that way, so I'd have spells to help us get Excalibur back."

Rachel groaned loudly as the Jia golem took a step back in surprise. "What? You can't be serious!" the doll said.

"Do you know how *dangerous* that was, New Kid?" Rachel asked, glaring down at him. "You could have died! What if the book had protection against that? What if it was too much for you? Because from this side, it definitely looked like your head was going to explode. Think about what would have happened if Jia hadn't been here!"

"What made you do such an insane thing?" the Jia golem asked.

"I wanted to . . . to help get Excalibur back," Fort said, rubbing his head. "I decided that even if I'm not as powerful as you two, I still need to step up and help. And I thought this might be a way to do it, help you get the sword, and maybe even fight the Timeless One."

Rachel and the Jia puppet looked at each other, and Jia sighed. "We should have told him. *I* . . . I should have told you both . . . *everything*."

"Too late now," Rachel said, but her tone was more gentle than her words. She reached down to help Fort to his feet. He stood up a bit shakily, a wave of dizziness threatening to overtake him, but with Rachel's help, he steadied himself, and handed Jia's puppet back to her. "You're staying here, though. You're in no shape to come with us."

What? Was she joking? "No, I can *do* this!" he said. "Please, let me help. I can make a difference in there!"

"And all you did was make yourself a liability," Rachel said, giving him a sympathetic pat on his shoulder. "Look, I get that you want to be there for us, but you can't take shortcuts and expect them to work. This is just like when you stole spells to avoid getting kicked out of the school in the first place!"

"That wasn't exactly my choice," Fort said, looking down at the Jia golem with more guilt than he'd expected. "Sierra did that to me."

"Because you were desperate to stay," Rachel said. "Just like you can't wait to send Ember to Avalon. But this is what happens when you don't think things through."

Ember, who had been prancing around happily, abruptly stopped and looked at Fort strangely.

"We *could* have used your help, yes," Rachel continued. "But you would have been great the way you were. Now—"

"Rachel, just give me to him," the Jia golem said. "I'll make sure he's okay, heal his pain if it comes back. We *do* need him."

"Please, Rachel," Fort whispered, hating to practically beg, but not knowing what else to do.

Rachel scrunched her eyes closed in annoyance. "We're going to be fighting our way through half the TDA, not to mention any students Colonel Charles has guarding the sword," she said to the Jia puppet. "Yes, we need him, but not if he's going to hold us back in a fight."

"Oh, we're not going to be fighting," Jia said, her little sculpted smile widening. "Because while I've been stuck here, I think I came up with a new plan."

- TWENTY-SIX -

THE COTTAGE'S DINING ROOM *HAD* been wrecked. Fort stared guiltily at the various cleaning instruments fixing his damage, wishing he could remember doing it. Whatever was in his head now was a *lot* more dangerous than he'd thought.

Though weirdly, the memory of that strange, comforting feeling was there too. He wasn't sure where it had come from, or why it now made him feel almost relaxed when thinking about magic, like his problems weren't quite as bad as he'd thought they were, but the feeling wasn't unpleasant, and right now, he could use anything that wasn't straight-out panic.

"In there," the Jia golem said, pointing her little hand into one of the side rooms. "We need a mirror."

They passed through a doorway into what looked like a bedroom, complete with bed, bureau, and large, full-length mirror. "Okay," the golem said, as Rachel put her down on the bed. "Fort, I'm going to use some of the magic I've been studying on you, so don't be alarmed."

Fort's eyebrows rose, and any comforting feeling he was getting from the magic in his head disappeared. "Um, what? You're going to make me a puppet?"

The Jia doll rolled her eyes. "That's not all I've been working on. This is Corporeal magic." Her hands began to glow with a blue light. "I'm going to make you both look like TDA soldiers, so we can sneak around without anyone knowing it's us."

Whoa. She could do that? Of course Fort knew she was able to change Ember from a dragon into a cat, but somehow it seemed stranger to just modify their looks.

"What about their uniforms?" Rachel asked. "I didn't know you could do clothing."

"It's easy, as long as I use cotton clothes, or anything that used to be alive," the golem said. "Doesn't work on anything human-made, like polyester." She pointed at the lone bed in the room. "I tried using it on my sheets last night while we were training, just in case anyone looked in."

The bed began to glow with blue light, and the sheets formed into what looked like a Jia-sized lump, rising and falling as if Jia were curled up beneath them, sleeping.

"Creepy," Rachel said, her eyes widening as she started to smile. She looked at the doll, and her smile faded. "Um, nice job, though."

The golem looked away sadly as the sheets faded back to their normal shape and color. "Thanks. Ready, Fort?" Jia asked, and, this time, gestured at him.

Instantly Fort's T-shirt and pants changed into a soldier's uniform, just like the ones the TDA wore at the Oppenheimer School. "Um," he said, holding up some long sleeves. "I think you made it a bit too big."

"That's because I'm not done," Jia's golem said, and now her blue light shone over his body. A weird feeling spread throughout his legs and arms, and the room shrank a bit around him—no, wait, it wasn't the room. He had *grown*. And now the uniform fit perfectly.

"Whoa!" Rachel said, looking at Fort in surprise. "He looks completely different! You should *keep* this new face, Fort." She grinned at that.

Fort reached up to touch his mouth and cheeks, then quickly moved to the mirror. A stranger looked back at him, and for a moment, Fort couldn't believe this wasn't some kind of magic mirror.

Instead of his normal brown hair, now he had short blond hair, buzzed almost to the scalp. His face looked nothing like his own, instead resembling a man in his twenties, at least.

And he had so many muscles! He flexed, wondering if he could beat up Colonel Charles now. Probably not, since he had no idea how to fight, at least not without a staff, thanks to Sergeant Tower's training.

"Fort's a private, but I'm going to make *you* a major," the golem said to Rachel. "That way you can order people out of our way if you need to."

"Perfect," Rachel said as the blue Healing light bathed her. "I've been ordering people around my whole life anyway. Hey, do you want to go higher in rank, maybe? I'd be okay with general, honestly."

As Fort watched in astonishment, Rachel's hair shrank into her head, and her face shifted completely, both adding more lines around her eyes and mouth while also shrinking her cheekbones. When Jia had finished, the woman standing before him looked like a completely new person, nothing like his friend.

"I, ah, made you less pretty, so you wouldn't stand out as much," Jia told her as Rachel went to look at herself in the mirror.

Though Rachel didn't turn around, Fort could see her blush in the mirror. "That's, um, nice of you to say. Your golem's pretty cute, by the way."

This time the golem turned red, which itself was a trick, considering it was made of wood, and Fort hid his smile in spite of the situation. Whatever it took to bring these two back together was fine by him. Still, the room had gone silent now, and someone needed to talk. "So, um, don't we have a sword to steal?"

"You, *quiet*," Rachel said, and Fort instantly recognized her angry look, even on the new face. "You're lucky to be here, with all that nonsense in your head. Do *not* mess this up for us, Fort. I need to be able to depend on you." She pointed at the golem on the bed. "Now put Jia in your pocket so we can get moving."

Fort did as he was ordered, sliding Jia's golem into his front chest pocket. From there, she could peek out if she needed to but otherwise stay hidden.

"How are we going in?" Fort asked.

"My room is actually open," Jia said. "Since they're holding me in the cafeteria. You can open a portal there."

"One second," Fort said, and moved back out to the dining room, where Ember was watching the cleaning process. *"Hey, Ember, stay here and don't eat anything, okay? We can go hunting when I get back."*

The dragon looked up at him and nodded, looking far less excited than she had the last time he'd said that. But at least she understood him clearly and seemed to be going along with it, which was all he could ask. He nodded back, then returned to the cottage's bedroom.

There, he opened a teleportation circle to Jia's bedroom. Fortunately, the TDA had isolated her in her own room, so there were no roommates to worry about, and the room was empty. Also, it was incredibly clean, which made Fort feel guilty about the state of his room back at his aunt's house.

Though to be fair, some of that was Ember's fault.

Rachel moved to the bedroom door and put her ear up to it, listening carefully. "We're good," she said, then slowly opened the door, peeking out into the hall. She gave a slight nod to Fort, then pulled the door all the way open and stepped out. Fort followed, closing the door behind him and canceling the portal, just in case anyone came looking for Jia.

"They usually guard my room," Jia said, sticking her head out of Fort's pocket as they moved down the hall toward the rest of the school. "But since I'm in the cafeteria now, there's no one else in this section, so we should be good to go until the elevator. They don't let me near any other students, which is bad, because I might have gotten Sebastian or one of the others to help us."

"I doubt it," Fort said. "He's probably enjoying Agent Cole being in charge."

"*Shh,*" Rachel said, giving him a dirty look as they reached the elevator, and she clicked the button. "I don't want to take a chance that you cast some random spell by accident."

"It's all under control," he said, not mentioning the ocean of vocabulary swirling around in his head and the pain still throbbing at the back of his skull. "Don't worry—this is all going to be fine."

The elevator dinged, and the door opened.

Colonel Charles and a man in a business suit were standing inside.

- TWENTY-SEVEN -

FORT'S ENTIRE BODY FROZE IN SHOCK AT the sight of his former headmaster, and his mouth dropped open. He fumbled for something to say as the colonel just stared out at them, like he was trying to place them.

"In or out, Major," Colonel Charles said to Rachel. "We don't have all day."

"Yes, sir," she said, awkwardly stepping into the elevator. "Sorry about that, sir."

Fort followed right behind, her movement snapping him out of his paralysis. The doors closed, and he turned to face the front, trying not to look at the colonel or whoever the man in the suit was if he could avoid it.

"What floor?" the man asked.

Rachel threw a look at Fort that told him she had no more

idea than he did about where the sword was. "Level four, sir," she said, apparently improvising. "We were ordered to guard the weapon that just appeared, but I'm told the location was changed for security purposes."

"You were told wrong," Colonel Charles said, and the hair on the back of Fort's neck bristled at the suspicion in his voice. "It's still in the trophy room."

The trophy room? Did he mean the room with the dragon bones? "So, floor thirteen, sir?" Fort asked, keeping himself facing forward.

"Do I need to *walk* you there, Private?" the colonel said. "I didn't realize I was your personal guide around the base."

"No, sir!" Fort said, pushing the button for floor thirteen. "Sorry, sir!"

He felt a pull on his arm, and he turned to find the colonel staring at him closely. "Your voices sound familiar, but I can't place your faces," Colonel Charles said to them. "What are your names?"

"Major . . . Paine, sir," Rachel said, somehow keeping a straight face.

In spite of the situation, Fort let out a quick laugh before immediately catching himself as Colonel Charles whirled on him, glaring suspiciously. "Sorry, sir," Fort said quickly. "I had something caught in my throat. Allergies."

"You should go to the medical bay once we're clear from lockdown to get something for them, soldier," the colonel said, still staring intently at Fort. "And your name?"

"Private, ah, McHenry, sir," Fort said quickly, blanking on everything except the various names of forts from his American history book. At least it sounded real, not like *Major Paine* next to him.

"I don't remember seeing either of you on the duty roster," the colonel said. Just then the elevator dinged, and the door opened.

"We were just transferred here, sir," Rachel said quickly. "After the London situation, to cover for the soldiers still recovering. We heard about your, ah, heroic actions there, sir, and might I just say, we're all in your debt?"

Fort almost laughed again, but this time at how much she was pushing this. He glanced at Rachel disbelievingly, but she looked completely sincere, so hopefully there'd be no way for the colonel to know she was mocking him.

"Thank you, Major," the colonel said, then nodded at the open doors. "This is your stop." With that, he then turned back to the man in the suit, who seemed bored with their conversation. "Our timeline has changed, and we'll be leaving for Berlin tonight. I've got the assets secured, and from here, the Gathering Storm will be—"

And then the doors closed, cutting off whatever he was saying.

Rachel leaned back against the wall, a huge grin on her face. "Well, *that* was fun!"

"What were you thinking?" Fort hissed at her, trying to keep his voice down as he could see other soldiers at the end of the hallway now. "Major *Paine*?"

"Hey, read some history," she told him. "Thomas Paine was one of America's founding fathers!"

"Oh, I know," Fort said, his mind filling with all kinds of details. "He wrote *Common Sense*, a pamphlet that called for independence from Great Britain. And John Adams was quoted as saying about him, 'Without the pen of the author of *Common Sense*—'"

"Wow, did you use that spell on Wikipedia, too?" Rachel asked. "C'mon, McHenry, we've got a job to do."

He sighed, but saluted her and hurried to follow her down the hall. "Still, Colonel Charles could have known you were mocking him."

"Good," she said. "I want him to know. I *hate* the man. But I don't look anything like me. Even if he was suspicious, there's no way he'd know it was Rachel Carter, who's home right now with no memory of this place." She grinned. "Though I'm sure he's going to go back to his office and look up Major Paine!"

Fort groaned. She wasn't wrong, and as soon as the colonel found there was no record of Rachel's snarky made-up name, he'd sound the alert. And if the TDA didn't know exactly when thieves were showing up to steal the sword, they did now. Or would, in a matter of minutes.

"Let's just grab the sword and get out of here," he said, not bothering to hide his annoyance.

"You shouldn't even be here," Rachel told him as they rounded the corner, only to stop. "Where is this room, by the way? I've never been to the one in *this* school."

Fort moved past her to lead the way, knowing how to get there by heart after using the room to study.

The last time he'd been there, he'd run into Gabriel, the colonel's son, having no idea that Gabriel was after the same thing Fort was, to find a missing relative. But that was before Gabriel had threatened to kill him if he didn't take them both back to the Dracsi world, so the last thing he wanted to do was remember how much he'd liked the other boy at one point.

Of course, with their luck, Gabriel would probably be waiting there in the trophy room too. His father, the colonel, had brought him back to the school during the London attack, using Gabriel's Space magic to teleport TDA soldiers into the city.

"There," Fort said, pointing to the end of the hall, where a large, bank-vault-like door stood slightly open. "That's it."

"Okay," Rachel said, stopping him a ways back. "We go in there, say we're replacement guards, and then get as close as possible to the sword. Then you teleport it and us out of here. No fighting, no hurting soldiers or our old classmates. Got it?"

"Got it," Fort said. "What do we do if they know we aren't supposed to be replacing anyone?"

Rachel reached into her pocket and pulled out a number of miniature wooden sculptures of monsters. "Jia's got us covered," she said with a smile.

Fort raised an eyebrow. "Aren't they kind of small?"

"They'll grow," Jia said from his pocket. "Trust me."

Rachel took a deep breath, then nodded. "Let's go, then. Follow me."

She strode down the hallway like, well, like an officer in the TDA, then paused at the door one more moment. Finally, she

232

grabbed the handle and pulled it wide. "Major Paine and Private McHenry reporting for guard duty—" she started to say, only for her mouth to drop open.

Just behind her, Fort saw what had stopped her and couldn't think of a word to say either.

Facing them in the room were at least two squads of TDA soldiers, each one holding lightning rods aimed right at the door.

And then Fort laid eyes on the sword. Excalibur was encased in some sort of transparent glass box, though only two people guarded it. One was Agent Cole, the federal agent who'd hunted Sierra down, then returned to the Oppenheimer School to run it in Dr. Opp's place.

And the other was Fort's best friend, who he thought had been lost in time.

"It's them, Agent Cole," Cyrus said, nodding at the door. "These are the two thieves I told you were coming for the sword."

- TWENTY-EIGHT -

"TAKE THEM DOWN!" AGENT COLE shouted, and the TDA soldiers immediately fired their lightning rods straight at Fort and Rachel.

Fortunately, Rachel was faster. She used her magic to yank the concrete floor up between them, letting the electrical spikes strike the rock instead. "Out!" she yelled at Fort, while throwing something from her pockets into the room.

Fort knew better than to argue and quickly leaped back into the hallway, preparing a teleportation portal. There was no time to think, but that *couldn't* have been Cyrus, could it? The last Fort had seen him, William had taken over Cyrus with Spirit magic and had had Cyrus send himself into some distant time, only coming back when William sent word it was okay.

And considering William had lost his magic shortly thereafter, that time wasn't coming up anytime soon. So if Cyrus had brought himself back, why come here, back to the Oppenheimer School? He had to know that Agent Cole and Colonel Charles couldn't be trusted.

Rachel slammed the vault door shut just in front of him, bringing his attention back to the present. "Move!" she said.

Only when Fort *tried* to move, he found he couldn't. His legs, his arms, everything was frozen in place, like he'd been paralyzed. But how—

A group of Oppenheimer students appeared at the end of the hallway, each one of them glowing with blue Healing light from having used a Paralyze spell on them. "Nice job, everyone!" shouted Moira, one of Fort's former classmates. "Now put them to sleep! Agent Cole wants to question them!"

But before the students could attack, a large blue sphere formed around them, and suddenly Fort found he could move.

"Get us out of here!" Jia's golem said, leaping to the floor as she freed Rachel from the paralysis spell as well. "I'll hold them off!"

Fort started to open a teleportation portal, but before he could, the floor suddenly gave out from under them, and they tumbled into darkness, the blue protective ball still surrounding them.

They landed hard, but whatever the ball was, it saved them from any broken bones. Unfortunately, it seemed to have shocked the little golem enough to disrupt Jia's attention, because the wooden doll fell to the floor, completely limp now.

"We've got incoming!" Rachel shouted, and Fort looked up to see more students, this time with glowing red hands.

Destruction students. They'd been the ones to take out the floor beneath them. *This* wasn't good.

Dozens of fireballs came crashing down from the floor above like some kind of apocalyptic rain, followed right behind by several of the students. Rachel managed to knock the fireballs out of the way with a nearby concrete wall, but two of the other students, boys that Fort recognized as Bryce and Chad, shot a few thousand gallons of water straight into her chest, sending her flying into the opposite wall.

Fort got a portal open before they could do the same to him, and he leaped through it, emerging right next to Rachel. "I'm taking us back to the cottage!" he hissed at her, opening another portal as the Destruction students advanced on them.

"No, get us back to the sword!" Rachel shouted, electrifying the water now pooling on the floor. Chad and Bryce, both walking through the puddles, got hit by the electricity and went sprawling to the floor. "We'll never get another chance at this if Cyrus is up there!"

Fort gritted his teeth but knew she was right. He pulled a teleportation portal down over the two of them, and they appeared in the dragon bones trophy room, where Fort expected to find a few dozen TDA soldiers waiting for them.

Instead, there was absolute chaos.

Monstrous golems of all different sizes were attacking the soldiers, like cursed dolls in some horror movie. Some were almost as big as a person and shaped like some kind of terrifying beast covered in fur and bristling with fangs, while others really did look human, just lifeless and awful.

Most of the soldiers were screaming in terror, trying to get the golems off them, but Jia's practice had paid off as she kept them all moving in different directions at once, attacking with the golems' hands, feet, or whatever they had, as well as her own magic.

These were what Rachel had tossed into the room, like a grenade of eerie puppets. And it made sense why Jia hadn't returned to the golem they had, if she was controlling this many at once!

"The sword!" Rachel shouted as Agent Cole grabbed the

transparent glass case to make a run for it. Fort opened a portal, and Rachel leaped through, then pulled the nearby wall out to grab Agent Cole, imprisoning her in the rock.

"Cyrus!" the agent shouted, and Fort and Rachel both turned in surprise to find their friend disappearing into nothingness, leaving behind just a flash of a shadow. Uh-oh.

"Where is he?" Rachel shouted to Fort, taking down two nearby TDA soldiers as the rest tried to reach their leader. "Do you see him?"

Fort quickly opened portals all around Rachel, but a stray lightning bolt sizzled into his leg, and he toppled to the floor, everything going dark for just a moment. He heard Rachel shouting from a distance and, somewhere behind him, the vault door opening again, but his head was ringing, and it was so hard to concentrate. Also, somehow it was getting harder to breathe, like the air was thicker than before.

Wait, no, the air *was* actually thicker. As Fort's head cleared, he found himself in the middle of a strange fog, far too dense to see through and weirdly almost solid. He could still breathe, but it took some effort, and he could feel the thick air sliding down into his lungs uncomfortably with every breath. What *was* this, and who—?

A blurred shadow gradually slowed into something resembling Cyrus, and Fort realized what was going on: This was one of Rachel's new tricks for fighting the Timeless One. She'd made the air in the room almost solid, and it was slowing Cyrus down.

Unfortunately, it wasn't helping Fort much, though, and he struggled to open a portal in front of Cyrus but missed as the other boy flashed right past it, still moving too quickly to catch. He heard Rachel shout in surprise as if from a great distance and realized the fog must be messing with the sounds, because she hadn't been too far before.

But before he could figure out what had happened to her, the air thinned out, revealing all of the Oppenheimer students now surrounding Fort. Next to Agent Cole, Cyrus had the box with Excalibur, and Rachel slumped to the floor next to him, apparently unconscious.

"Take him!" Agent Cole shouted, and all the Oppenheimer students turned to unload on Fort at once.

"No, *STOP*!" he shouted, not sure what else to do.

Only he didn't say "stop" in English.

The entire room froze in a shimmery black light, and Fort's eyes widened as he realized that he'd done this, using his new magic. He'd stopped time for the entire room.

And then he collapsed to the floor, completely exhausted.

Apparently, just knowing the magic words didn't mean he had the power to cast such a powerful spell. And it wouldn't have helped that he wasn't born on Discovery Day.

Still, even entirely devoid of energy, Fort almost laughed at the absurdity of everything as all around him, various students were just moments away from unleashing their magic on him. All he had to do was get to his feet, grab the box with Excalibur, teleport out with Rachel, and they'd be home free!

Fort grunted, then pushed himself up to his knees, then to his feet. As he stood, the room swayed dangerously, and Fort grabbed a nearby student to steady himself. Not wanting to faint, he quickly regained his balance, then stumbled over to where Cyrus waited with the box.

"I don't know what you're doing here," Fort said to his frozen friend. "But we're going to need to talk about this later." With that, he reached out a hand to take the box.

Cyrus grabbed him by the wrist before he could.

"Hey, Fort," the other boy said, smiling slightly. "How about we talk about it *now*?"

- TWENTY-NINE -

"WHOA!" FORT SHOUTED, LEAPING backward in surprise, then almost falling back to the floor when the room began to dance again. "Cyrus, you're awake?"

"Of course," his silver-haired friend said, then reached out to help support him. "I knew it was coming, so was prepared with my own magic. Are you okay?"

"No!" Fort shouted, but let Cyrus help hold him up. "I'm *not* okay. What are you doing here? You're helping Agent Cole now? Rachel needs that sword to take down the Timeless One!"

Cyrus's smile faded. "You don't know everything that's happening here," he said. "But to be fair, there's no reason you should." He raised a glowing hand, and without thinking, Fort immediately raised his own, ready to defend himself, only for Cyrus to give him a sad look. "Really, Fort? I'm not going to

241

fight you. I just wanted to make you look normal again. It's weird talking to a stranger."

Fort slowly lowered his hands, having almost forgotten about Jia's disguise spell. The glow of black Time magic surrounded him, running Jia's spell in reverse, and a moment later, he had shrunk back down to Cyrus's height.

"There," Cyrus said. "That's better."

"Fine," Fort said. "Now tell me what you're doing here. I thought you were lost in time after everything in London! And where is Ellora? She should have come back with the sword."

Cyrus nodded. "She did. The Healing kids put her to sleep right as she appeared. Agent Cole is holding her for now, until the UK takes her home."

"We can't let them," Fort said. "Not after how they treated those students before!"

"I'll make sure she's okay," Cyrus said. "But that's not why we're here—"

"And you still haven't said how *you're* back!"

"It wasn't hard, actually," Cyrus said with a shrug. "I assume you took away William's magic with the sword, because I was myself again by the time I arrived in the future. His spell must have broken when he lost his power."

"So why didn't you come back when I took William down?" Fort asked. "And why are you *here*? The TDA aren't the good guys, Cyrus. If we let them have Excalibur, who knows what they'll do with it. We barely stopped Colonel Charles from starting a world war over my father, remember?"

Cyrus sighed. "I do remember, of course. But I can see what's to come, Fort. Colonel Charles isn't the issue today. Right now, there are bigger worries."

"What's a bigger worry than the Old One of Time?" Fort asked, raising his eyebrows.

Cyrus paused for a moment. "Fort, I'm going to ask you to trust me. If you've ever thought of me as a friend, listen to me now. What I'm about to ask you is for the good of everyone. Do you understand me?"

"Okay, yes, I understand," he said, though he wasn't sure he did. "Just tell me."

Cyrus looked him in the eye. "I need you to leave the sword here, Fort."

Fort took a step back in shock, not even sure what his friend was saying. "I hope you're joking, Cyrus, because that's *insane*. There's no way I'd ever leave it here, not with Colonel Charles or Agent Cole. But even if they weren't going to use it, we still need it to use against the Timeless One. If we don't, humanity is going to suffer, not to mention that the faerie queen will throw us in her prison for the rest of our lives."

Cyrus winced. "I know you had no choice, but the fact that you made deals with her is a huge problem. You believe the TDA isn't on your side? The faerie queen is your actual *enemy*. She wants to return here, Fort, to bring her children back where she thinks they belong. That faerie girl isn't just here for a dragon. She's learning about modern-day humanity too, so the queen will have an advantage when she comes back to push humans out of her former land."

Fort's eyes widened. "*That's* why she's here? I knew the queen hated that they were exiled, but no one said anything about pushing humans out for the faeries to come back." He pictured Xenea and her complete disregard for all things human and wondered if it could be true.

But then he remembered her face while she watched the movie and how she wanted to see it again, in spite of that doing nothing for her mission. She didn't seem like the kind of person who'd go along with a war, not from what little he knew about her. "I don't know," he said, shaking his head. "Maybe the queen does want to come back, but I'm sure we can figure out a way for that to happen without anyone getting hurt. Besides, the only reason Xenea is here is because I made a deal for my father."

"Which the *queen* suggested," Cyrus said. "But even that can wait for now. You need to know what's happening with the Timeless One and Merlin. You're being thrown in the middle of a game between two all-powerful creatures, a game that's been going on for thousands of years. And the only way to keep you safe is *not to play*."

"A game?" Fort said, frowning. "What kind of game?"

"The kind where humanity lives or dies depending on who wins," Cyrus said. "*That's* how serious this is. But they can only play through their pawns, which right now are you, Rachel, and Jia. If the three of you refuse to play, the game can't continue."

"But Merlin's on *our* side," Fort said, feeling even more confused now. "He helped King Arthur. And he wants to stop the Old Ones, who I know for a fact want us all destroyed."

"Merlin's doing those things so he can *win*," Cyrus told him. "None of you matter to him, not compared to his game. And if you do finally succeed in using that sword on the Timeless One, then the whole future is going to be in horrible danger."

Fort rubbed his forehead, not understanding. "None of this makes sense, Cyrus. Are you trying to tell me we *need* the Timeless One?"

"In a way, yes," Cyrus said quietly. "There's a lot you don't know about him. A lot Merlin wouldn't tell you, though he did tell Jia and Rachel. Do you want to know what he's hiding from you, what he swore the others to secrecy about?"

This got Fort's attention, striking right through all the confusion of the past few minutes. "You know what the secret is?"

Cyrus nodded. "Merlin's trained all the Artorigios, right?" he said. "And the first six all faced Emrys, the Old One of Time, and lost. But Merlin himself has never tried to fight Emrys. Why do you think that is?"

Fort shrugged. "What, are you going to tell me that's part of the rules?"

"It is, but not the way you think," Cyrus said. "Merlin *can't* fight Emrys, because if he does, all of time could be destroyed. So they came up with the game, these two lifelong enemies. Merlin would train a human to face the Old One using an Avalonian sword, something that could actually hurt an Old One, while Emrys agreed to let Merlin train the human and wait for Merlin's pawn to be ready. The game hinges on the fact that Emrys doesn't believe a human can ever win, while Merlin thinks they can. Regardless, Merlin has seven chances, seven human Artorigios, to face Emrys. All Merlin needed was for *one* human to win, but so far, he's zero for six. And Rachel is the last one. After that, Emrys wins."

"Which still sounds like a bad thing to me," Fort said. "Not to mention that if we just skip out on whatever game those two are playing because you say so, then the faerie queen will—"

"*Forget* the faerie queen!" Cyrus shouted, his face contorting with anger. "She doesn't matter, not in this. Merlin's the dangerous one, and you're falling into his trap! Do you think he gave you a book of magical spell words *just* to talk to your dragon? Who suggested you Learn the whole thing, so you'd take it all in? He did! He can see the future, Fort! Everything that's happened so far has been according to his plan!"

Fort blinked in shock. "He . . . knew? But why would he—"

"Because he's lost six of these matches against Emrys," Cyrus said, shaking his head. "He knows Rachel will lose too, even with Jia at her side. But he knows you, knows that if you've got the power, you'll stand by your friends no matter what. So he secretly makes sure you've got the magic to do just that. He arranged for it *all* to happen."

Fort just stared at him for a moment. "No. He told me *not* to fight! He's made it pretty clear that if I help them, we will lose. Why would he tell me that if he secretly wanted me to fight?"

"Because if you hadn't felt so down on yourself, and looking for some way to help, you might not have used Learn on the book of magic," Cyrus said, sighing. "He knows how to manipulate people, Fort. He's done it six times so far."

Fort's mouth felt dry, and he couldn't believe this was all true. "But . . . he *couldn't* have known. It was all coincidence. I only have Ember because of D'hea freaking out at the tar pits. Without her, I would never even have needed the book of dragon language—"

"Who do you think made sure that dragon egg in the tar pits hatched before D'hea got there?" Cyrus said, glaring at him. "You don't get what I'm saying. Merlin's been around for an *eternity*. He can arrange things hundreds of years in advance, and *has*. And now he's manipulating you, too! And I can't let that happen. I won't let him change the fate of this entire world just because he thinks knows best!"

"No, that's not possible," Fort said. "No one could plan things out to that level. He couldn't be human!"

"Yes!" Cyrus shouted, slapping his shoulder. "Now you're finally getting it."

Fort swallowed hard, not liking what that sounded like. "Getting what?"

"That he's *not* human," Cyrus said. "Merlin looks like one, just like you looked like a soldier a second ago, but he's not."

Fort felt his entire body go cold. "Then what is he?"

"What do you think?" Cyrus said. "He's an Old One."

- THIRTY -

CYRUS'S REVELATION HIT FORT LIKE A punch to the stomach. "Merlin . . . is an *Old One?*" he said, barely able to say the words. "But—"

"That's how he's manipulated humankind for centuries," Cyrus said. "I've *seen* it, Fort. That's the real reason I was in his cottage, to learn as much as I could about him, and to see if I could stop his plan. But he knew what I was doing and pulled some strings so I'd be sent away by William. It's no coincidence that Sierra woke William and the rest up when she did. Merlin had everything exactly where he wanted it, using his own magic to send the other Carmarthen students back to the precise moment he wanted them, before Sierra and Damian could get the book of Time magic."

Fort fell back against one of the frozen soldiers, feeling faint again. "But . . . *you* brought us to him," he said quietly. "*You* told me to bring the book of Spirit magic to his cottage! You had us in the home of an Old One, and thought that was okay? Cyrus, what were you thinking?"

The other boy looked away. "I knew he wouldn't interfere, not directly. You three were too important to him. And I needed to know what was coming next." He turned back to Fort sadly. "I'm so sorry I couldn't tell you all of this at the time, but he knew I was trying to stop him and would have sent me away before William did if I'd revealed what I knew."

"You're *sorry*?" Fort shouted. "You just told me the guy who's been training Jia and Rachel for *months* is an Old One!" He paused as that fact really sank in. "I ate his *stew*! So did my poor baby dragon!" He turned away, gritting his teeth. "Which one is he, Cyrus?"

"Pardon me?" Cyrus sounded confused by this. "What do you mean?"

"Which Old One is he?" Fort said. "What's his magic? We'll need to know if we're going to fight him. That, and how he got back to our planet. If Merlin found a way to return after they were all exiled, we have to make sure none of the rest can follow him." He looked up at the ceiling, thinking out loud. "He knows Time magic, but that can't be his specialty, since the

Timeless One is already the Old One for that magic. Unless there are multiple Old Ones of each type?" He shuddered at the thought. "If that's the case, we might be in real trouble—"

"Merlin wasn't exiled," Cyrus said. "He's always been here. But it doesn't matter, because you don't *have* to fight him. You couldn't even if you wanted to—he's far too powerful. To beat Merlin, all you need to do is keep this sword away from Rachel—"

This threw Fort again. "Wait, go back. I thought they all were exiled. All but the Timeless One."

Cyrus sighed deeply. "Fine, okay, yes, you're right," he said. "All but the Timeless One *were* exiled." He rubbed his temples. "I suppose I *do* have to explain this. Let's back up a minute. Have you ever heard the stories about how Merlin lives backward in time? That part made it into the King Arthur tales and is basically true, if not very descriptive."

"Backward in time? What does *that* mean?" Fort said.

"The easiest way to imagine it is that he's born in the future, lives his life in reverse, and dies in the past. Are you with me so far?"

"Not even a little bit," Fort said, trying to wrap his head around how that could be possible. "Does everything just look like it's moving backward to him then?"

"Yes, but he just uses Time magic to align himself with the rest of us whenever he needs to manipulate events."

"So he *does* know Time magic?" Fort said. "Does that mean there are multiple Old Ones?" He winced. "If we have to face two Old Ones of Spirit magic, we're done for."

"I'm getting to that," Cyrus said, sounding almost miserable. "Merlin does live backward: He was born at the end of time and, assuming he doesn't get killed along the way, will live until the very beginning. But think about how long that is, Fort, between the beginning and end of everything. *Trillions* of years, if not more."

"I don't see how this—"

"I'm saying, in *that* long a time, immortals can change. You've grown and progressed even in the months since I've met you, Fort. And even someone as eternal as an Old One can evolve, become someone new, especially over so many millions of years."

Fort groaned at trying to follow this. "Cyrus, what are you saying? That Merlin isn't the same person he was when he was younger? I don't get how this has anything to do with which Old One he is."

"That *is* what I'm saying, and it matters here," Cyrus said, looking like he was suffering from his own headache now. "Over that long a time, we're not talking about changing small things, like going from loving cakes to hating them. After a few hundred million years, anyone could change dramatically, to the point that they might not even recognize their younger self. They'd be almost an entirely different person."

"Just tell me what you're trying to say!" Fort shouted, getting more confused by the minute.

"I'm *saying* that Merlin is an Old One, and has been on our world for all his life. And I'm also saying that only the Timeless One was left here when the rest of his family were exiled. Do you see now?"

Fort just blinked a few times, only for Cyrus's point to finally click, and his mouth dropped open.

"What?" he shouted. "No. *No way.* No!"

"Merlin *is* the Timeless One," Cyrus said, nodding. "And I know how that sounds, believe me. But when someone can live for an eternity like the Timeless One, and use Time magic to travel to any point in history, you can see how the same creature can—"

"Can what, *fight* himself?" Fort said, his headache now back and pounding almost as bad as when he'd learned the book of magic. "How can that even be possible? And *don't* say Time magic, because that just makes me more confused!"

"The Timeless One is Merlin's younger self, literally millions of years younger," Cyrus said. "And they want different things. Younger Emrys, that's the Timeless One's real name, he wants the other Old Ones to return to this world, whereas Merlin wants to rule everything by himself. It's for this reason that they can't fight each other directly, because if older Emrys destroyed his younger self, it'd create a time paradox, and probably rip apart the whole universe."

Fort's eyes widened with horror. "Oh, *of course!*" he shouted. "Because we can't have one Old One fighting himself. That'd be too strange!" He groaned loudly. "*Two* Timeless Ones? Seriously? Now we have to use Excalibur on both of them?"

"No, that's the whole reason I'm telling you this!" Cyrus said, leaning in close. "Fort, you *can't* face the Timeless One. Merlin is setting you up. He doesn't care if any of you live or die. All he wants is to defeat his younger self, so he can win. If you and the others try to fight the Timeless One, you'll—"

"Lose?" Fort said.

"Yes, almost assuredly," Cyrus responded bitterly. "But even if you beat him, then Merlin will still be around to take over

JAMES RILEY

the world. The only way to keep *either* of them from besting the other is to refuse to play. They'll keep each other in check, which is the best we can do for a being of such power."

Fort stared at him for a moment, lost in his thoughts, then slowly nodded. "Okay. I think I finally get it then."

"You do?" Cyrus asked. "So you agree with me? You won't play his game? You'll leave the sword here?"

Fort looked at his friend, the only one who wanted anything to do with him from the moment he'd arrived at the Oppenheimer School. As much as he'd never really understood Cyrus, Fort had always been so thankful for him just being there and not thinking worse of Fort for being less powerful than the others.

And he'd seen Cyrus's magic firsthand and knew it was real. Cyrus really could see everything he'd claimed to have seen, and Fort couldn't imagine his friend had any reason to lie about it all. Not to mention that it made an awful sort of sense: Of course Merlin wouldn't want Rachel or Jia to tell Fort that their trainer was actually the Old One they intended to fight. He still didn't know why his friends had stuck with Merlin, but he could ask them that later.

For now, Cyrus needed an answer.

Fort took a deep breath, then opened his mouth to say—

"Don't," Cyrus interrupted, wincing. "I saw you making this choice but hoped you'd listen, given our friendship." He sighed deeply, down to the bone. "I could stop you, Fort. I think we both know that."

His hands began glowing with black light.

Fort took a step backward, knowing that he'd never have a chance to stop Cyrus, not if the other boy really wanted to keep him from the sword. A flurry of magical words passed through his mind, but none made sense, none would stop a Time magician as powerful as Cyrus—

"And I *want* to stop you," Cyrus continued, "for the sake of everything. But not if it means I'd have to hurt you. I won't do that. Not for anything."

The light faded from his hands, and Fort blinked, not having seen this coming at all.

"I have to hear it from him, Cyrus," Fort said quietly. "I heard everything you said, but I can't let this go. I have to take the sword and get the story directly from *him*."

Cyrus nodded and slowly smiled at Fort. "The very first time we met, you told me we'd end up being the best of friends, and that our friendship would change everything. You probably don't remember that, but it's true. And I hope that's still the case."

Fort nodded, even though he remembered *Cyrus* saying they'd be best friends, not Fort himself, but he didn't want to argue the point. "I'll be back, Cyrus. And if Merlin admits to it all, maybe I can figure out a way to fix this. I'm sorry—I really am."

And then, before Cyrus could respond, Fort teleported himself, Rachel, the Jia golem, and the sword away.

- THIRTY-ONE -

FORT LANDED ON THE GRASS OUTSIDE the destroyed cottage, with Jia's golem, Rachel, and the case with Excalibur in it appearing right beside him. The clearing was empty, which made sense, as he'd left Ember inside the cottage, but still, everything felt eerily silent.

Instead of thinking about it, Fort turned to the others and raised his hands up over Rachel and Jia's golem. *"Start!"* he yelled in the language of magic, hoping that would cancel his Stop spell.

Nothing happened.

Uh-oh. Fort tried a few more phrases, from *Restart Time* to *Move Again, My Friends!* but nothing seemed to work. Finally, he gave up, realizing that maybe this was for the best. After all, Rachel and Jia apparently already knew Merlin's secret, so it was fitting that Fort face the Old One alone now, to confront him about it.

Which meant there was no putting off what had to happen next.

Fort took a deep breath, then opened the case with Excalibur.

The last time he'd held the sword, it'd set him on fire after judging him unworthy. Jia claimed that the sword had changed its mind by the time Fort had taken down William in his monstrous, Spirit-magic-filled form, but he knew he couldn't count on those good feelings anymore.

Still, if the sword's whole purpose in life was to take down the Timeless One, Fort intended to help it with that. So maybe it could listen to reason for once.

"Listen, Excalibur," he said, his hand pausing in the air just over the sword's hilt. "I know we got off to a bad start, but I want you to know that I'm on board with your whole mission. I'm happy to be your partner here and let you do all the work. Together, we can take away the Old One's magic, okay? But I'm going to need you to not burn me alive in the process. Deal?"

Fort paused, but there was no response from the sword. After a few seconds, he rolled his eyes, not sure what he'd been expecting. Still, after everything else, a talking sword shouldn't have been out of the question.

"Deal!" someone shouted, and Fort leaped backward in surprise, only to realize the voice came from the door knocker. "Ha, did I get you?" the imp shouted.

"*No!*" Fort shouted back, lying completely. "And hey, did you know you're answering doors for an Old One?"

"Times are tough," the imp said. "And an imp's got to work."

"Well, I'm sorry to say you're going to lose your job," Fort said, his hand still hovering over the hilt. "Because I'm about to take Excalibur inside and use it on Merlin."

"Like I haven't heard *that* one before," the imp said, which didn't sound good.

Still, whether the sword was going to judge him or not, he'd wasted enough time. Fort spread his fingers out wide, closed his eyes, took a deep breath, then quickly grabbed the sword, wincing in anticipation.

Shockingly, he didn't feel anything but the cool hilt of the sword, so he happily opened his eyes, only to yelp in surprise as he found flames running from the tip of the blade toward the hilt, coming straight for his hand.

"Ahh!" he shouted, but didn't let go. He'd used his Healing spell on his hand before, and would just have to do it again.

But before the flames reached his hand, they seemed to

pause at the cross guard of the sword—and *stopped*. He slowly lifted Excalibur up out of the box and stared at it in amazement. "Are you really not going to burn me?" he asked.

The flames pushed down toward the hilt once more, and again Fort flinched. But just like the last time, they paused, then pulled back up to the blade.

Apparently that was his answer? If so, the sword *had* found a way to talk.

"Aw, it likes you!" the imp door knocker shouted. "Doesn't think you're worthy, granted, but it likes you. That's adorable."

"Do you . . . speak its language?" Fort asked, holding the sword out for the door knocker to see.

"It's a sword—it doesn't *speak* a language," the imp said, giving Fort a questionable look. "No, I've just seen more than one Artorigios here, and it isn't always the biggest fan of them. Respects them, sure. They're heroes, after all, and worthy of wielding it. But you, it seems to have taken a shine to. Otherwise it'd let the flame burn you."

Fort looked down at the hilt, just an inch away from the flames. He could feel the heat on his hand, but not in an uncomfortable way, which was odd, considering how hot the fire had been last time he'd held the sword. Even now, waving his other hand a few inches over the sword felt far too close, given the flames' heat.

"*Thank* you," he said to Excalibur, and meant it. He'd never had a sword want to be his friend before, even if it didn't think he was worthy of carrying it. "I hope I can win your respect through what we're about to do."

The sword's flames intensified for a moment, then diminished back to their previous state. Fair enough.

Fort picked up the ruined door from the ground, held it in place with his free hand, then pulled it open with the hand holding Excalibur, ready for anything. Merlin could see the future, so he had to know Fort was coming. He braced himself. . . .

But the only one inside the cottage was Ember, curled up in dragon form on the table, the pot of stew now lying on its side on the floor, half-eaten and licked clean.

"*Ember, come out here,*" Fort said in the language of magic, and the dragon looked up at him in surprise, then quickly stood and slunk out the doorway.

"*Hello, Father,*" she said to him. "*I am glad you've returned, as I'm hungry and wish to go hunting. Do you still intend to take me?*"

Fort winced. "*Uh, not just yet. I have to take care of something inside, but I need you to wait out here. Can you do that for me?"*

The little dragon tilted her neck to give him a questioning look, before getting excited as she noticed Excalibur's flames. *"What do you have to take care of? Is it burning something? Because I would very much enjoy burning something just as much as hunting!"*

"No, it's not burning anything," Fort said quickly, trying to hide the flaming sword behind his back, then giving that up as pointless. *"This is for, uh, decoration."*

She gave him a suspicious look, and he knew he wasn't fooling her. *"Whatever you say, Father."* She turned to look at Rachel and Jia's golem. *"I assume I shouldn't hunt the other human and the possessed sculpture, then? They would not be much of a challenge in their state?"*

"Right, no hunting them!" he said quickly, eyeing the inside of the cottage. *"In fact, you should watch over them for me. Can you do that? Can you be a good girl and protect them?"*

She snorted, a little plume of fire rising from her nose. *"Don't speak down to me, Father. I'm almost three days old, after all. But I will protect them until you return."* She paused. *"Though if you don't return, then we shall see what we shall see."*

Fort snorted. *"I will return, in just a few minutes. Okay?"*

"Whatever you say, Father," the dragon said, and settled in around Jia's golem protectively. At least Fort hoped it was protectively.

He turned back to the door and slowly stepped through, closing it behind him.

"Merlin! Come out and face me!" he shouted in English again, holding Excalibur up.

"Forsythe?" Merlin said, appearing out of nowhere in a burst of black light. "Ah, you have the sword. Are we that far along already?"

Fort wasn't sure what that meant but aimed Excalibur right at the old man. "I don't know what you're talking about, but you and I are going to have a talk. I think it's time for the truth, don't you, Timeless One?"

Merlin smiled. "Ah. *That.*"

- THIRTY-TWO -

YES, *THAT*," FORT SAID, HIS FLAMING sword aimed straight at the old man. He knew it wouldn't exactly be much of a threat to Merlin if the man was still in a different time, if this Merlin before him was just a hologram, but there was no way to know that now. Besides, it couldn't hurt to show the Old One that the sword was letting Fort wield it, just in case Merlin decided to try a spell on him. "Now tell me *why*. Why you've lied, why you're using humans for your sick little game, and what happens if you win. I want to know *all* of it."

"You spoke to Cyrus, then," Merlin said. "Good. I was beginning to wonder when he'd show back up. Funny how that boy can consistently knock things off schedule, yet still somehow manage to be late when *I'm* waiting on him."

Fort narrowed his eyes. "Cyrus doesn't matter. I want to know why you're having us fight your younger self."

"Cyrus doesn't matter?" Merlin said, his eyes twinkling with amusement. "If you say so. Still, did you know that none of this was supposed to happen yet, Forsythe? Rachel was meant to face the Timeless One as a fully grown adult, after magic had been back for over two decades. Remember, none of the other Artorigios were children. Why would I ever send an apprentice against someone so powerful?"

"I don't know why you're doing it to begin with!" Fort shouted. "Whatever game you're playing here—"

"Is a game to save *humanity*, Forsythe," Merlin said, sitting down in one of the chairs around the dining room table. "And is only a game so that there are rules to follow, rules for both sides." He patted a chair next to him. "Have a seat, boy. I intend you no harm. You can put down that ridiculous sword before it sets the cottage on fire."

"I'm good standing, actually," Fort told him. "And this sword is protecting me, so nice try."

Merlin sighed. "Forsythe, do you really think that sword could save you if I wanted to hurt you? I have access to all time. If I chose, I could keep you from ever being born. That's the power of Time magic." He patted the seat again. "But I am not my younger self. I only want to protect humanity, not see it punished, as he does."

"So you *admit* you're an Old One!" Fort shouted, feeling victorious at catching Merlin so easily.

"Of course I am," Merlin said. "What do you think I told Rachel and Jia on the first day of training?"

"Right, the secret!" Fort said, gritting his teeth. "Jia wanted to tell me, but Rachel wouldn't let her."

Merlin raised an eyebrow. "Interesting. You think *this* is what I asked them not to share?" He slowly smiled. "But yes, I told them from the start. They had to know every strength, every weakness of their opponent. And one rather large weakness is that the Timeless One's older self is their ally, if they were only able to accept me as such. It took them each a few days to come around, but eventually they did, though it took showing them my history." He shrugged. "If I knew you'd handle it so calmly, perhaps I'd have shared this with you, as well."

"Don't get sarcastic with *me*, Merlin," Fort said, glancing back at the door to where his friends were still frozen outside. "They should have told me, so I'd have known not to trust you. No wonder you had me reading a book of magical language without warning me. You probably wanted me to set myself on fire!"

"I'm afraid *that* was entirely on you," Merlin said, leaning back. "And I imagine they didn't tell you because they knew what you would think, especially as they themselves had thought the exact same thing when they found out. They also learned to trust me again, and took my word that you would find out when you were meant to."

"I don't believe it," Fort said, shaking his head. "There's no way they'd trust an Old One."

"Then why come back for training?" Merlin asked. "Perhaps that bears considering. Still, I *didn't* mean for you to find out just yet, but as I said, Cyrus has a talent for sending my plans off schedule." He smiled. "And vice versa."

"What plans?" Fort shouted, not liking any of this, but especially not that his friends did seem to have trusted Merlin. "What is this big game between you and your younger self?"

Merlin looked away for a moment, as if he were collecting his thoughts. "You and Emrys share one thing in common," he said finally. "You both experienced losing your families when you were very young. Emrys will be born in the far future on a world from where his family has been exiled for millions of

years, never knowing what it was like to have their companion-
ship. All he wants in this universe is to bring them back, much
like you felt with your father."

"I'm *nothing* like an Old One!" Fort shouted. "His family—
your family!—wants to wipe out humanity so they can rule
over our world again. You're monsters!"

Merlin looked slightly hurt. "I didn't say it was *exactly* the
same thing. But you may wish to look at things from his perspective in the future. It might help with what is to come."

"And what's that?" Fort said. "What's your part of the plan here?
Why are you even fighting against your younger self? Because I
don't buy that you're really on our side just because you got older,
like you flipped a switch and all of a sudden turned good."

"Oh, definitely not," Merlin said, folding his arms. "I'm easily as capable of horrible acts as he is. But as I aged, I had the
good fortune to meet some humans, and it opened my mind
to the . . . *consequences* of my actions. In fact, I became such
good friends with one that I decided I couldn't go through with
my original plan, and instead helped humanity exile my *own*
family in the past."

Fort rolled his eyes. "And I'm just supposed to believe you
did all this?"

Merlin gestured toward the door. "You can ask Jia and Rachel. I showed them everything I've done, so they could witness it for themselves. As your kind was learning magic from dragons, I worked with two of my more sympathetic siblings to send our family away. It caused a bit of a ruckus, you might say—a bit of a civil war in my family. But it led to a golden age here on Earth for your kind."

Fort frowned, not understanding how this was possible. An Old One had become friends with humans and so worked against his own family? That didn't track, not with what he'd seen of the monsters before. They'd tried to kill him several times, not to mention brainwashing Michael, Colonel Charles's son, and attempting to take over the world with the Dracsi. None of that really spoke to them being particularly *sympathetic*.

"So now you're playing a game with your younger self throughout time, trying to keep him from bringing your family back?" Fort said, furrowing his brow.

"Oh, yes, that, but it's become even simpler at this point," Merlin said. "After realizing I'd never let him bring our brothers and sisters back, he's decided I must be erased from existence completely. If I'm gone, then the Old Ones will never have been exiled, and his family will exist all the way to the ends of this world, even to his birth."

Fort opened his mouth to respond, then realized he had no idea what to say to *that*. Instead, he focused on something Cyrus had mentioned. "I thought you couldn't hurt each other, or the world would explode."

"Indeed," Merlin said with the hint of a smile. "He knows that if he tries to destroy me directly, I will defend myself, creating a paradox with unknown consequences. So instead of potentially wiping out all of existence, we agreed to a contest, one with rules that each must follow. I would only operate through chosen heroes, my Artorigios, with a sword created by the greatest smiths in Avalon." He snorted. "Can't tell you what I had to pay the queen of the faeries for *that*. Helped her save her entire race by de-aging them into children, and she *still* blames me for it."

Fort frowned. That part was definitely true, since the queen had explained things pretty much the same way. But Fort still couldn't bring himself to believe that Merlin was trying to help humanity. "If you're an Old One, why did you decide to help send your family away? Especially if you didn't have them when you were younger, like you said?"

"Because unlike my siblings, *I* can see all of time," Merlin said, looking away. "When I was younger and saw them only from a distant time, I justified the horrible things they did because of their exile, and their right to self-preservation. But as I grew older and saw more of their history, I knew that there was a darkness in them from the start, born of rage, arrogance, and fear. They wanted all the power of magic to themselves, and would destroy any race that could possibly stand against them."

That sounded more like the Old Ones Fort was used to. But he wasn't here to figure out why the monsters did what they did, just to learn how to beat them. "Even if Jia and Rachel confirm all of this, it doesn't matter," Fort said. "Cyrus told me that the only way to win is not to play your game. Then neither you nor the Timeless One would gain an upper hand."

A brief flash of anger passed over Merlin's face. "Perhaps Cyrus wasn't as honest with you as you believe. If an Artorigios does not appear to face the Timeless One at the proper time, then my younger self automatically wins. I will be wiped from existence, and the Old Ones' exile will never have happened. In that event, the very best case for your species is that you return to an eternity of servitude, assuming my siblings don't just destroy you altogether."

The matter-of-fact way Merlin described the end of humanity made Fort's blood run cold. "Cyrus wouldn't lie to me," he said quietly. "And considering you come from a family of horrible monsters, I'm going to believe him over you anyway."

Merlin nodded, then spread his hands. "If so, there's nothing I can say to convince you. And the rules bind me in what I am allowed to reveal as well. But I would suggest you take a look at your friend, and his plans. Where has Sierra gone? And why have you seen nothing of Damian since the attack on London?"

"*You* sent Sierra away!" Fort shouted, not wanting to even think about Damian. "You said she had something she needed to be doing!"

"She is as much a part of this as you are," Merlin said. "Just not in the same way. She won't need to face the Timeless One. Instead, she works on what is to come next."

Fort growled in frustration, not liking any of this. *Sierra?* he shouted in his mind. *Please, if you can hear me,* say *something. I need to know you're okay, and what you're doing! It's* important!

But again, there was no response.

"You won't hear from her," Merlin said. "You can't. She and Damian aren't presently in this time. They've been sent to the near future, where they're retrieving the remaining books of magic."

What? Sierra had been sent to the future? But how? *Why?* "It's so convenient that these 'rules' keep you from telling me more," Fort said, raising Excalibur again. "Maybe I should touch you with this sword if you keep refusing to tell me everything, how about *that?*"

"Then you would take my magic from me permanently, and I would *still* refuse," Merlin said. "The rules are there to save all of reality, not for your annoyance, Forsythe."

Fort stared at him for another minute, then lowered the sword, having no idea what to think about any of this. "So if we face your younger self and win, then what happens?" he asked quietly. "Wouldn't you lose your magic too?"

"It would appear that way," Merlin said, his eyes twinkling slightly. "But don't worry about me—I'll be just fine when all is said and done."

"I *wasn't* worried about you!" Fort said, even more confused now. "And Cyrus said you'd take over if we beat the Timeless One for you."

Merlin smiled. "Unfortunately, if I told you what is to come, or *how* to beat the Timeless One, then I would again be forfeiting the game, and my younger self would win. But you know all you need to know, Forsythe. Consider what I've said now, and what I told you before: You cannot fight Emrys, the Time-less One. You don't have that kind of power. Once you accept that, you'll have learned all you need to know."

And with that, he disappeared, leaving Fort alone in the cottage.

- THIRTY-THREE -

FORT WALKED THROUGH THE IMP'S door and back into the clearing, Excalibur still flaming in his hand, his mind reeling with everything he'd just heard. Was any of it even true? Why would Merlin have hidden his true identity from him if it was?

Okay, yes, finding out Merlin was an Old One was bound to make anyone suspicious of the old man—old *monster*, really. But he'd told Rachel and Jia. So why keep it from Fort?

"Are you well, Father?" Ember said, coming up to him with a slightly worried look in her eyes. *"I did as I was told, and kept this sad human and disconcerting doll from harm."*

He couldn't help but smile at that. *"Thank you, Ember. You did great."*

A small burst of fire exploded from her nostrils, and she grinned, showing a row of razor-sharp teeth. *"Of course I did,"* she said, but still sounded proud of being praised. *"Will you release them from their spell now with your weapon of undoing?"*

Weapon of . . . *oh*. Fort almost slapped himself in the forehead, which would have been dangerous while he was holding a flaming sword. Of course he could have used Excalibur to unfreeze them from the beginning! It'd worked back in London, but in the panic to see if he could pick it up to begin with, he'd completely forgotten about that.

"Yes, um, I believe it's time," he said to Ember, trying to make it sound as if he'd always intended to wait. *"But thank you for the reminder."*

She tilted her head and raised an eyebrow, which made Fort feel uncomfortably like she saw right through him. *"You are welcome, Father. Not that you asked for my help, of course."*

Just what he needed, his baby dragon turning into a sarcastic teen dragon.

Carefully he brought the flaming sword down close to Rachel first, making sure not to let the sharp side of the blade touch her. If he cut her by accident, she'd lose access to magic forever, so he moved as slowly as he could. As soon as the flat of the sword touched her, she immediately came to life.

"Fort!" Rachel shouted, staring at the sword. "What happened? How did you get Excalibur? What happened to Cyrus? Where's . . ." She glanced down at the golem on the ground next to her and immediately panicked. "Jia! Is she okay?"

Fort pressed the sword to the doll, but nothing happened. Why hadn't it freed her from the Time spell?

Or wait, did it undo too much and take away Jia's original spell on the golem? If so, they'd have no way of communicating with Jia, and she could be in trouble, now that they'd stolen the sword!

"Hey," shouted a voice from inside the open cottage door. "*There* you both are. Took me forever to get out of the bag I left this in!"

They both turned to find a duplicate golem standing in the doorway, waving at them.

"Jia!" Rachel shouted, and ran to her, picking the golem up and hugging her close. "You're okay!"

Whatever problem the two of them had had seemed to be less important at the moment, and Fort for one wasn't going to jinx it by saying anything.

"Yup, still in the cafeteria," she said, hugging Rachel back. "What happened? I lost access to all my golems at once, like they were completely shut off!"

"I'll get to that," Fort said. "They didn't blame you for the sword being stolen, did they?"

The golem shook her head. "Agent Cole came by to interrogate me, but she didn't seem to expect much. From what I can tell, they must not have been able to see through the disguises. I don't think they know *who* it was. But she had Cyrus with her." The golem paused. "I had no idea he was even here, but that explains a lot."

"Yeah, we had a fun run-in with him," Rachel said, still hugging the golem close.

But Cyrus being there for Jia's interrogation sent Fort's mind spinning again. Cyrus had clearly known who was underneath the disguises, but he hadn't told Agent Cole. Why not, if he was on her side? And if he wasn't, did that mean he really was there to try to keep Fort, Rachel, and Jia from facing the Timeless One?

"He's the reason the sword showed up early," Fort said. "And *he* knows it was us. But I guess he's not going to turn us in, which is lucky."

Jia sighed. "I'm not sure it's luck, Fort. You still don't know everything that's going on right now—"

"I know that Merlin is the Timeless One," Fort said, giving

her and Rachel a long, guilt-inducing look, which wasn't easy to do with a wooden puppet. "Why didn't you tell me?"

Rachel and the golem traded glances. "You know I wanted to," Jia said, looking away miserably. "I've . . . had too many problems with keeping secrets from the most important people in my life." She looked up at Rachel. "I'm so sorry, Ray. I should have told you from the beginning that I'd made a bargain with the faerie queen. I just couldn't let a world war break out if we failed, and if she could stop it somehow . . ."

"I know," Rachel said, wincing a bit, but still holding tight to the golem. "It's about time I let that go. You did what you thought was best, and I guess I just don't like things being kept from me. But you're allowed to have privacy. And who knows? Maybe the queen *did* help us out."

"Wait, what?" Fort said, blinking rapidly. "That was your deal with the queen, that she'd keep the war from happening? But she did that by making sure my dad couldn't use magic anymore. Which means . . ."

"Which means she played you both," Rachel said, sighing. "She got a two-for-one deal. By fixing your dad, Fort, she accomplished Jia's deal too, but we still owe her twice."

Fort shook his head, realizing now that Rachel had been

right all along. It really didn't pay to make deals with the Tylwyth Teg. "So what was your payment, Jia? What else is she going to get out of us?"

Jia's golem looked down at the ground. "I'm not allowed to say. That was part of the deal, and why I didn't mention it to begin with. But it won't hurt anyone or mess with our world at all. I told her I wasn't willing to make things worse just to keep the war from happening!"

Fort noticed that Rachel had tensed up during this last part, but she let out a long breath and nodded. "Like I said, not a fan of secrets, but I trust you, Gee. And if you say the price for stopping the war isn't that bad, then it's probably worth it." She raised the golem to look it straight in the eye. "But next time, we *talk* about this first!"

Jia's golem smiled shyly. "Deal."

Fort sincerely was happy they were getting along again, but still, there were bigger things at the moment. "Can we get back to Merlin being an Old One and you not telling me?"

Rachel lowered Jia to the ground, coughing uncomfortably. "Well, he said you'd find out when you needed to, so we didn't think it'd matter just yet," she said, not looking at him. "Plus, you still needed to learn Ember's language, and I can't see you studying in an Old One's house, can you?"

"No, which is why you should have *told* me!" Fort shouted. "I would have figured out some other way to deal with Ember."

"What do you mean, deal with me, Father?" the dragon said.

He winced. *"Nothing. We'll talk about it later."*

She hissed, then turned away and slunk back into the cottage to take another bite out of the stewpot.

"So tell me the truth now," Fort said, turning back to Rachel and Jia. "You both trust Merlin, and think we need to fight the Timeless One? Because Cyrus said we should just skip the whole thing, and then neither of them would win."

"Of course he'd say that," Rachel said, then yelped as Jia pinched her leg with the golem's tiny little wooden hands. "Hey!"

"He's got his own stuff going on," Jia told Fort. "And no, *you* still shouldn't fight the Timeless One, but we need to. Merlin is hiding some things, but he is on our side, on humanity's side. So yes, we're going to fight Emrys."

"Why did you pinch her?" Fort asked, raising an eyebrow. What were they hiding about Cyrus?

"To prove that I'm not a dream," Rachel said quickly. "She thinks she must be imagining me sometimes, I'm so perfect."

"That's true," Jia said, then pinched her again, making Rachel shout out.

Fort bit his lip, wanting to ask again what they weren't telling him, but instead just handed Excalibur to Rachel. "Well, this is yours. At least we got it back."

As soon as she took the hilt, the flames disappeared, and Rachel grinned. "I love this thing," she said, swinging it around a bit.

Fort watched her play for a moment, then looked back into the cottage to where Ember was almost through with the pot and searching for more metal to eat. Rachel and Jia were still definitely keeping things from him. But none of it made sense. Between what they had accidentally revealed, and everything Merlin had told him, it was like none of these pieces actually fit the puzzle.

Not unless the puzzle was of a completely different picture than he'd been expecting.

As Rachel continued practicing with Excalibur, with Jia offering commentary, Fort went silent, considering everything he'd been told or picked up from hints that Jia or Rachel had provided. Clearly, *someone* wasn't to be trusted, but the one person he suspected most seemed to have the trust of his friends.

And the person they *didn't* seem to trust . . .

Wait. *Wait.*

Fort's eyes widened as things suddenly began to make sense. If this *was* a jigsaw puzzle, then the picture coming into view wasn't the one he'd thought, not at *all*. Not if what Jia and Rachel had told him was true, and if he couldn't trust them, then nothing made sense.

And the idea that had just come to him *did* fit everything he'd learned. But it also was something he didn't want to believe, not even a little bit. His whole body felt cold, and he truly didn't want to pick at this thread. If he was right, everything he'd known since first going to the school would have been a lie.

But that wasn't exactly new, was it? Dr. Opps, Colonel Charles, *everyone* had lied to him from the start.

Fort swallowed hard. Even the idea that it could be possible made him want to throw up. But it all fit, and he couldn't just ignore it! Why did it have to be . . . couldn't it have . . . *ugh*!

He sighed heavily, really hoping he was wrong about all of this, but worrying he wasn't. Maybe that's exactly why Merlin, Jia, and Rachel were trying to hide it from him, even if they weren't doing a great job of it. Whether it was the rules of the game, or just not wanting Fort to get hurt, it didn't really matter. If he was right, he almost wished he *hadn't* figured it out.

But it was too late to stay ignorant. There was no going back to how things used to be, not anymore, no matter how much it might hurt or make him feel completely empty inside.

"I have to get back home," Fort said to Rachel and Jia, then looked down at the golem. "Are they releasing you back to your dorm room?"

"Already in the process," Jia said, nodding.

"Good," he said. "Then I'll see you both tomorrow night. *Come on, Ember. We're going home.*"

She huffed indignantly but walked out of the cottage and sat down next to him, waiting for him to open a portal.

"Where are you with everything, Fort?" Rachel asked, giving him a worried look. "I know that was a lot to take in, about Merlin. Took me a few days to be okay with it."

"Me too," Jia said.

"I don't know that a few days will change anything," Fort told them. "But I do think I have some decisions to make."

"Okay, New Kid," Rachel said, looking at him sadly. "Come back tomorrow night, and we can talk it all over if you want . . . well, anything we're allowed to say."

Fort snorted but gave her a small salute. "I'll be here. See you two then."

And with that, he teleported himself and Ember back to his bedroom, knowing he had a big choice to make.

Because if he was right about everything, the only way their battle against the Timeless One would work out was if he *did* face the Old One at Rachel and Jia's side. And for the first time, he wasn't sure he could.

THIRTY-FOUR

FORT LAY IN HIS BED, WATCHING AS Ember finished off the remnants of his aunt's exercise equipment. The dragon had already eaten through enough that he'd just decided to let her have the rest, especially since cat food was clearly not going to do the job anymore.

"Will we hunt tonight, Father?" she asked him after swallowing the last bit of dumbbell. *"You did say we'd do that soon."*

Fort shook his head, lost in his thoughts. *"I have a lot to think about tonight, Ember. I'm sorry."*

She licked her lips, not looking happy. *"Does this mean that it is okay to break a promise?"*

That got Fort's attention. *"No, it's not, and I* will *take you hunting,"* he said. *"It's just that I have a problem, and I am not entirely sure what to do about it."*

"A problem?" she asked. *"Maybe I can hunt and kill it for you."*

"No, that's okay," he said quickly, smiling at her. *"It's just a decision I have to make about something."*

A look of both anger and worry crossed her reptilian face. *"What decision?"* she asked, and her voice sounded less confident than usual.

"There is an . . . enemy," he said. *"At least, I think. And my friends, the two girls you were just protecting, they're going to fight it. But they don't think I should fight it too, because they worry about me. But I believe I have to, even if . . . I don't know that I can."*

Ember's eyes narrowed, and a little plume of smoke began to rise from her mouth. *"They insult you, Father. I will destroy them for this!"* She began to flap her wings. *"With me at your side, you have the power to take down any foe!"*

"No, they're not insulting me!" Fort said, jumping off the bed and trying to pin her wings back down so she wouldn't make even more noise. The last thing he needed was for his dad or aunt to come by and see how his kitten was doing, only to find a dragon as big as Fort. *"They care about me and don't want me to be hurt. And I do have the power to face this enemy, but I don't know that I can fight. Because . . . well, a lot of reasons. The old man in the cottage—"*

"*The man?*" Ember said. "*He is no human, Father. Were you not aware?*"

Fort snorted. "*Not until earlier, no. I wish I could have talked to you a few days ago.*"

Ember rolled her eyes. "*You are not as intelligent as I am. But I do not hold it against you.*"

"*Thank you,*" Fort told her, half sincerely. She purred loudly, even as a dragon, and rubbed her scaly head against his cheek. "*Anyway, he told me some things I didn't know, and it led to other things, and now I don't know what to do.*"

"*Ask me,*" Ember said. "*I shall tell you. Enemies should be burned, then eaten. There is no need to think on it further.*"

"*It's not that easy,*" Fort said, not really sure how to explain it.

"*Why?*" she asked.

He growled in frustration. "*I just have to think, okay? Things are so complicated, and I was supposed to use this magic to get you to Avalon, but now I've learned that so many other things were happening, and—*"

She took a step back, suddenly looking at him with a mixture of anger and fear. "*No, Father. I do not wish to go to that place. I wish to stay here, with you.*"

Ugh. This was the last thing he wanted to be talking about

at the moment, not with everything else going on in his head. *"I'm not sending you right now, but someday you will have to go, Ember. There are other dragons there, and they can take care of you better than I can."*

"Please, Father, don't do that," she said, backing away now, pulling her head in closer to her body as she crouched down low. *"I hear you talk about it with the humans and know what you say. I know you intend to send me away, and it hurts me, Father. I do not wish it!"*

Her words hit him like a punch to the gut. *"Ember, I don't want you to leave,"* he said, moving over to her and hugging her close. He held her for a moment, then pulled away. *"But it's better for you that way. Humans and dragons live very differently."*

"Then I should live as a human," Ember said, and he noticed her cheek scales were now wet. *"I do not mind!"*

"No, that's not who you are," Fort said. *"Another dragon I know lived as a human, and I'm not sure it was all that helpful, to be honest, considering how he turned out."*

"You are sending me to this other dragon?" Ember asked, not looking happy about it. *"But you imply he is not worthy of me."*

"No, I'm not sending you to him," Fort said quickly. *"But you're right, he is definitely not worthy of you. That's why the dragons in*

Avalon will be better, because they live as dragons."

"But you *are my father, not them!"* She shook her head vio-lently.

"Ember, I'm not," he said, and she froze at his words. *"You were . . . created by another dragon. I just promised to watch over you for him. And I think this is the best way to do that."*

She looked like she might be about to start sobbing. *"Then you would break that promise, because you could not watch over me if I am no longer around. Please, Father, I do not want to leave you!"*

"It's just the way things have to be," Fort told her quietly, his heart breaking as he said it. *"I wish it wasn't that way, but there's nothing I can do."*

She looked at him, her eyes drooping now with sadness. *"There is something you could do, but you won't do it. You do not care about me."*

"That's not true!" Fort said. He reached for her, but she pulled away. *"I care deeply for you, Ember, and only want the best for you!"*

"Then let me stay with you!" she said, and he found himself at a loss for words. *"That is what is best for me!"*

"I can't, *because that's not how things work!"* he said a little too

loudly, feeling terrible about all of this. *"I'm sorry, Ember, but there's nothing to argue about here. You're a dragon, I'm a human, and you can't stay here!"*

His words caused her to tremble, and she bowed her head low, nodding. *"Then I will not interfere with your human life any further, Father,"* she said, turning away. *"I shall leave now, to honor your wishes. Even if you did not fulfill your promises, I will."*

Fort felt like he was going to throw up. *"Ember,"* he said, shaking his head. *"You don't have to go now. We have time—"*

She looked up at him and blinked, tears running down her cheeks. *"Good-bye, Father,"* she said.

And then she disappeared in a burst of green light.

"Ember?" Fort said, pushing to his feet. *"Ember, where did you go?"* He searched the room but knew it was pointless. His dragon had just teleported away somewhere, and wherever she had gone, she didn't want him to find her.

Because she thought he didn't want her.

Only nothing could be further from the truth. Over the last few days, he'd come to care deeply for the little dragon and knew he'd be devastated when he had to send her away.

But now she'd left on her own and thought he didn't love her. This was the worst possible way it could have gone.

There is something you could do, but you won't do it, she had said.

Well, she was right about the first part, but not the second. He might not know what to do about the Timeless One and Merlin, but he did know he couldn't let Ember leave, not like this.

"Find Ember," he said in the magic language, putting all of his will into it. He didn't know if the spell would work, but—

Wait, there she was. And she hadn't gone far.

In fact, she was just across the road from his house. That made sense, since Ember hadn't seen very much of the outside world yet.

But unfortunately, she wasn't alone. Someone had already found her.

Someone who was staying in the park across the street.

Fort's blood ran cold and he swore, then teleported after her.

- THIRTY-FIVE -

"XENEA!" FORT SHOUTED AS HE PASSED through a portal to the park outside his bedroom window.

The faerie girl stood under a streetlamp just inside the park, Ember floating unconscious in some sort of magical prison in the air right in front of her.

"Look what *I* found," Xenea said quietly, giving Fort a strange look. "Turns out you had a little dragon hiding in there all along. Who would have thought?"

A chill went through Fort's body. "She's not *yours*, Xenea," he shouted, running over to the faerie girl. He reached out to Ember, to free her from the glamour . . .

And went flying backward like he'd been hit by a Dracsi.

Fort slammed into the ground a good ten feet away, the breath knocked right out of him. He tried to say something, but he didn't have the air and had to wait until he could catch his breath before pushing to his feet, staring at Xenea in surprise. "What . . . what did you just do?"

"You were trying to take the queen's dragon," she said, raising one eyebrow. "Why would I just let you do that?"

"She's *no one's* dragon!" Fort shouted, walking more slowly toward Xenea this time, trying to bring to mind a spell to use on her if he needed to. "She's her own dragon, but *I'm* watching over her, so give her back—"

"No, I don't think so," Xenea said. "To any of that. Because before I grabbed her, I could see in her mind that *you* sent her away. Not to mention that you were supposed to be helping me find her, according to your deal with my queen. You're lucky I'm feeling forgiving, or I'd tell her you broke your bargain."

This stopped Fort dead. If he angered Xenea any further, and she told the faerie queen Fort had broken his deal, there was no telling what she'd do to his father.

But he couldn't let Xenea take Ember, either.

"I *didn't* send her away," he started to say, then stopped, sighing. "Okay, yes, I did, sort of, but it all came out wrong. She wasn't ready to go yet, and I didn't want her to."

"I thought you didn't own her," Xenea said, raising the other eyebrow now.

"I don't!" Fort shouted. "I was just trying to get her to safety, find her a home with her own kind."

"Sounds like she didn't agree with that," Xenea said with a sneer. "Typical selfish human: send away a helpless creature who loves you because they're an inconvenience." She shook her head in disgust. "I knew those move vees were a lie. You all pretend you want to be good, to be heroes, like the woman who burned up aliens. But deep down, none of you are willing to actually step up and *do* something. You just want to hide away, hoping someone else will take care of things. Well, someone else did, Forsythe. Go home, and be thankful for my mercy."

Xenea turned to go, Ember floating behind her. But before she could, Fort leaped forward, reaching out to grab her shoulder. "Wait, Xenea, I don't—"

The magical blow this time was even more powerful, and it slammed him all the way across the street. "Good-bye, human!" he heard Xenea shout from the park as the world spun around him.

"*No!*" he shouted back, unsteadily rising to his feet and

shaking off the force of her hit. He dizzily teleported himself back to where she stood, even though the world seemed to be swaying back and forth before his eyes. "You're *not* taking Ember," he said, trying to clear his head. "I was wrong. She knows enough to decide for herself, and if she wants to stay—"

This time, it wasn't magic that hit him, but Xenea's fist, right in his stomach. He doubled over just as she kicked out, knocking him backward for a third time with her foot. "Nice try, human!" she shouted. "I'll give the queen your regards!"

Fort gritted his teeth and teleported in front of her one more time. He could barely stand now but lifted his hands up to defend himself. "Give . . . her . . . *back*," he whispered.

"Why do you care?" Xenea asked, kicking out again. Fort managed to dodge her foot, but another magical blast hit him square in the chest, sending him back to the ground. "You wanted her to be given to the dragons, and I'm taking her." She sighed. "I'll even make sure she's not hurt, if that's what you're worried about. So stop fighting to keep her, or I'll have to stop holding back!"

Holding *back*? Fort's mind spun with how powerful Xenea actually was, but that didn't stop him. "No," he said, only to get hit again. "I didn't—" Another hit. "I—"

"You don't even *know* what you want!" Xenea said, and launched an enormous blast at him.

"Enough!" Fort shouted in the language of magic. The force of whatever spell he'd just cast dissipated Xenea's blast and left her staring at him in wonder, even as he dropped to his knees, completely out of energy. "I *do* know."

"And what's that?" she asked him.

"I want . . . to *protect* her," he said, just hoping he didn't fall over. "To protect them all. My dad, my friends, people I don't know. None of them deserve what they're going through. And it's like you said in the movie theater. Even if I'm not the most powerful, I can still help. I can do something. And so I'm going to—I'm going to keep doing something, keep coming after you until you give Ember back. And then *she* can decide when she's ready to go to the dragons, if ever. And I'll figure out a way to keep her safe until then."

She watched him with narrowed eyes for a moment, then snorted. "*There.* Was that so hard?"

Her words almost knocked him over again. "Wait, what?"

"You've had this coming since I met you," she told him, giving him her hand to help him up. "Seriously. It's been all I could do not to slap you in the face most days. You should hear yourself!"

"You just beat me up . . . to prove a point?" Fort asked, almost too tired to be so amazed.

"I didn't beat you up, you large baby," she said, rolling her eyes. "But one thing I've noticed about humans is that you're fairly hardheaded, so it can take something equally as hard to get through to you. Thank you for finally admitting you were wrong."

Fort just stared at her in shock. "So you'll give me Ember back, then?"

"Give?" Xenea said, and laughed. "Have you met me? No, but I will make a *deal* for her."

Fort's mouth opened and closed in disbelief, before he finally nodded. "Done. Whatever you want, I'll find a way. Just give her back, *please*."

Xenea's eyes widened. "No one's ever agreed to *anything I want*." She went silent for a moment, then gritted her teeth in frustration. "Three things, Forsythe! Number one, you will find that older, teenage dragon for me, as you said you would."

"Done," Fort said again. "Gladly, even."

"Two!" Xenea shouted. "Until I receive said older dragon, you will take me to the move vees until we've seen every one about aliens."

Fort laughed in disbelief. "Okay, sure. That might take a while."

"Well, I'm starting to get used to the smell, so maybe that's not so terrible," Xenea said with a sniff. "And three? You *cannot* tell any of the Tylwyth Teg how easily I let you off the hook here. I'm *far* too nice for my own good."

"Easily?" Fort said, every inch of his body aching from her attacks. But seeing her start to get angry again, he quickly agreed. "Definitely easily. I'll tell them you took everything I owned and more."

"Good," Xenea said, and floated the dragon over to him. "You're lucky I'm warming up to you, Forsythe," she told him, giving him a suspicious look. "My queen would throw me in the dungeon for centuries if she ever learned I gave you a dragon for so little. But even I could tell Ember was better off here, with you."

Fort put out his arms, and Ember floated into them. Then, abruptly, Xenea's glamour ended, and the full weight of the dragon dropped into Fort's hands, knocking him back to the ground.

Fortunately, the blow wasn't enough to even disturb the dragon, so as soon as he had pulled himself together, he raised her head in his hands and gently said, *"Wake up, Ember,"* in the language of magic.

The dragon opened her eyes and looked up at him in surprise. *"Father? Why have you come for me?"*

"Because he was *wrong*!" Xenea yelled.

"Because I was wrong," Fort said to Ember. *"I was scared for you, here in my world, and thought you'd be safer with your own kind. But if you want to be here with me, then I will protect you and watch over you until you decide on your own that it's time to leave."*

A tear began to slide down Ember's cheek. *"I may stay with you? For as long as I wish?"*

"For as long as you wish," Fort said, trying not to think about how he was going to make that work. *"You were right, that I had a choice, and I made the wrong one. Now I'm going to make up for that. Maybe we can find you a place of your own, where you'll have room to hunt and grow, but I can see you every day like we do now."* An idea came to him, and he lit up in spite of the horrible pain in his body. *"A cave, maybe! I know a good one, where no one will find you."*

"As long as I may still spend time with Father, then that is suitable," Ember said, her voice thick with emotion as she

hugged him with her long neck. *"Perhaps we should celebrate me being home with a hunt?"*

He hugged her back tightly. *"Let's go talk to Merlin again. I need to tell him I'm going to face the Timeless One alongside my friends, no matter what happens."* He looked over at Xenea. "You want to come?"

She laughed. "Are you joking? *I'm* not going to get myself killed fighting one of the eternal ones. But I'm impressed that you're going to." She saluted him. "Good luck with the aliens, Human Female Captain."

Fort saluted her back, then teleported himself and Ember away.

- THIRTY-SIX -

THEY LANDED IN THE CLEARING OUT-side Merlin's cottage, giving Fort a minute just to prepare himself. He knew he was in for an argument at the very least, and maybe more. Merlin might even try to stop him by sending him elsewhere in time, so Fort had to be ready with his own magic.

He still hadn't come to grips with what he'd figured out about the Timeless One, Merlin, all of it. But there was no way he could let Rachel and Jia face the Old One alone. He had to be there, if just to keep his friends safe.

All of his friends.

With Ember at his side, Fort walked over to where the door lay on the ground and reached down to pick it up.

"Be warned!" the imp said as he touched it. "There was an intruder in the cottage, which was extremely *not* my fault!"

Fort looked over at the imp in alarm, then quickly leaned the door against some debris to hold it up and opened it.

Inside, the cottage now matched the exterior's destruction. Any illusion that the cottage had been a cozy little cabin in the past was now gone. Smoke filled the air, and alarms blared as Fort stepped inside. A horrifying creaking noise came from the ceiling, like it might collapse at any minute.

The living room where earlier Ember had been eating the stewpot was now completely wrecked. Where once the holographic system had shown a wooden dining table, now was revealed to be a futuristic plastic board, split in half. The fire was gone, replaced by an elaborate food maker of some kind, which itself was now on fire, smoke filling the room due to there not actually being a chimney.

"The other two humans were here," Ember hissed, her eyes half-closed against the smoke. *"Them . . . and something else."* She growled low and threatening.

"Jia? Rachel?" Fort shouted, covering his mouth as he picked his way through the smoke. But there was no answer, and the creaking above was only growing louder.

Ember grabbed his sleeve with her teeth and pulled him to a

stop. *"We must go,"* she said. *"It was one of the eternal ones. Do not worry, though, Father. I will protect us."*

She stared at him intently, her eyes glowing with Corporeal magic, and a blue sphere of light appeared around them, which helped with the smoke, at least. Fort took a step, and the sphere moved with him, so he quickly made his way to the room where Jia had given them their disguises, hoping to find his friends there.

Unfortunately, the room no longer existed. The door now led to nothing but black space.

"Merlin?" Fort shouted, and the old man appeared in front of him, at least in part: His hologram was glitching so badly that Fort could barely make Merlin out.

"He . . . them," Merlin said, his voice going in and out.

"He took them?" Fort said. "Who, the Timeless One? Was your younger self here?"

The glitchy Merlin nodded, then seemed to rub his forehead. The hologram disappeared, and in its place was a solid version of the magician. "There, that's better," he said, looking much more tired than the hologram had. He pushed his way into the blue bubble, which Fort assumed Ember had allowed him to do. "We should leave this place, though, as it won't exist for much longer."

"I saw the bedroom, or what used to be the bedroom," Fort said. "Is the whole cottage going to disappear?"

Merlin nodded. "He made it so this space will no longer exist. I think he hoped you wouldn't be able to find me in time. Come, boy. I'd rather not be crushed by a disappearing moment of time, if you don't mind?"

Fair point. Fort led the old man back to the front door as the cottage began to shake all around them. The trembling grew so bad that Fort lost his footing at one point, and Merlin toppled over on top of him.

"Quickly now, boy!" Merlin shouted, and Fort teleported the three of them straight to the front door and out into the clearing, just as the cottage collapsed into a tiny singularity behind them, then blipped out altogether.

And then the remains of the front door began to disintegrate as well, as did the rest of the rubble from the exterior of the cottage.

"Sir!" the imp shouted as the dissolving began to approach it. "Might I have a word, *quickly*?"

Merlin reached a hand out, and the imp detached from the disintegrating door with a sigh of relief. It crawled over the ground to reach Merlin's leg, then hugged his shin closely. "*Thank* you, sir," it said to him.

"I'd hardly let you be hurt, Quimbly," Merlin said, bending over to pat the imp on its head. "You did your job well, and now you must return to your proper time."

The imp let out a quiet sob, shaking his head. "I *never* thought I'd be done with visitors," it said, before giving Fort a nasty look. "They were so rude, sir. So very, very rude!"

"I know, Quimbly," Merlin said. "Manners truly are a lost art."

"I'm sorry if I was rude, ah, Quimbly," Fort said, feeling bad now, in spite of everything else that was happening.

"You *should* be, young man," Quimbly said, sticking out its tongue.

Merlin smiled slightly, then waved a hand, and the imp disappeared. "Now, Forsythe, to the business at hand: As you know, my younger self wasn't due to face off against Rachel until just under a year from now, but it seems he's discovered a bit of a loophole."

Fort sighed. "Let me guess. Did he pull them into the future by a year?"

Merlin coughed, his face turning red. "Yes, well, ah, you see, I never really considered that he'd try *that*. He's not breaking any rules, per se, as he's still battling them at the proper time, technically, but he's cutting off any preparation and training they could have made between now and then. They're just not ready." He began to mumble to himself. "Should have made it clear that he'd have to let time advance naturally, instead of bringing magic into this. It's the principle of the thing, you know?"

Fort rubbed his temples, not really believing this. "For someone who can see through time, you've sure been surprised a *lot* by him."

"Well, he is quite intelligent, if I do say so myself," Merlin said with a shrug. "And I have been putting a stop to his plans for almost ten thousand years now. Perhaps *some* credit is due?"

"Sorry," Fort said, not meaning it. "But we need to figure out how to get them back. They're not ready to fight him."

"Agreed," Merlin said, "but I'm afraid it's not that simple. As I said, he's not breaking any rules, and, therefore, he has every right to face them now, in the future. Rachel has Excalibur, and that's the only true condition."

"But you said yourself that they're not ready yet!" Fort shouted. "You can't just leave them there. If he can bring them there, you can bring them back!"

"To do so would put me in conflict with my younger self,

and I'd risk destroying the universe," Merlin said, shaking his head. "No, I'm afraid there's very little I can do."

He went silent, giving Fort a long look.

"You can show me where he is, can't you?" Fort said. "I know the rules say I'm not supposed to be involved, but you can still show me, and I can get to him myself. I have to *try*, at least!"

The edges of Merlin's mouth curled into a smile, but his tone was still deadly serious. "Think carefully about what you're asking, Forsythe. Even with your knowledge of magic, you still don't have enough power to defeat him. If you fight, you *will* lose, all of you. My family will return, and either enslave or destroy humanity altogether. Are you sure you wish to do this?"

"I am," Fort said, not knowing if he was lying or not. "It might not work, but I think I have an idea. Now that I know who the Timeless One really is."

Merlin smiled fully now. "That's my boy."

"Ember?" Fort said, turning to his dragon. *"I can't ask you to come with me, as it's going to be incredibly dangerous. But—"*

"We hunt," she said, grinning widely. *"I'm interested to see what an eternal one tastes like."*

Merlin flinched at this, giving the dragon a worried look. "Ah, right, well then," he said, as black Time magic glowed all around him. "Good luck then, Forsythe. You will most assuredly need it."

"Thanks," Fort started to say, but Merlin was already gone as a new vision surrounded Fort and Ember, a vision of the location of the Timeless One.

Fort looked around at a destroyed world, and he swallowed hard, suddenly doubting all of his choices. Everything was devastated, a dead world that didn't look like it could even support life.

This couldn't be just one year from now . . . could it?

If it was, all the more reason to face the Timeless One and stop this destruction.

"Here goes nothing," he told Ember, then stared at the desolate destruction in front of him and whispered, *"Travel to this time. Please."*

And just like that, they did.

- THIRTY-SEVEN -

THE VISION WAS ONE THING, BUT THE reality was even worse.

Fort and Ember arrived in a land under a dark, menacing red sky, a bit like during a sunset, though the sun still hung high in the sky. The land around him was destroyed, barren, but not *completely* unfamiliar. What Fort at first mistook for rock was actually the remnants of a city.

Though almost everything had been ground down to pebbles, here and there a surviving bit of civilization showed this place had once held life: A broken neon sign that advertised a diner. Metal shelving next to a hollowed-out steel box.

Could this truly have all happened in a year? What kind of power would have been needed to destroy the world like this?

Fort turned around slowly, looking for life, only to jump as

Ember headbutted his arm. *"There,"* she said, and held out a claw to point off to his left.

He looked in that direction and found what could have been a skyscraper, somehow still standing in the rubble of the rest of the city. But as he stared at it, he realized this wasn't a building like any he'd seen before.

It almost looked like a strangely futuristic castle, like something out of a science-fiction movie. The castle seemed to be made of a kind of black stone, a material that absorbed light, as it didn't seem to shine in any way.

But the shape, the design was all wrong. There were turrets jutting in unnatural directions, almost looking uncomfortably *pointed*, even from this far away. The whole castle had an air of sharpness to it, in fact, and it made Fort sick to even look at.

"Father!" Ember shouted, leaping forward several feet and bristling at something Fort couldn't see. *"I can feel them!"*

Again he looked in the direction she was facing, and off in the distance, he saw a burst of black light against the red sky.

"It's the humans," Ember said to him, not taking her eyes off the scene in the distance. *"Them . . . and one of the eternal creatures."*

Fort nodded and started to open a teleportation portal, only to pause, considering things. Right now, they had the element of surprise . . . and not much else. They had to use that as best they could.

"Ember, listen to me," he said to the dragon, squatting down before her. *"I promised you a hunt, and that's what we're going to do. I'm going to teleport us over there behind the Timeless One. If we can sneak up on him, I want you to try to put him to sleep, paralyze him, anything that will stop him, okay?"*

She looked disappointed. *"I cannot use my teeth or flames? That is hardly a hunt as I understand them."*

"If it comes to teeth and flames, I think we've already lost," Fort told her. *"Also, whatever you do, stay away from Rachel's sword, okay? It can really hurt you."*

"So I should burn her if she gets too close, then?" Ember asked, sounding a little too hopeful for Fort's liking.

"Not even by accident, Ember," he said, giving her a stern look. *"Promise me."*

She sighed. *"I won't burn the sword girl."*

"Or the other one! Don't hurt Jia or Rachel in any way. Promise!"

"Fine! I will not harm any of the humans, or use my teeth or fire on the eternal one. Unless it becomes necessary, *correct?"* She

looked up at him with such hope that he couldn't help but smile.

"Fair enough," he told her. *"Just be careful, okay? I don't want you getting hurt."*

She laughed hard at this, which didn't make him feel any better. *"Whatever you say, Father."*

"Okay, I'm opening the portal . . . now," Fort said, and did just that.

Without a moment's pause, Ember leaped into the air, flying straight through the portal with Fort just behind her. They emerged behind a cloaked figure that floated a few feet above the ground. That *had* to be the Timeless One.

Right in front of the figure, Jia and Rachel both looked ready to fight, with Rachel aiming Excalibur at the Old One.

"Now!" Fort shouted, and Ember released a burst of blue light right at the cloaked figure's back. At the same time, Fort shouted, "Freeze!" in the language of magic, hoping that would paralyze the Timeless One.

Ember's and Fort's spells hit the Old One at the same time, and the cloaked figure toppled to the ground, unmoving. It landed hard in the dirt and rock, and just lay there as Rachel and Jia stared in surprise.

"I'm here to help!" Fort shouted, running over to them. "Rachel, now's the time. Can you get to him?"

But neither of the girls moved. As Fort reached them, he turned to look behind him, wondering what was going on.

The cloak on the ground was dissolving away into black light, leaving nothing behind.

There hadn't been anything beneath it.

"You can't surprise someone who can see through time," Rachel whispered to him as she turned in a circle. "Where did he go?"

"Fort, what are you *doing* here?" Jia asked, morphing herself in various places. First dragon wings much like Damian's grew out of her back, and her fingers merged together to form hard, scale-covered fists. Her arm muscles increased to something beyond a bodybuilder's, while huge fangs grew from her mouth. Entirely creepy all around, but exactly the kind of person Fort wanted by his side against an Old One.

"I'm here to face him with you," he told them. "I couldn't let you do this alone. And I can help, I promise!"

"And if we lose because of you?" Rachel asked, raising an eyebrow. "I mean, Merlin sounded pretty clear. . . ."

"He had rules to follow," Fort told her, ignoring what she

was implying about his lack of power. "You two just have to trust me, okay?"

"Can we discuss this when we're *not* facing an Old One?" Jia said. "He's here somewhere. He brought us here for a reason."

"YES, I DID," said a voice behind them. Ember whirled and launched herself at it as Fort and the others turned, but the little dragon was far too slow: The Timeless One caught her in a Time spell and froze her in place, the beginnings of a plume of fire emerging from her mouth. "I WANTED YOU TO SEE YOUR FUTURE."

As Fort saw the Timeless One for the first time, he felt a horrible chill go down his spine. The creature seemed to have no body, and not much of a face, only a sort of melting infinity sign where his eyes would be. One hand emerged from the mostly empty cloak in a vicious-looking metal glove, while the other seemed to be entirely made of bone.

"Whatever this is, it'll *never* happen to our world," Rachel shouted at him, aiming Excalibur at the Timeless One.

"AH, BUT YOU DON'T GET IT," the Timeless One said. "THIS *IS* YOUR WORLD, NOT EVEN A YEAR FROM YOUR PRESENT. THIS IS THE WORLD I HAVE MADE, AND ONE THAT YOU CANNOT AVOID." He waved a hand, almost proudly. "YOU SEE, THIS IS THE WORLD WHERE MY FAMILY HAS *RETURNED*."

And off in the distance, several glows appeared on the horizon: orange, red, and yellow. The colors of Spirit, Elemental, and Mind magic.

- THIRTY-EIGHT -

I T'S *NOT* GOING TO HAPPEN!" RACHEL shouted, though Fort saw her looking off into the distance at the light of the other Old Ones nervously. "I don't care if we're ready to fight you or not, we *will* take you down." She stepped forward, Excalibur shining in the burning sun.

"We have to get him before the others arrive," Fort said quietly to the others.

"OH, THEY WON'T INTERFERE," the Timeless One said. "THAT WOULD BE AGAINST THE RULES. BUT DON'T WORRY—YOU STILL WON'T WIN. DIDN'T MERLIN EXPLAIN? WHATEVER YOU DO TO *ME* NOW, THE FUTURE IS SET. I HAVE ENSURED MY FAMILY WILL RETURN, WHETHER I'M AROUND FOR IT OR NOT. YOUR DRAGON FRIEND DAMIAN HAS ALREADY FOUND THE SIX BOOKS AND OPENED

A PORTAL TO MY FAMILY'S WORLD. *THIS* IS THE RESULT OF HIS BATTLE WITH THEM."

Fort's eyes narrowed. Well, that basically confirmed his worst suspicions, which made him doubly glad he was here.

"It can still be changed," Jia said, her hammerlike hands glowing with blue magic. "If we have to find the book of Time magic ourselves, we'll *fix* this!"

The Timeless One began to laugh. Rachel growled in fury, then leaped straight at him, the ground beneath her feet rising up to push her to his level. She swung Excalibur at him, but the Timeless One disappeared in a blur of black light.

He instantly appeared behind her, and she tried to swing out with the sword, but the earth holding her up began to crumble with age, infused with the Old One's Time magic. She started to fall, and the Timeless One swung out with his gloved hand—

Only to pass right through her.

Rachel grinned. "I've been practicing, you old jerk," she said, then gestured.

A circle of Rachels appeared all around them, each one holding a sword, all aimed at the Old One.

"ILLUSION? WELL DONE, CHILD, YOU'VE LEARNED

TO MIX ELEMENTAL AND MIND MAGICS," the Timeless One said, and Fort's eyes widened. *This* was what Rachel had been training in? "BUT ILLUSIONS CAN'T HURT ME."

"Maybe not," all the Rachels said together. "But they can sure distract you."

The Timeless One spun around at her words and struck out with his armored hand. Someone invisible cried out in pain, and the real Rachel dropped to the ground, nursing her now wounded arm.

"No!" Jia shouted, and her body split into a dozen copies, each one heavily armored and sprinting at the Old One. Was this another illusion? But no, the first one struck the Old One, who defended himself with a bubble of Time magic, much like the one the Carmarthen Academy students had made. The second Jia struck, and the third, and each one's blow struck the bubble.

But how was she doing it?

The last Jia looked over at Fort, now that there was no room left to attack the Old One. "Golems," she said with a smile, and Fort finally understood: This wasn't Jia here, but a life-sized puppet, one she'd just duplicated using the same magic.

"AWAY!" the Old One shouted, and the golems began to

disintegrate with age, falling apart before Fort's eyes, a shroud of darkness appearing where he'd been floating.

"Can't see the future . . . if you can't see," Rachel said from the ground, then used the rock beneath her to push herself to her feet. Once again, she turned invisible. . . .

But she reappeared as time reversed itself completely. The shroud of darkness disappeared, and this time, the Timeless One appeared next to the final Jia golem, his armored hand holding her in the air.

"SURRENDER, OR SHE WILL PAY FOR YOUR ARRO-GANCE," he said to Rachel.

"That's not really her, genius!" Rachel shouted, but Fort could tell that his threatening even a golem that looked like Jia had enraged her.

"THIS MAY NOT BE HER, BUT SHE IS CONNECTED TO IT," the Old One said, and slowly disintegrated the golem. "WHICH MEANS I CAN FIND HER, EVEN THROUGH YOUR ILLUSION."

Again time reversed, but this time only for the golem, spiraling backward until Jia appeared out of nowhere, holding a tiny doll in her hands. Rachel must have cloaked her in illusion to keep her safe.

"No!" Rachel shouted, and tried to use the ground to hurl herself between the Timeless One and Jia, but the rock fell apart beneath her as the Old One aged it into nonexistence.

"Don't worry, Rachel!" Jia shouted. "The Old Ones hate Healing magic, remember?" Her hands lit up with blue light. "I'm going to make him wish he'd never been born in the future!"

The Timeless One's face broke into a grin. "THAT WAS MY BROTHER, KETAS, WHEN HE INHABITED YOUR FRIEND'S BODY. HEALING MAGIC DOES NOT HARM US OTHERWISE."

And then he shot a spiral of black magic straight at Jia.

"YOU CANNOT WIN," he said, now using his Time magic directly on Jia. She began to age quickly, passing through her teenage years to adulthood, then gaining wrinkles and stooping, her muscles disappearing. She tried to strike out at him, but the Timeless One grabbed her hand and wrenched it painfully. "YOU ARE SIMPLY NOT READY TO FACE ME."

"*Restore Jia!*" Fort shouted in the language of magic, then turned to his dragon. "*And free Ember!*"

Jia's age immediately returned to normal, and she smiled again at the Timeless One as Ember set his cloak on fire. "Are you sure about that?" Jia said, and swung out with hammer-hands just like her golem had.

The Timeless One disappeared in a blur, and Jia followed a second later, glowing blue, which meant she must have used her Corporeal magic to speed up her own movements like Merlin had suggested. Rachel thickened the air around them, just like she'd done in the Oppenheimer School, which made it tougher to breathe, but it worked: The Timeless One slowed down just enough for her to strike out at him with Excalibur.

He disappeared right before the blade touched him, appearing a few feet back.

"I KNOW ALL OF YOUR TRICKS!" the Old One shouted, and Jia skidded to a stop on the ground a short distance away, her enhanced muscles and speed reversed through Time magic. The air also thinned back out, and the Timeless One disappeared and reappeared next to Rachel, holding a horrible-looking sword of his own. "I HAVE FOUGHT SIX ARTORIGIOS ALREADY. YOU THINK MERLIN COULD TEACH *YOU* ANYTHING THAT HE DID NOT ALSO SHOW THEM?"

As Rachel frantically defended herself with Excalibur against the Old One's sword, Fort raced over to Jia and helped her to her feet. "Are you okay?" he asked. "I can try to heal you. . . ."

"I'm good," she said, wincing as Healing magic flowed through her body. "But we're not winning here. Do you know any spells that could take him down?"

"I can definitely try," Fort said, and turned back to the fight. The might of the Timeless One had pushed Rachel to one knee, and she was on the verge of losing. *"Duplicate Rachel!"* Fort shouted in the language of magic.

A thousand tiny Rachels appeared all around her, as Rachel stared at them in surprise.

Okay, that wasn't exactly what Fort had intended. But at least they weren't illusions this time.

The new army of Rachels pointed their tiny swords up at the Timeless One and shouted something too high-pitched to understand, though it sounded like some kind of war cry.

"Fort, what is—" Rachel shouted, but cried out in pain as the Timeless One swung his sword, narrowly cutting into her shoulder.

She dropped Excalibur for just a moment, but that was enough: The Timeless One seized his opportunity and froze her in Time magic.

"No!" Jia shouted, and used her magic to restore Rachel, but the Timeless One struck out in the midst of her casting, knocking her backward to the ground. The spell worked, though, and Rachel regained her sword, even as the tiny versions of herself all ran at the Timeless One, not even able to reach him.

"PATHETIC," the Old One shouted, and sent the tiny Rachel clones away into time. "GIVE UP NOW, OR I WILL DESTROY JIA." Another Timeless One appeared, holding his skeletal glove to Jia's neck as Rachel pushed to her feet.

"Let her go!" Rachel shouted, then gasped as more Timeless Ones appeared around her, each one moving in a blur to strike her with their armored gloves. She blocked as many as she could with Excalibur and tried to form a shield with the ground around her, but the Timeless Ones were too fast, and again she fell to her knees.

Fort teleported over to her as quickly as he could and grabbed the sword from her hand, just as another Timeless One attacked. He managed to block the Old One, the sword mercifully not burning him again, then teleported them both, as well as Ember and Jia, away to the black castle in the distance, hoping to get some breathing room.

The multiple Timeless Ones were waiting for them. One of them grabbed Jia right back.

"THERE IS NOWHERE YOU CAN RUN, NOWHERE YOU CAN HIDE FROM ME," the Old One told them. "YOU ARE THE FINAL OBSTACLE TO BRINGING MY FAMILY HOME. ONCE YOU ARE BEATEN, MERLIN WILL GIVE UP HIS RIDICULOUS CHALLENGE, AND I WILL HAVE THEM *BACK*!"

"You won't beat us," Fort said quietly, handing Excalibur back to Rachel and moving to stand in front of her. "You and I both know this."

The Timeless One began to laugh. "YOU WERE NEVER MEANT TO BE HERE IN THE FIRST PLACE. MERLIN SOUGHT TO CHEAT, BUT *I* HAVE ALWAYS OUT-PLAYED HIM. NO MATTER WHAT POWER YOU HAVE, YOU DON'T YET HAVE THE KNOWLEDGE TO USE IT!"

"Oh, I'm not here to use my magic," Fort said.

This made the Timeless One pause. "THEN YOU ARE EVEN MORE USELESS THAN YOUR FRIENDS SUS-PECTED."

"Maybe," Fort said, looking up at the Old One with a raised eyebrow. "But why don't we stop playing games, *all* the games. Come down here and face us as your *true* self."

"Fort, no," Rachel whispered. "You don't know who he is. This isn't the time—"

"It's exactly the time," Fort told her, then turned back to the Timeless One. "And I do know who he is. It was pretty obvious all along, wasn't it, buddy?"

The Timeless One went still, then floated down to the ground. He raised his hands to his cloak, then pulled it off his head, revealing a mass of curly silver hair, and a very familiar face.

"Hey, Fort," Cyrus said, smiling darkly at him. "Be honest: How long have you known?"

- THIRTY-NINE -

FORT HAD KNOWN, HE'D *KNOWN*, THAT it had to be Cyrus. All the clues, all the hints from Jia and Rachel, Merlin, even Cyrus himself only made sense if the silver-haired boy was the Timeless One, Merlin's younger self.

And yet, seeing Cyrus here in this desolate world made Fort have to fight to keep from vomiting.

He so badly wished he'd been wrong. Fort had made so many other mistakes, why was this the one thing he'd gotten right?

This was his *friend*, the first person to actually welcome him at the Oppenheimer School. Cyrus had been his confidant, the one he had shared his fears and secrets with from the start. And it devastated Fort to see he was right, that Cyrus had been manipulating them all from the beginning.

"Really, when did you realize?" Cyrus asked again, as Fort

hadn't been able to even speak, seeing his former friend standing there wearing an Old One's cloak.

"It doesn't matter," Fort said quietly. "I just wish things . . . were *different*, Cyrus. It didn't have to be this way."

"No, it *always* had to be this way," Cyrus said, his smile fading as he stared at Fort. "It was the only way I'd ever get my family back. I'd think you of all people would understand that, Fort. What someone would go through to have their loved ones home."

"How did you find out?" Rachel asked from the side of her mouth, her focus on Cyrus still. "We promised Merlin we wouldn't tell you!"

Fort smiled sadly. "Yeah, you were both pretty terrible with that," he said. "You gave away tons of clues, especially after I found out Merlin was the Timeless One." He looked up at Cyrus, barely able to keep his voice from betraying his feelings. "Sorry, *your* future self. Once I found out that Merlin—who looked human—was an Old One, then I realized his younger self might look human too. Plus, Merlin kept mentioning that you, Cyrus, had different plans from him, and you mentioned visiting his cottage trying to find out what *he* was up to, so it all fell into place."

"Well, I'm happy to drop all the melodrama at least," Cyrus said. He shrugged the cloak to the ground and took off his armored glove, then pulled the bones off his other hand, revealing that it was some kind of magical covering, with his real hand beneath. "And yes, I'm the younger self of Merlin, the Timeless One, the Old One of Time, all of that." He waved his hand absently. "Phew. I really was getting tired of all the secrecy!"

"Merlin thought that if you knew, there was no telling what you might do," Rachel said to Fort, her eyes on Cyrus. "I didn't even think you'd be here with us, but in that case, it was kinder for you not to find out Cyrus was an evil eternal monster."

"Hey!" Cyrus shouted as the other Timeless One, the version guarding Jia, took off his cloak as well, leaving another Cyrus standing there, though this one kept his gloved hand on, still threatening Jia. "Did you call Fort evil for wanting to bring his father home? Because that's all *I'm* trying to do! And before you go blaming me for everything, the rules for the game with my older self stipulated that I couldn't bring them back myself. All I've done is push you people in a direction you were willing to go."

"So you're saying you're not to blame for this?" Fort said,

nodding at the desolate landscape around them. "You weren't responsible for wiping out *humanity*?"

Cyrus sighed. "Humanity isn't destroyed or anything. You're all living below the ground, serving the Dracsi, like the dwarfs." He shook his head. "And you're all *happy*, thanks to my sister, Q'baos. As far as any human knows, you've *always* worshipped my kind, and you'd do anything for us."

"You used *Spirit* magic on everyone?" Rachel shouted, holding Excalibur up again. "I'd take you down just for that, even if I didn't have to!"

Cyrus gave her a pitying look. "Except you couldn't. I've been going easy on all of you, because as much as it pains me, I've grown fond of you over the last months. Something like pets, I imagine." He looked over at Ember. "You must understand that now, huh, Fort?"

Ember hissed angrily, but Fort motioned for her to back down, which she did, though she didn't look thrilled about it.

"Anyway," Cyrus continued, sounding almost as devastated as Fort felt for some reason. "Win or lose, it doesn't matter. Like I said, this future is already done. There's no way to stop it. I sent Sierra and Damian to get the last books, telling them that Damian was the only one who could defeat the

Old Ones. And of course, being Damian, he believed it." He cringed. "Turns out one dragon doesn't do very well against my family."

As much as he hated Damian, Fort winced at that. "Then we'll go back and stop Damian before he brings the Old Ones back," he said. "There's nothing you could have done that we can't undo, right?"

Cyrus raised an eyebrow. "Nice attempt, Fort. What, you think I'm just going to tell you my whole plan? Do you have any idea how many *centuries* I've been working on this? How many problems I've had to fix, because you humans could never just do what I wanted you to do? And you've been the *biggest* problem, Fort! You're not even supposed to be here. Merlin and I agreed that you'd be spared, kept from this fight. It was in the rules!"

That explained a few things to Fort, though why Cyrus would care about him when he'd been lying this whole time was another mystery. "I wish *you* weren't here either, Cyrus," Fort said quietly. "I really do. I thought we were friends."

Cyrus growled softly, then looked away. "Humans and an Old One, friends? Like I said, at best, I saw you as pets." He still didn't look at them. "But if it helps . . . I did make sure you and your family are treated well, here in the future. You're not serving us in the underground. I got you out before that. A weakness in myself, I suppose."

"Oh, isn't that *sweet*?" Rachel said. "And what about the rest of us, Cyrus? What'd you do to me and Jia?"

"I would have helped you *too*, but you wouldn't accept it," Cyrus said, turning back now in anger. "You and Jia insisted on fighting, until there was nothing else I could do. Even now, hearing that, you're *still* going to insist on stopping me. And you can't! But why would that change the great Rachel's mind? You just *had* to take the sword, didn't you? All you needed to do was get the book of Spirit magic from the faerie queen, but instead you volunteered to be her final hero."

"And I'd do it again," Rachel said.

"You might have had a chance, too, if we'd done this when you were older," Cyrus said with a shrug. "That sword is far more powerful than you even know. It could *kill* one of my kind. Which is why I can't let you use it."

Before Rachel could move, three versions of Cyrus appeared out of nowhere, one of them holding a huge, glowing hammer. Two of them struck Rachel at the same time, sending Excalibur flying from her hand. The third, standing right where the sword landed, lifted his glowing hammer and brought it down hard on the blade.

The resulting explosion knocked them all from their feet. When the ground stopped spinning, Fort pushed himself back up and gasped.

Excalibur now lay broken in two, flames sputtering on the broken blade before gradually fading out.

"There," Cyrus said, as the other Cyruses disappeared. "Now it's *completely* over, and you've lost. Do you want to give up now? Here." He gestured, and Jia reversed in time back over to them. "See? I'll even give you Jia back."

Jia gave Rachel and Fort a sad look. "Well, this isn't going so great, huh?"

"We're not done," Fort told them, turning back to his former friend.

"Actually you *are*, if you'd just listen," Cyrus said. "I will once again offer you *all* the chance that no other human is going to get: Stand down and stop fighting, and I'll make sure you and your families are all okay. But keep this up, and you'll all be sent to the underground with the rest of humanity."

Jia snorted, then raised her hammer-hands. "I always knew

there was something off about you, Cyrus. I liked you, but *something* wasn't right."

Cyrus rolled his eyes. "Rachel? Do I even need to ask?"

Rachel bent down and ran her hand over the ground, infusing it with her magic. Seconds later, she picked up a steel sword, formed from what was left of the earth below them. "Nope, you can guess my answer."

Cyrus nodded, then turned to Fort, giving him an almost pleading look. "You don't have to go along with them, Fort. You were *never* one of them. Neither of us were. Do what's best for yourself and your family. I can give you the life you always wanted. And all you have to do is surrender, here and now. This can all be over for you!"

Fort just stared at Cyrus, not knowing what to say.

"Can't decide?" Cyrus said. "Really? Well, maybe you need more incentive." He gestured, and a glowing black window opened, showing Fort a cozy little living room with a mother, father, and son all watching television. And to Fort's horror, he recognized all three: One was himself, one was his father . . . and one was someone he'd only seen in pictures.

"I can give you more," Cyrus continued as Fort stared in disbelief. "Your mother didn't need to die when you were born.

I can fix that, Fort! All you need to do is stand down, and you can have everything you ever wanted!"

Fort moved toward the window, his mouth dropping open. He slowly put a hand up to it, not able to believe his eyes. "Mom?" he said quietly, staring at the woman in the living room.

"Fort," Rachel said. "Listen to me. Look around you. *This* is the world she'd be living in—"

"It's the world you'll *all* be living in, and nothing can change that!" Cyrus shouted, his face turning red with anger as the black Time window disappeared. "Now, Fort, tell me your answer, or pick up a weapon and fight. Either way, this is going to end once and for all."

His mother. Cyrus had shown him his *mother*. So many emotions filled Fort's head it felt like a riot going on, and he could barely think, let alone deal with this.

But if there was one thing he had learned by now, it was not to make deals with strange creatures.

Fort wiped his arm over his face, then nodded. "Okay, Cyrus," he said, then walked over to where the broken blade of Excalibur lay. He leaned over and picked up the hilt, just a bit of the blade still attached, and looked at Rachel. "You're going to need this still," he said, and handed it to her. She took it, dissolving the sword she'd made.

She took it, staring at him. "You're doing what he says?"

Fort looked at her, then at Cyrus. "No. But I don't have the power to stop him, not with magic. He's too strong."

"Wise boy," Cyrus said, nodding. "Now step aside so I can finish this."

"We can't give up, Fort," Jia said softly.

"I know," Fort said. "And I'm not." And with that, he moved between the Old One and his friends, then turned to Cyrus and beckoned the boy to come at him. "Ready, Timeless One? Let's do this."

- FORTY -

CYRUS STARED AT HIM IN SHOCK. "YOU would stand against me, still? After everything I've offered you?"

"I've never met . . . my mother," Fort said, trying to sound confident in spite of his voice cracking with sorrow, "but I . . . I have a feeling she'd ground me for *years* if I ever joined you."

"You have *lost*!" Cyrus shouted, his anger now combined with something else, something Fort almost thought sounded like regret. "I destroyed Excalibur and brought my family home. What more do I have to do to show you?"

Fort just smiled sadly. "I guess you'll have to take me down, Cyrus. If you can."

Rage flooded over Cyrus's face, and he floated up into the air once more. "Maybe you'll change your mind when you see what happens to Rachel and Jia." His hands glowed with black Time magic, and he aimed them at Fort's friends.

But Fort just spread his arms out, putting himself between the Timeless One and the others. "If you want them, you'll have to go through me first, Cyrus," he said.

Cyrus's eyes widened, and he blipped out in a burst of black light, appearing right in front of Fort. The Timeless One grabbed Fort by his shirt and lifted him into the air as if he weighed next to nothing. "*Why* are you making me do this?" Cyrus shouted, sounding almost uncertain. "I don't want to hurt you!"

"I'm not making you do anything," Fort said, not resisting. "I'm not fighting you, but I won't stand aside, either. You're going to have to take me out if you want them."

Cyrus screamed in frustration and tossed Fort aside, but Fort quickly opened a teleportation circle and reappeared right in front of his friends.

"That's not going to do it," Fort said, realizing he might regret taunting his former friend. But this was the one chance they had. There had to be a reason both Merlin and Cyrus wanted Fort kept out, a reason why Cyrus kept offering him things to make sure Fort wasn't hurt. And Fort suspected he knew what it was.

Merlin had said that a friendship with humans had turned him around on his own family. If that were true, it meant that maybe the Cyrus whom Fort had known in the Oppenheimer School wasn't entirely an act.

There was no way to know for sure, but this was the only power Fort had now. Even with all the magical spells in the world at his fingertips, he still couldn't match Cyrus's power, not without years of practice.

But maybe he didn't need to, not if the Cyrus he'd known was even partly real. And he had to believe that at least a bit of the boy he'd known existed in the Old One. Fort had seen too much of that Cyrus to buy that it was all manipulation.

Even so, it was still a huge risk, betting the future of humanity and his world on Cyrus's friendship. It was also his only chance.

Cyrus's eyes turned black with magic, and he screamed again, the land around them shaking as the rest of his family grew closer, their magic getting brighter. "If this is your decision, then let it be on you!" he shouted, and sent magic streaming at Fort.

The spell struck Fort in the chest and knocked him to his knees. Agony erupted through his body as he stared down at his hands in horror, the skin wrinkling, his fingers gnarling painfully, as his body weakened all around. Hair grew over Fort's eyes, white hair, and he struggled just to hold his head up.

But in spite of the pain running through his limbs and chest, he managed to look Cyrus in the eye. "Is this . . . what you want?" he asked, his voice shaking with age.

Cyrus stared down at him, almost in shock. *"No!"* he shouted. "I didn't want . . . I tried to protect you, Fort. I've been doing that since the start! Since I couldn't bring my family back directly, I needed *you* to wake Sierra, which would lead to Damian coming back as well. That's why I had Dr. Opps bring you to the school!" He cringed. "But I knew we'd be friends, and I never wanted you to be hurt." He looked away as Fort fell back to the ground, too weak to stand. "But you just wouldn't *listen*. You weren't meant to find your father, or go rescue him. There was never supposed to be a second dragon. None of that was according to my plan, and I should have removed you then, when I realized you weren't controllable. But I couldn't! Because I *understood*, Fort. I knew why you couldn't stop trying to save your dad, just like I've never given up on my own family! We're the same, you and I, and for that reason, I couldn't raise a hand against you."

"Well . . . you've done it . . . now," Fort said, laying his head against the dusty ground. "I hope . . . you did . . . the right thing."

A moment passed, then black magic flooded over Fort once more, and instantly he felt his strength return. "I *hate* you for forcing this on me!" Cyrus shouted, floating right in front of Fort now. "I tried scaring you, I tried bribing you . . . what will it *take?*"

Fort stood up straight, marveling at how his muscles all worked again. Then he looked at Cyrus and smiled. "You can't do it, can you?"

Cyrus roared, his hands still glowing. "What I *can* do is remove you from time! If you won't listen to reason, then maybe a few thousand years in the future you'll see things differently!"

Fort shrugged, hoping this was going to work. "You do what you have to do, Cyrus. I understand what it feels like to want your family back so much you'd do anything. But I learned the hard way that hurting other people to get what you want is never worth it."

Something flashed, almost too quick to see, and for a moment, Fort worried that Cyrus had noticed it. But the other boy seemed too angry to have caught it, and Fort let out a huge breath, then moved one step to the right as quietly as he could.

"Then you learned the wrong lesson," Cyrus said. "Because I would do anything for *my* family. Maybe you'll agree when you've missed yours as long as I have. Good-bye, Fort. I'll check in on you in a few thousand years."

And then Cyrus unleashed his magic on the boy standing directly in front of him.

The black light passed directly through Fort, not touching him.

Cyrus floated backward in shock. "What . . . ?"

And then Rachel appeared out of her own illusion and sliced the broken blade of Excalibur over the back of Cyrus's hand, just enough to cut him. "Sorry, Future Boy," she said, dropping the rest of her illusions, revealing Fort just to Cyrus's left. "You really shouldn't believe everything you see."

- FORTY-ONE -

CYRUS SCREAMED IN HORRIBLE PAIN as the sword bit into him. He grabbed his hand and clutched it to his chest, then dropped to the ground, writhing there as black Time magic exploded out of him, morphing the land around them into several different eras: One looked like some kind of prehistoric world, while another showed cities and highways, just like home. A third was even more desolate than the land had been one year from the present, and a fourth . . .

Fort gasped as he stared at the fourth time period, reaching a hand for it.

But then the Time magic disappeared, sending everything back to the postapocalyptic land of the Old Ones.

"My . . . my magic!" Cyrus cried, reaching up toward the sky. "I can't feel it. What have you done? *What have you done!*"

Rachel dropped Excalibur as she stared at Cyrus in silence, shaking her head, and the sword disappeared, as did the rest of the destroyed blade a few yards away.

Jia grabbed Rachel's shoulder and pulled her around for a hug, and both of them began to shake as if in relief.

Fort bent down over Cyrus, though, as Ember approached, sniffing the silver-haired boy.

"He has lost his power," she said. *"Now may I eat him?"*

Cyrus's eyes widened, and he tried to push himself away from the dragon but was too weak to move.

"No," Fort told her. *"I think we might still need him. He was right, after all . . . even beating him didn't stop his family from returning. We need to figure out where Damian and Sierra are and keep them from bringing the Old Ones back."*

"It'll never work," Cyrus said quietly, still staring at Ember in fear. "You can't change the future, Fort, no matter what you do. And believe me, they won't have any mercy on you like I did. They'll destroy you *and* your loved ones, and you'll *deserve* it for what you've done to me!"

Fort grimaced, as Ember licked her lips. *"Please, Father? Just a bite? He annoys me."*

"Keep her away from me!" Cyrus shouted, pointing at the

dragon, only to yank his hand back as Ember nipped at his finger.

"No, Ember," Fort told her, but he had to think about it for a moment. *"At least, not yet."*

And then he stood up to go check on his friends, leaving Cyrus to think about *that*.

"We need to get out of here," Fort said to Jia and Rachel, and they released their hug, both with wet eyes. "The other Old Ones won't hold back now that they've seen Cyrus lose."

"Can you use a Time spell to get us home?" Rachel asked.

"I can try," Fort said, but before he could, a black glow surrounded them all, and a moment later, the Old Ones' time had disappeared, replaced by the clearing around Merlin's cottage.

Only, there was no cottage there now, not even the destroyed remnants of one. Instead, it looked as if no cottage had ever existed there, as the ground was undisturbed.

Rachel separated from Jia and walked over to where the cottage used to be. "One last gift from Merlin, getting us home," she said, turning around and smiling slightly. "I guess our apprenticeship is over?"

"It looked like the queen took Excalibur back," Fort said. "So we shouldn't have to worry about her anymore."

"You should!" Cyrus shouted, but went quiet as Ember bared her teeth at him.

"So what now?" Fort asked his friends. "What do we do with him?"

"I'm down for throwing him into a volcano," Rachel said, glaring at the silver-haired boy. "Or letting Ember eat him."

"Yes, we should do as the heroic girl says!" Ember shouted, and Cyrus winced.

"I think we might still need him, if we're going to keep Sierra and Damian from bringing the Old Ones back," Fort told them, not mentioning that he didn't have the heart to let them hurt Cyrus. Even after everything, it was hard to look at the other boy and not see the version of Cyrus that had been his best friend. But right now, he had to ignore all of that and concentrate on what was to come. "He might not have his magic, but he still knows what's coming."

"Which I'll never tell you!" Cyrus shouted, in spite of Ember's hissing. "Do whatever you want to me—I've already won!"

"Volcano it is!" Rachel shouted, and readied her teleportation slap bracelet.

Then she froze in a glow of blue light.

"Rachel?" Fort said, not understanding, only to go still himself. He couldn't move his arms or legs but was still able to watch as Jia moved freely over to Cyrus, giving both Fort and Rachel a sad look.

"This was the deal," she said softly to them as Cyrus flinched away from her. "This was the bargain the queen made. She wanted the Timeless One, and in exchange, she'd keep us from going to war."

Fort tried to say something, to stop her, but his mouth refused to move. *No!* They couldn't give Cyrus to the faerie queen, not like this. As much as he hated his old friend for what he'd done, Fort still couldn't stomach just handing him over to his worst enemy, a faerie who'd hated him for thousands of years. Especially not without magic to protect himself!

A shimmer in the air appeared to Jia's right, almost in the shape of a tall human of some kind. It reached over Cyrus, who tried to push himself away, but the shimmer was too quick. "Fort!" Cyrus screamed. *"Please—"*

And then the shimmer and Cyrus disappeared together.

Jia immediately released them from her spell, and Fort felt control return to his body. He ran over to where Cyrus had lain and bent down, making sure this wasn't some illusion, some sort of glamour.

Then he looked up at Jia, who was covering her mouth like she might throw up.

"Was it worth it?" he asked quietly. "Tell me it was worth it. Tell me that the queen didn't just trick us all."

She looked down at him and shook her head, then began to quietly cry as Rachel hugged her close.

Fort sighed, rubbing his forehead. Maybe Xenea could find out what happened to Cyrus, try to keep him safe, but he doubted it. The faerie queen had been holding a grudge against Merlin/Cyrus/the Timeless One for centuries, and now that she had her old enemy in her hands, Fort didn't think she'd ever be willing to release him.

And that meant they had no idea where Damian and Sierra were in time, or when they'd be reappearing with the books of magic, ready to summon the Old Ones.

"We *might* be in trouble," Fort said, standing back up.

"Nothing new about that," Rachel said, as she let go of Jia and turned to him. "Got any ideas?"

Fort swallowed hard, hating what he was about to say. "Just terrible ones. We're going to need help. And there's only one place left to find it."

Rachel groaned, shaking her head. "They'll never take us back."

Fort nodded. "I know. But we still need the TDA and the other students at the Oppenheimer School." He looked up at Jia and Rachel. "Hiding magic away for over a thousand years didn't keep the Old Ones from coming back. If we can't stop Damian before he summons them, then this time, we'll have to *destroy* magic altogether."

EPILOGUE

A TALL HUMAN MAN APPROACHED the throne, trembling with each step. The queen beckoned him forward, looking impatient, so the man hurried a bit.

"I have done as you ordered, Your Majesty," Fort's father said to the faerie queen, bowing low. He nodded at the new "sculpture" next to her throne, that of a silver-haired human boy frozen in time. "You have the Timeless One for whatever revenge you desire. Now may I return to Avalon for good?"

The queen gestured, and the changeling magic disappeared, turning a human man back into a faerie boy, the very same faerie who'd accused Fort of injuring him back during the humans' trip to Avalon. "I could not look at you like that for one minute longer," the queen said. "It's bad enough that I must keep the boy's actual father in stasis here, but I did promise the boy I'd protect the man and must live up to my end of the bargain. Now, *report*. What have you learned?"

"Fort . . . the boy, he has a young dragon, just as you suspected, Your Majesty," the faerie boy said. "Xenea knows of it, but is letting him keep it for some reason. I haven't yet figured out why. Instead, she awaits the return of the older dragon."

The queen's eyes narrowed. "Perhaps she was the wrong choice for this task. I shall punish her upon her return." She tilted her head. "But you have done well, my son. Not only have you given me my greatest enemy, but you have been a great source of information."

The faerie boy nodded in thanks, then paused. "Your Majesty, I live to serve you. Might you take back the memories and feelings you gave me, then? I find it . . . *difficult* to betray Fort—the boy—when I have his father's emotions and know their history."

The queen raised an eyebrow. "You suggest that serving me is a problem?"

The faerie quickly raised his hands in protest. "Of course not, Your Majesty! I will do anything you ask! I merely was requesting—"

"You will have your reward when I am finished with you,"

the queen told him coldly. "Now, return to our former world, and continue your information gathering. Things seem to be coming to a head there, and it might create the chance we've been looking for. If humanity and the eternal ones go to war, perhaps the Tylwyth Teg will find an . . . *opportunity*." She smiled, and the faerie boy shimmered as her magic changed him back into Fort's father. "Now, go. I dismiss you."

The human-looking faerie bowed low, then turned to leave.

"Child?" the queen said, making the faerie freeze in place just before he left. "Don't let your human memories and emotions get the better of you. I wouldn't want to have to punish you like poor Xenea."

"Of course not, Your Majesty," Fort's father said to her. "No matter what human feelings I have, I am loyal only to you."

"As it should be," the faerie queen said, then sent her faerie back to Earth in a shimmer of glamour magic. "As it should be."

Then she turned to stare at her newly acquired prize, a slow smile crossing her face. The eternal one's punishment had been coming for over a millennium, but there was no need to rush it now.

After all, with the Timeless One in her power, she had all the time in the world.

ACKNOWLEDGMENTS

Whoa, I did *not* see that coming! Fort's father is a changeling? Who knew! (Well, okay, I did, because I can't just let Fort have a happy moment. I'm so mean.)

Originally, I'd planned on Revenge of Magic being a seven-book series, one for each book of magic. But as we've been going, all the story I wanted to tell kept coming out faster than I'd planned, probably because Fort was so impatient. So instead of seven books, the next book, Revenge of Magic: *The Old Ones*, will be the final book in the series . . . mostly because there won't be any story left to tell if the Old Ones make it back. Whoops!

That said, thank you *so much* for sticking with me this far, and I hope you enjoyed book four. None of these would exist without the following people, who all deserve more thanks than I can ever give them: Corinne, my own personal magic, Michael Bourret, my agent, and my two editors at Aladdin, Liesa Mignogna and Anna Parsons, whom you can thank for Xenea getting even more screen time than she would have.

I also need to give all my thanks to Mara Anastas, my publisher at Aladdin; Chriscyntheia Floyd, deputy publisher; the marketing team of Alissa Nigro and Caitlin Sweeny; Cassie Malmo and Nicole Russo in publicity; Elizabeth Mims; Sara Berko; Laura DiSiena, the designer of the book; Michelle Leo and the education/library team; Stephanie Voros and the sub rights group too; Christina Pecorale and the whole sales team; and especially to Vivienne To, still making my books look much better than they deserve with her cover art.

Well, there's no delaying things any further . . . as some famous doctor once put it, we're in the endgame now, so see you in Revenge of Magic: *The Chosen One*!